This book should be returned to any branch of the
Lancashire County Library on or before the date shown

MIC   0 2 SEP 2015   Brooks HAC

PICK   26 OCT 2015

HANS   1 6 NOV 2015   1 8 OCT 2017

BW2   2 0 NOV 2017

ES2   Taylor

2 2 JUL 2013   1 1 MAR 2016   0 9 NOV 2018

DML

KX

WEST   3 1 MAY 2016

           - 9 NOV 2016
           - 2 DEC 2016

                              AFC

Lancashire County Library
Bowran Street
Preston PR1 2UX

Lancashire
County Council

www.lancashire.gov.uk/libraries

LL1(A)

THE JOYS OF MY LIFE

The new novel in the Hawkenlye series

May 1199. Abbess Helewise has been summoned by Queen Eleanor to discuss the building of a chapel at Hawkenlye Abbey. Meanwhile, Sir Josse d'Acquin is on the trail of a group of mysterious knights rumoured to be devil worshippers. As Helewise heads for home, Josse follows his quarry to Chartres, where he meets the last person he expects: Joanna. And she has grave problems of her own...

Alys Clare titles available from
Severn House Large Print

The Paths of the Air

THE JOYS OF MY LIFE

A Hawkenlye Mystery

Alys Clare

Severn House Large Print
London & New York

This first large print edition published 2010
in Great Britain and the USA by
SEVERN HOUSE PUBLISHERS LTD of
9-15 High Street, Sutton, Surrey, SM1 1DF.
First world regular print edition published 2008 by
Severn House Publishers Ltd., London and New York.

British Library Cat

Clare, Alys.
  The joys of my li:
  1. d'Acquin, Joss
  2. Helewise, Abb
  3. England--Soci
  4. Detective and
  I. Title II. Series
  823.9'2-dc22

ISBN-13: 978-0-7278-7830-4

Printed and bound in Great Britain by
MPG Books Ltd, Bodmin, Cornwall.

For Davey, Lisa and Charlie
with much love

Wafna! Wafna!
quid fecisti, sors turpissima?
nostre vite gaudia
abstulisti omnia!

Alas! Alas!
What have you done, atrocious fortune?
You have taken away
All the joys of my life!

Carmina Burana,
cantiones profanae

(author's translation)

Prologue

March 1199

The evening air was still. The day had been unseasonably hot, with a definite hint of summer. Now, as the sun went down beyond the low hills on the far side of the Tardoire River, the temperature was rapidly cooling and it was clear that it was barely spring, let alone summer.

The bareheaded man in the fine woollen tunic stood on a hillock in brooding contemplation of a field whose rich brown earth had been turned ready for sowing. The ploughing had been more than a month ago and still the empty earth lay patiently waiting. Above the field, a mile or so distant, a castle sat upon a slight rise. It was in a state of siege; two trebuchets stood before it, and gaping holes in the soaring walls gave testament to the accuracy and force of the missiles that had been repeatedly hurled from the siege engines' slings. Nearby, a stoutly constructed wooden structure on wheels stood waiting for the morning, when the sappers would utilize its protective shelter to creep up to the walls and continue

7

the process of undermining them. Back in the besiegers' encampment lay the scaling ladders, ready for deployment as soon as the castle's resistance had been sufficiently worn down for a forced entry.

The man in the tunic scratched his head vigorously – he was not much bothered with bathing even at the best of times, and living under canvas with limited access to hot water did not rank anywhere near *best* – and winced as his dirty fingernails raked off scabs from infected head-lice bites. He sniffed at the sweet evening air, noticing wryly that the stench of his unwashed body easily overcame the scent of fresh young grass, and then raised his eyes to stare up at the castle.

Curse the man! Could he not appreciate that holding out so determinedly was merely postponing the inevitable? And the longer it took, the angrier the besiegers would be when finally they took the castle. 'I *will* take it,' the man in the tunic murmured, 'and I will do so before any rival claimant arrives to argue about who owns what. *I* own the lot, and that's an end to it.'

Abruptly making up his mind, he leaped down – he was congenitally unable to keep still for very long and he had been standing on his mound for all of three minutes – and strode back to the encampment. He hollered for the captain of his mercenaries, waiting impatiently while the man came hurrying out of the mess tent.

'My lord?'

The man in the tunic stared at him, taking in the strong body and the sense of barely restrained violence waiting for an excuse to break out. The captain's face was at first glance impassive until one looked into the deep, dark eyes, where ruthlessness was as easily read as capital letters on an illuminated manuscript.

'I want to reconnoitre,' the man announced.

The captain of the mercenaries suppressed a sigh. He had accompanied his master all around the castle walls that morning; the only difference now would be that the sappers had dug a little further beneath the walls and the hole beside the left-hand gate tower was slightly larger. The besiegers had not had a great day. 'As you wish, my lord,' he murmured. Then, 'I will fetch your sword and your armour.'

The man waved an impatient hand. 'There's no need for that. I've rarely seen it so quiet up there.'

'You must at least wear your helm,' the captain insisted. Then, because he knew you did not insist with a man of his master's calibre, he added, 'Please, sire. I am responsible for your safety and it is not wise to take unnecessary risks.'

'Oh, very well.'

The man stood tapping a foot in irritation,

but the wait was short. Very soon his captain reappeared proffering the heavy iron helm and the close-fitting leather bonnet worn beneath it. The man put them on. Then, picking up his shield more out of habit than from any sense that he would need it, he strode off out of the encampment and along the wide track that his besieging force had made across the pasture.

The castle might well have appeared quiet – the lookout towers and the defensive positions on its battlements seemed deserted, for many of those inside were sitting down to their meagre evening meal, and all of them were complaining because there was less to eat today than there had been yesterday and the meat was rotten – but the tranquillity was deceptive for, hidden behind the stout walls, several men stood up on the fighting platform keeping careful watch on the scene below. One man had his eyes fixed on the pair walking towards the castle, their manner so relaxed and casual that it was an insult.

The man was an archer, his weapon the deadly crossbow, whose bolts were so savage that they had been known to enter a knight's leg and penetrate deep into his horse's side so that he was pinned as fast as a man nailed to a cross. He was a fine archer, one of the best.

He watched the two men far below. Despite their nonchalant air, the archer noted with ironic amusement that they kept out of bowshot. They were obviously inspecting the day's damage. He waited, biding his time. One of the men was helmed and fully armoured, the westering sun glinting off his chain mail and studded gauntlets. The other man bore a shield – the archer strained his eyes but could not make out the device – and he wore a helmet. Otherwise, he did not appear to be dressed for fighting.

A slow anger began to burn in the archer's breast. He thought grimly, how *dare* they amble along down there as if the castle had already fallen and its occupants were no longer a threat? They have put us through a miserable and frightening fortnight of siege, and all because of one man's greed! Well, we have not fallen yet and there is still plenty of heart in us. We shall defend ourselves for as long as it takes.

The two men below, heads together as they talked, had strayed closer to the castle. The archer placed a bolt in his crossbow and, resting the front of the bow on the ground, put his foot in the little iron stirrup and wound the handles that pulled the bowstring taut. Then, raising his weapon to eye level, he stepped back up on to the platform and, leaning on the wall, aimed at the men below.

The armoured man stepped into the archer's sights but then moved away again. The other man was standing with his left arm raised, indicating something on the wall

11

beside him. For a few precious moments he stood quite still and the archer had a perfect shot. With luck the bolt would enter beneath the upraised left arm and pierce the man's heart, killing him. Even if luck were not on the archer's side, there was no chance that he would miss. The crossbow was utterly steady as the archer took aim, drew a calm breath and then, when the moment was perfect, released the bolt. It flew down straight as a die and, finding its mark, buried itself deeply just above its victim's left armpit.

The archer stood back – instant retaliation was always a possibility and he was better off out of sight – and a grim smile spread across his lean face. That'll teach them not to wander up to a besieged castle like ladies on a May Day outing, he thought. That'll teach them not to underestimate an arbalester of *my* quality! With a swift glance over the parapet – the wounded man was kneeling on the ground, his pale tunic already stained with blood – the archer left his post and went in search of a celebratory mug of ale.

The wounded man was in a great deal of pain. With his captain's support he managed to get halfway back to camp before the faintness caused by loss of blood overcame him, at which the captain left him lying on the ground while he sprinted for help. He swiftly returned with a horse and cart, and the man suffered agonies while they loaded him up on to the cart and bounced him back to his tent. They begged to be allowed to inspect the wound but, beside himself with pain and fury, the man would not let them.

'Go and take the castle!' he roared. 'Attack and keep on attacking, and don't stop till it's ours!'

'But, my lord—' began the captain of the mercenaries.

The wounded man turned bloodshot eyes on him. Drawing a ragged breath, he hollered, 'Get on with it!'

Late that night, the captain tried to extract the iron arrowhead, but it was buried deep and the muscles around it were powerful and firm. The captain's first attempt succeeded only in removing the arrow shaft, which broke off, leaving the head embedded. Several more attempts were necessary, each one further mangling the torn and bloody flesh, before at last the bolt was out. The man, all but unconscious from shock and blood loss, fell back into an exhausted sleep that was as deep as a coma.

At first he seemed to revive. He was strong and he firmly believed that it would take more than an arrow in the shoulder to do him any lasting harm. As time passed, though, his body began to grow warm, then hot, until he was burning with fever. Streaks of dark, sinister red stood out along the veins of his left arm, the stench of putrefaction filled the air, and he knew without being told that his blood was poisoned and it was going to kill him.

Between the hallucinations and the delirium of high fever there were moments of lucidity during which the man had time to think. What was I doing here? he asked himself on one such occasion. Why did we have to take the castle? With an effort he remembered the reason, recalling how, a month or more ago, they had come racing to tell him of the crock of gold unearthed by a ploughman. The tale had swiftly grown and the crock of gold had become a huge golden statue of an emperor seated with his wife and children around a jewel-encrusted table.

Where was the treasure? Had his troops found it when they stormed the castle? The man tried to bellow for his captain, but his bellowing days were over and all he managed was a croak, for his mouth and throat were parched and his lips cracked and bleeding. The servant attending him must have heard the feeble whisper, for he bent down low over his master, careful not to let his disgust at the smell show on his face.

'My lord?' he enquired softly.

'Tr–treasure,' the dying man managed. 'They've found it? Wh–what is it?'

The attendant briefly considered a kind lie but decided against it. 'No sign of any treasure as yet, my lord,' he murmured. 'I am very sorry.'

No sign of it, the man thought. Ah, well.

He slumped back against his blood- and pus-stained pillows and wearily closed his eyes.

He lasted the best part of another week, for he had always been a fit man, strong and hardy. He used the time to set his affairs in order, arranging for his succession and for the disposal of his body. He confessed his sins; he said farewell to his beloved mother. Then, late in the evening of 6 April, he gave up his spirit and the forty-one years of his life came to an end. The day was a Tuesday and appropriate, the chroniclers would later say, for Tuesday was dedicated to Mars, god of war.

And Richard the Lionheart of England, who died from septicaemia following a futile treasure hunt that failed to turn up a single gold coin, had been a warrior all his life.

Part One

The Island

One

The five travellers were in no fit state to go before a queen. Their journey had taken three weeks and, although the sea crossing had mercifully been calm and uneventful, since coming ashore nearly a fortnight ago they had encountered wet weather that had soaked them and turned the roads to mud, swiftly followed by sudden hot sunshine, which had burned their faces, raised clouds of dust and attracted a million newly-hatched flies to settle on their sweaty skin. The inns had been full to bursting – it seemed that everyone was on the roads just then – and what accommodation they had managed to find had been filthy, the food poor and anything resembling decent wine or ale quite unobtainable.

There had been a brief respite at the great abbey of Fontevrault, where they had been offered clean beds, warm water for bathing, servants to help brush the mud off their clothing and excellent food. They had, however, believed Fontevrault to be their destination and so their pleasure in its generous welcome was mitigated by discovering that they were faced with a further hundred miles or more on the road. The first few hours' travelling had swiftly cancelled out most of the good that Fontevrault had done.

Nevertheless, they had received a royal summons and, dirty, weary, hungry, flea-bitten or not, they must obey. They had pressed on uncomplainingly and now they were close to their journey's end. Abbess Helewise glanced at her four companions and, suppressing a moan of distress at their appearance, turned her mind to the problem of how on earth she was to spruce them up.

The summons had reached Hawkenlye Abbey a month ago. Like everyone else, the nuns and monks had still been reeling from the terrible news of King Richard's death. He had died like the great and noble man he was, some said, fighting and defeating the vicious and tyrannical lord of a castle some-where in the Limousin, wherever that might be. One version of the tale added the em-bellishment that the tyrant had been an infidel, and such was local ignorance of the great world beyond Hawkenlye that nobody thought to ask what an infidel lord was doing with a castle in the middle of France. Others – the very few with contacts in high places – heard and believed a version that was closer to the truth, but they had the good sense to keep their mouths shut.

Then, in the middle of April, the messengers had come, three of them in the livery of Aquitaine. They had demanded to see the abbess and had presented her with Queen Eleanor's letter. It was the queen's wish, the letter announced, that a chapel should be built at Hawkenlye Abbey, dedicated to the well-being of the soul of her dear son King Richard. Stunned, Helewise read on and swiftly learned that, the queen being unable to come to Hawkenlye, its abbess must go to her at Fontevrault to receive her instructions.

Go to Fontevrault, Helewise thought, her mind already buzzing with frantic planning. Leave Hawkenlye – leave England! – and cross the seas to France. Attend the queen herself and then come back here to build a chapel. Dear God, how am I to achieve all this?

My emotion and distress must not show, she told herself then. She sat quite still, her head lowered as if she still read the queen's words, and waited until she felt calm. Then she looked up, gave the senior messenger a serene smile and said, 'I shall set out for Fontevrault as soon as arrangements can be made.'

The first thing she did was send word to Sir Josse d'Acquin, for she could not contemplate her mission without him. Good friend that he was, he must have read the urgency behind the carefully bland summons and he arrived at Hawkenlye ahead of

21

the lay brother who had gone to fetch him. As soon as he understood what they must do, he began making practical and concise plans. A small group was best, he advised, for a great gaggle of people always took longer to get anywhere. Could she manage with just one nun?

'Of course,' Helewise had said, instantly deciding on young Sister Caliste.

They would take two lay brothers, Josse went on, and he suggested Brother Saul and Brother Augustus. Smiling to herself – for these two brave and loyal men would have been her choice too – Helewise sent for Sister Caliste and the brethren to break the news.

She had always judged Sir Josse to be a man skilled at organization but even so she was surprised at his swift efficiency. Within days he had found good mounts for all five travellers – the sturdy Horace for Sir Josse, the golden mare Honey for the abbess, the Hawkenlye cob for Brother Saul and borrowed horses for Sister Caliste and Brother Augustus – and a pack animal to carry supplies of food, drink, a rudimentary medical kit, spare clothing and various other bundles and bulging bags whose purpose, Helewise thought, would no doubt become clear as they went along. All too soon it was time to depart. There had been a special service the previous day, during which the community prayed for the travellers, but

22

Helewise snatched a moment to go alone to the abbey church, where she fell to her knees and begged the Lord's help and protection for her companions and herself while they were away from Hawkenlye.

She kneeled, eyes closed, hands clasped, in the cool, silent church. Then, just for an instant, she thought she sensed something, a sort of brief pressure on her head. With a smile, she opened her eyes, got to her feet and hurried outside. Josse was holding her horse and he stepped forward to help her into the saddle. Then he swung up on to Horace's back and turned to her. She nodded and he led the way out through the abbey gates and off on the long road south.

They crossed the English Channel from Hastings to Honfleur, on the mouth of the Seine, and then turned south through Normandy and Anjou, stopping when they could in the relative safety of the busy, hectic towns – Lisieux, Alençon, Le Mans, Tours – and when nightfall found them out in the lonely countryside, putting up in whatever rural household would have them. Finally reaching Fontevrault, that renowned and wealthy abbey where Eleanor of Aquitaine now spent her days, they were greeted with the news that the queen was no longer there. She had left but a few days ago, Abbess Matilda informed them, bound for her castle on the island of Oléron. She had left orders that the Abbess Helewise and her party were to join her there.

Helewise glanced nervously at Josse, who had given a very faint shrug as if to say, don't ask me! So, summoning her courage and telling herself firmly that she too was an abbess, she said to the abbess of Fontevrault, 'My lady, I do not know where this island may be found. Is it far?'

Abbess Matilda looked at her sympathetically. 'It is off the coast near La Rochelle, and perhaps a week's journey. Less if the roads are dry.'

A week! Helewise kept a serene expression and said calmly, 'I see. In that case, we shall set out immediately.'

Abbess Matilda reached out and clasped her sister abbess's hands. 'A day will make little difference. Stay with us this night. Let us tend you and your horses. You can bathe, rest and recover some strength. Then we shall replenish your supplies and see you on to your road.'

Helewise hesitated. She sensed her four companions urging her to accept the kind offer and in her head she heard again Abbess Matilda's words: *A day will make little difference.* With a smile of sheer relief, she said, 'Thank you, my lady. We accept.'

As they rode out the next day, she urged Honey on so that she drew level with Josse. Sister Caliste rode ahead, while Brother Augustus and Brother Saul brought up the rear with the packhorse. There was nobody near enough to overhear, but it was still in a carefully soft voice that Helewise spoke. 'Sir Josse,' she said, 'what do you think of this, of Queen Eleanor having left the safety and sanctity of Fontevrault for some island castle?'

Josse frowned. 'I have been thinking hard, my lady, yet have come up with no satisfactory answer. Undoubtedly the queen has much to occupy her in these uncertain times, for although it appears that King John's succession is not to be contested, there are many matters for Eleanor's attention.' His frown deepened. 'I could have understood had she gone to some city such as Niort, or Poitiers, or Tours, where urgent matters of State might be addressed. Yet I asked around at Fontevrault and was told that Oléron is a desolate place with few inhabitants and barely a sizeable building other than the queen's castle and— My lady?'

Helewise was nodding in sudden comprehension. 'I believe I can help, Sir Josse,' she said. 'Our dear Eleanor has just lost her favourite son. Unlike most people, she has not the luxury of privacy, for the death of a king demands the attention of one such as she. Yet she is human too and perhaps her grief has overcome her. You describe this Oléron as a lonely spot where few people dwell; where better for a queen to withdraw and mourn in privacy?'

Now the travellers were south of the great port of La Rochelle, out in the midst of an area of flat marshland that seemed to go on for miles in each direction. The day was warm and sunny, although the soggy ground produced strange mists that snaked up around the horses' feet and legs. Insects whined and buzzed in clouds around the heads of both humans and animals, and the irritable swishing of the horses' tails was a constant background sound. Presently the road led up over a low humpbacked bridge and, at the top of the rise, the view opened out before them.

Sister Caliste, riding in front, called out, 'I can see the sea!'

Josse slipped off Horace's back and hurried to stand beside her. 'Aye, you're right!' he exclaimed. 'And there's an island over there, straight in front of us, maybe a mile off the shore.'

'Is it Oléron?' Helewise demanded urgently. Just then she did not think she could bear it if he said no.

He turned, gave her a very sweet smile and said, 'I believe so, my lady. We'll have to go on to the coast, find a boatman and ask, but I have been following the instructions that the monks at Fontevrault gave us and I am all but sure that at long last our destination is in sight.'

Helewise set up a brief prayer of thanks.

Then, looking round at her companions, she said, 'The queen awaits us. There is no dwelling, religious house or even lowly cottage where we may seek help, but I notice that this bridge crosses a stream.' Already Josse and the lay brothers were eyeing her dubiously. 'Sir Josse, take Brother Saul and Brother Augustus down there to the far bank. Sister Caliste, you come with me along this side of the stream to that stand of willows.'

Josse said, 'What are we all to do, my lady?'

She fixed him with a direct look. She said firmly, 'Wash.'

Quite a long time later, the five travellers reassembled on the road. Helewise cast a critical eye over her companions and was surprised and pleased at what she saw. Her own and Sister Caliste's ablutions had been modest and prim; carefully back to back beneath the concealing willows, they had stripped to their chemises, washed as best they could and then put on clean linen and wimples. Caliste had rubbed the mud from the hems of their robes and banged the dust from their veils, and the two of them had dressed again and stood back to inspect each other. The effect, Helewise concluded, was not bad under the circumstances. The three men, however, had outdone them. Judging from the hoots of laughter and the loud splashing noises that she and Sister Caliste had tried to ignore, Josse and the lay brothers had apparently plunged right into the water. Now they stood with wet hair, decidedly damp garments and sheepish expressions, but all three looked as if they had just stepped from a bathhouse.

'Excellent!' Helewise exclaimed. 'And Brother Augustus has even removed some of the dust from the horses. Well done! Now, before we have a chance to get dirty again, let's go and find the queen.'

They reached the shore and soon found a narrow inlet where several boats were tied up to a wooden jetty. Josse found a group of seamen crouched over a cooking fire on which something savoury was stewing, and one of the men confirmed that the island across the water was indeed Oléron. Standing up, he pointed to a grim and forbidding fortress that stood on the point directly opposite. 'That's the castle,' he said, puffing out his chest. 'The *queen*'s castle.'

'Really?' Josse obligingly acted the part of a man overawed and deeply impressed. Then he said swiftly, 'Can you take us over there?' He turned to indicate his companions. 'We are five, with six horses.'

The man contemplated the group, rubbing a thumb across the dark stubble on his chin. He bent down to mutter with the other seamen and then, straightening, named his price. It seemed reasonable to Josse, although he guessed that the seaman was probably inflating his usual rate in the presence of unknowing strangers. More for form's sake than anything else, he offered two-thirds and in the end they settled on three-quarters. Then the man summoned a younger version of himself, who had to be his son, and, with two other men, they led Josse and his companions down the beach to a low, flat wooden craft with a broad beam and a single mast. Soon both humans and horses were standing on the salt-bleached deck as the seamen wielded their long poles and pushed off from the jetty.

It was less than a mile across the stretch of water to the island. Many sea crossings had never quite convinced Josse that boats were safe and he was glad of the abbess's presence beside him. They stood in the bows of the boat, staring ahead over the calm sea to the flat, green outline of Oléron, and he could sense her tense excitement. He did not think it was the crossing that was making her nervous.

He said, 'We have made good time, my lady. The queen will be surprised, I believe, to see us so soon.'

She looked up at him and he read gratitude in her face. 'Do you think so? Oh, I hope you are right – it seems so long since her messengers came to Hawkenlye and I have been anxious in case she is angry with me for delaying.'

Josse smiled. 'The queen is a great traveller. She understands better than most that nobody could travel from the south-east of England to the west coast of France in much better time than we have taken.' Impulsively reaching out to grasp her hand, he added, 'Stop worrying!'

She laughed softly. 'Very well!' Then – and he noticed belatedly that Sister Caliste and Brother Saul were watching – she extracted her hand and stepped a deliberate pace away.

They landed on the Île d'Oléron and stood looking around them. It was a long, thin island, lying at an angle to the mainland and stretching out roughly south-east to north-west. Eleanor's high-walled castle stood at the south-east corner; it was, Josse thought, staring up at it, the obvious place, for it commanded the straits between the island and the mainland. For some reason he felt a sudden deep shiver of apprehension. Something very bad had happened – or was about to happen – here.

He pulled himself together. 'Come,' he said bracingly, 'let us mount up and set a smart pace as we ride up to the castle.'

They set off, Josse and the abbess in the lead, and within a short time were approaching the narrow stone bridge that led over a deep gully to the castle on its headland. Guards stood at each end of the bridge and, on the far side, where an arched entrance led through the great wall into the courtyard beyond, an iron portcullis was poised ready for lowering. Arrow slits dotted the smooth stonework in a regular pattern and, high above, men could be seen on watch behind the crenellated walls. The castle gave the impression that it was bristling with weaponry and spoiling for a fight.

But that was fanciful, Josse told himself firmly. Wasn't it?

He dragged himself out of his strange mood and made himself pay attention to the abbess's exchange with the captain of the guard, who had stepped forward to bar their progress. Josse was about to offer his help but realized she did not need it; she was doing perfectly well on her own. The guard seemed impressed and, giving her a gallant bow, led the way across the bridge and in through the archway.

They were in Eleanor's castle at last.

Eleanor gave them a short time to refresh themselves and then sent for the abbess and Josse. Briefly – and ungratefully – it occurred to Helewise to wonder why Josse was summoned, since the construction of a new chapel at Hawkenlye surely had nothing to do with him. She put the unworthy thought firmly away as they entered the vast room and, deeply and reverently, she bowed before the queen.

Eleanor stepped down from the raised dais

where she had been sitting and took Helewise's hand. 'You have made good time, Helewise,' she said.

In a flash Helewise thought, you were right, Josse. Then she said meekly, 'We had a reliable guide, madam.'

'Yes,' Eleanor said, looking at Josse. 'I know.'

Helewise knew it was probably not the right thing to speak before being spoken to but she could not help herself. She stared into Eleanor's eyes; the queen's face was pale and drawn, and her deep-set eyes were shadowed with dark circles. 'I am so sorry, my lady, for your loss.'

There was a moment's absolute silence. Helewise, quite sure she had broken some rule of etiquette, was about to apologize when the queen gave a sigh and said softly, 'You too have sons, Helewise.'

'Yes, my lady.'

It was enough.

The queen seemed to shake off the outward manifestations of her grief. Straightening up and squaring her shoulders, she said abruptly, 'The new chapel is to be dedicated to St Edmund, who, like my dear son, died from an arrow shot. It is to be under the auspices of Hawkenlye Abbey, but I leave its exact site for you to decide, Helewise, in collaboration with the architect and the builders. I recall that the abbey does not have a great deal of available space within its walls and I would not have some existing building altered to make room. Within the chapel, the Hawkenlye community and the people will pray for the soul of King Richard.' She paused, looking wryly first at Helewise and then at Josse. 'Like all men, my son was a mixture of good and bad. He confessed his sins and was shriven before he died, but nevertheless I fear that many more prayers must be said for him before his soul may ascend to Our Lord in heaven.' She fell silent, the lines of deep grief once more very apparent on her face.

Helewise waited. Eleanor again brought herself back from the dark paths of grief to the matter in hand. With a peremptory 'Come!' she walked across to a wide oak table on which there were several large rolls of parchment. With Helewise and Josse either side of her, she unrolled the largest, revealing a beautifully drawn illustration of a small chapel. 'This is what I want,' she said quietly. 'Something simple, for my son was a plain man. Something for the ordinary people, who loved him.'

Helewise was not at all sure about *love*. It seemed to her that the unspoken opinion of most people was that the late king had cost them rather more than he was worth. This, of course, was no time to say so.

Eleanor was unrolling other parchments, showing them plans and elevations. 'You will go from here to the city of Chartres,' she said, 'where they are building the new cathedral on the fire-blackened ruins of the old one. There, you will find the stonemasons and the carpenters whom I have chosen to build my son's chapel and you will give them my written orders. Payment will be effected through the auspices of the Knights Templar, with whom I have arranged credit. It is my wish that work begin as soon as possible. I have already commissioned a similar chapel at Fontevrault, dedicated to St Lawrence, and it is my firm intention that prayers shall be said at both chapels within the year.'

It seemed a tall order. Helewise, briefly meeting Josse's eyes, guessed he felt the same, but then Eleanor was the queen, enduring, loved and respected; her people were long in the habit of obeying her.

'Very well, my lady,' Helewise said. 'It shall be as you command.'

Eleanor looked at her intently for a moment. Then she said simply, 'Thank you.'

Helewise sensed that they were dismissed. With a brief glance at Josse, she bowed low and began backing away from the queen. They had reached the great doors, which a silent statue-like guard opened for them, and Helewise was preceding Josse through to the vast open space beyond when Eleanor called out, 'Sir Josse! A word, if you please.'

His eyes flicked to Helewise's and she felt an absurd urge to giggle at the horror in his face. 'It is my turn to reassure you,' she whispered, pushing him back into the great hall. 'Stop worrying – you have done nothing wrong!'

Then the guard was gently but firmly closing the doors in her face. Whatever was in store for Josse, he was going to have to face it by himself.

Eleanor had dismissed her guard; she and Josse were alone. She went to sit on a low bench beside the empty hearth and beckoned to him to join her. After a moment's hesitation – was it right to sit beside a queen? – he obeyed, lowering his buttocks very cautiously in case she suddenly protested that it wasn't what she had meant at all and he should kneel at her feet instead. No such protest came.

After what seemed to the very nervous Josse a painfully long silence, Eleanor said, 'Sir Josse, why do you imagine I have come here to my castle on this backwater of an island?'

Josse cast around frantically for a diplomatic answer but all he could think of was the truth. 'We – that is, the Abbess Helewise and I – wondered if you might have sought a little solitude, madam, in which to grieve,' he said quietly.

'A gentle thought,' she replied, 'and, indeed, an accurate guess, for it is all too true that I have great need of such a retreat.' She

35

sighed. 'I have lost the staff of my old age, the light of my eyes,' she murmured, 'and it all but breaks me.' There was another pause and Josse felt her sorrow flow around him like a dark cloud. Then she said, 'But the luxury of solitary grief is not for one such as I. Why, even here matters of State occupy me and in the brief time that I have been on the island I have granted two charters and, when the blackness of my thoughts threatens to overwhelm me, I distract myself with a new project to set down once and for all a just and reasonable system of laws for maritime trade.' She fell silent, a frown creasing her face.

'I can think of nobody more fitted to—' Josse began.

As if she hadn't heard him, she spoke again, shocking him into silence: 'There are foul rumours concerning a group of knights who, so they say, have been indulging in devil worship,' she said bluntly. 'They sacrifice young boys and perform unspeakable sexual misdeeds.'

In a flash of understanding Josse recalled the moment of deep unease as he stood looking up at the castle. *Something very bad had happened here.* 'Aye,' he breathed. Then, eyes on hers, 'Was it right here, within these walls?' he asked urgently.

She looked at him, surprise on her face. 'No, but very close: on the island. How did you know?' Then, anger darkening her eyes, she hissed, 'Did somebody tell you?'

'No, madam, I swear it.' To his huge relief, she seemed to believe him. 'Just a sensation. I felt there was evil here.'

'You felt right,' she muttered.

'What has it to do with me?' he asked. 'Or with you, my lady? This is your island, I appreciate that, but—'

Again she interrupted him. 'I remember you, Josse d'Acquin,' she said. 'You came to our aid once before. Do you remember?'

'Aye, my lady.' Embarrassed, he lowered his head.

'I was preparing the way in England for my son's crowning and you helped to defend his good name. Well, now I call upon you to render to me the same service again.'

'Your son...? Madam, I do not understand.' Josse stared at her. He read something in her expression, something that made his heart thump in alarm, and he thought that perhaps he did understand after all.

'Yes, yes,' she said slowly. Then, suppressed fury sharpening her voice, 'Rumours, Josse, always rumours! So much has been said about my son King Richard, so much that is bad. *Evil*. So much that is untrue.'

'They are saying that he knew of this group of knights?' Josse asked tentatively.

'They are saying that he was one of them,' she replied brutally. 'They say he joined them in their foul, unnatural rites, that he

37

had carnal knowledge of young boys, that he came here, to this very island, not long before he died to lead one of their most frightful ceremonies–' she drew a shaky breath – 'that he was there to hear the terrible screams.'

'My lady, I...' But Josse was lost for words. He wanted to state firmly that he was quite sure there was no truth in the rumours, that the late king was innocent of the dreadful accusations, but he was not at all sure that he could speak the words and sound as if he were telling the truth.

'I have a mission for you, Josse,' the queen said quietly. 'When you have completed it, report back to me. I continue my progress for some weeks, but by mid-July I shall be in Rouen. I wish you to investigate these rumours and find out if there is any truth in them. If there is not, you are to arrest all those responsible for blackening the name of the king and bring them to me for trial and punishment.'

There was a long, aching silence.

Finally Josse said, 'And if there is?'

The queen's dark, unfathomable eyes stared straight into his. It was rather like being pinned to a wall. 'If there is,' she repeated, 'bury it. Bury it so deeply that it can never emerge.'

Two

The Hawkenlye party were treated with every courteous consideration during their brief stay at the Château d'Oléron. To Helewise's surprise, that evening Sister Caliste and the lay brothers were, like herself and Josse, invited to dine at the queen's table. Observing Helewise's amazement, Eleanor took her to one side and said, 'My dear, this, as I believe you perceive, is my retreat. I do not have to follow the rules of the outside world here and it is my wish to have a merry gathering. Let your good Sister Caliste and the brethren enjoy some luxury while they may.'

The queen had her wish. The simple diet of the Hawkenlye community did not include delicious and deceptively strong French wines and very quickly Brother Augustus and Sister Caliste emerged from their overawed shells and were laughing and joking as if they had known Eleanor all their young lives. Brother Saul, older and more conditioned to his lowly status, took longer to relax and it was only when the queen requested a song that he finally joined in the merriment. Helewise had never heard him sing solo before and the rich baritone that emerged from his thin, wiry frame was as much a revelation to her as it clearly was to Queen Eleanor.

When he finished – he had performed a faintly ribald song about a maid and a boy falling in love and the absurd course of the lad's courtship – the queen clapped her hands with delight, said she had heard nothing so good since she had been a girl in the sunny, romantic south and did Brother Saul know any more?

In the middle of the following morning, Helewise was ready to depart. The letters from the queen were safe in a small satchel that Helewise wore at her waist, and the parchments bearing the plans for the new chapel had been carefully rolled and stored inside protective lead cylinders. Brother Saul had been assigned the responsibility of getting them safely back to Hawkenlye.

Having taken her farewell of the queen, Helewise made her way down to the stables, where the others were waiting for her. Sister Caliste and the lay brothers were already mounted; Josse stood beside Horace.

'Ready, Sir Josse?' She smiled at him. 'We should make haste, for our business here is done and we must be on our way.'

'My lady, I am not coming with you.'

'Not...? But, Sir Josse, why ever not?'

He hesitated and she thought he looked awkward. 'I have ... The queen has asked me to fulfil a mission for her. It is a private matter.' He hurried on as she made to comment, 'Something that she confided in me yesterday.'

'When she called you back into the hall,' Helewise breathed. 'Of course.' Then a sudden flash of inspiration hit her and she realized that the queen had planned all this. Knowing Helewise, knowing the special place held by Sir Josse d'Acquin in the hearts of everyone at Hawkenlye, Eleanor had been fully aware who Helewise would ask to accompany her on this journey into the unknown. She reached out and caught hold of Josse's sleeve. 'Sir Josse, a word,' she muttered.

They walked a few paces away from the others. 'My lady?' Josse asked in a whisper.

'I realize that this matter must be sensitive and confidential, and that you are sworn to secrecy,' she whispered back, 'and I would not dream of trying to make you divulge any details. However, sensitive secrets habitually bring danger with them. Whatever you have to do, dear Josse, and wherever you have to go, take Gussie with you.'

'Gussie!' Josse exclaimed – too loudly, for the young man heard and his head shot up in alarm.

'It's all right, Brother Augustus,' Helewise called. Then, lowering her voice, she said to

Josse, 'I insist. I appreciate that you may not be able to tell him what you're doing but, please, at least accept him as a travelling companion.' Sensing that Josse was weakening, she added craftily, 'You would advise the same thing yourself, would you not?'

He laughed briefly. 'Aye, my lady, so I would.' He paused, frowning. 'Very well. I'll take the lad with me and I'll do what I've been commanded to do. I'll join you at Chartres if I can – I do not know how long my mission will take, but you, I imagine, will be in the city for a few days while you go about the task of engaging your workmen. If I miss you there, then I will meet you back at Hawkenlye.'

She looked at him. It all seemed very uncertain. It was undoubtedly a long way even to Chartres, never mind back to England, and suddenly the thought of all those miles, all those days, without his cheery, reassuring company seemed hard to bear. However, he had his orders and so did she.

She squared her shoulders and said, 'Very well, Sir Josse. God's speed, and may He keep you safe in His care until we meet again.'

She could tell he was touched by the same emotion – she read it in his eyes – but then he bowed low, saying gravely as he straightened up, 'And you too, my lady. Good luck.'

Then there was nothing else to do but give Brother Augustus his new instructions, remove two portions of the supplies and the spare clothing from the packhorse and, with Sister Caliste on one side and Brother Saul on the other, ride out of the courtyard, over the stone bridge and away.

Queen Eleanor planned to leave later that day. Well, that was understandable, Josse reflected, standing in a corner of the great courtyard and watching as the queen's luggage train was prepared. She had had her private talk with him and her business here was therefore done. Now she could go on to attend to some of the myriad other matters clamouring for her attention in these uncertain times as her youngest son, King John, took his brother's place. According to stable-yard gossip, Eleanor was heading first for Rochefort, then on to Saint-Jean-d'Angély and Saintes. 'She's got enemies all around her,' one of the grooms muttered to Josse, 'and she needs to make sure her own people will help her if she needs them.'

It seemed as good a summing-up of the position as any, Josse thought. Eleanor's situation – indeed, King John's situation – was the one thing every fighting man tried to avoid: facing two enemies at once. Now it was Arthur of Brittany over in the north-west and Philip of France in his heartland around Paris who threatened. Josse did not blame the queen in the least for hastening to ensure the support of her own loyal vassals.

43

Finally Eleanor's party was ready to leave and the queen descended into the courtyard. She was helped on to her horse and, as she turned to ride out across the stone bridge, she cast her eyes around as if for one last look. It seemed, though, that she had a more immediate purpose: spotting Josse, her tense expression relaxed and she beckoned him over.

He approached and made a low bow. Straightening, he said, 'Madam?'

Eleanor leaned down and said, 'Do you see the squat, swarthy guard at the far end of the bridge? Don't let him see that you are looking!' she added in an urgent hiss.

Slowly Josse ran his eyes all around the crowded courtyard as if assessing the number of people in the procession. Finally looking over at the bridge, he instantly picked out the guard to whom the queen referred. 'Aye, my lady,' he said softly.

'When all is quiet and the castle is abed tonight, seek him out. He lodges in a small house close to the port. On its door there is an iron hoop in the shape of a dolphin.'

Josse bowed again. 'I will, madam.'

She glared down at him for a long moment. Then she gave an abrupt nod, kicked the sides of her horse and set off at a smart trot across the courtyard and over the bridge. The long train of her attendants and her baggage snaked after her, leaving behind, when the last of them had gone and

44

the dust had settled, a sudden silence in the courtyard that seemed almost unnatural.

Josse decided that there was no need to involve Gussie yet, since there could surely be no danger in simply walking down to the harbour to have a chat with one of the castle guards. Accordingly, after supper that night Josse dismissed the young man with the suggestion that he turn in early and catch up on his sleep. Gussie did not need much persuasion; he was already yawning widely as he and Josse said goodnight.

Josse found a quiet corner at the end of the stable block and sat patiently watching and waiting. Guards came and went on their patrols and, as darkness fell, only a handful were left on watch. He had noticed the previous evening that they did not seem to be in the habit of lowering the great portcullis at night; presumably they felt that the narrow stretch of water between the island and the mainland was defence enough. Anyway, the queen would not have ordered him to slip out under cover of the dark if an iron portcullis stood in the way.

He noticed that the patrolling guards passed the bridge less frequently now. If he ran, he ought to be able to get out of the castle without being observed. Not giving himself time to worry about what might happen if they did see him, he stepped softly out of his corner, sprinted across the courtyard and over the bridge. Then he was racing down the winding approach to the castle, keeping to the shadows, and he knew by the silence that they hadn't spotted him.

He slowed to a walk, panting from exertion. The road led straight to the little harbour, where more of the sort of craft that had carried Josse and his party across the straits lay tied to the jetty. Opposite the water, there was a row of mean-looking dwellings that seemed to lean against the low cliff behind them. Some still showed a light, and Josse could hear the sound of voices. He walked slowly along the row and came to a door whose handle was decorated with a hoop in the shape of a leaping fish. Whether or not it was a dolphin did not seem important and he was prepared to take the queen's word for it.

He tapped on the door. Nothing happened. He tapped again, a little more forcefully, and suddenly the door opened. A fist closed on his tunic, he was dragged inside, and the door was closed quietly behind him. The room smelled dank, as if it were hewn from rock, and the air within was chilly. It was pitch black. The hand on Josse's tunic eased and there was a muttered apology. There came the scratch of a flint and a tallow lamp flared. In its light Josse saw that he was face to face with the swarthy guard.

'Did they see you?' the guard said, fear very evident in his low voice.

'No,' Josse said shortly. 'You know, then, why I have come.' It seemed the only explanation for the guard's furtive, frightened manner.

'Oh, yes,' the dark man said. Then, wearily, 'Wish I'd had the sense to keep my mouth shut.'

'But you didn't,' Josse said, 'and now I am tasked with hearing what you have to say.' And deciding whether or not you speak the truth, he could have added.

As if the man heard the unspoken thought, he said, 'It's true. It's all too true.' He sank down on to a roughly made bench that stood beside a flimsy table – those items and a low, narrow cot appeared to be the room's only furniture – and rubbed his face with both hands. A muffled sob escaped him, an unexpected sound in a man of his tough appearance, and he said, 'God help me, I wish I could say I made it all up, but I can't. As God is my witness, I saw what I saw and I would swear it before the highest authority in the land.' He gave a bitter laugh. 'And that'd be just what the new king would want to hear!'

Josse folded his arms, leaned back against the door and said, 'You'd better explain.'

The dark man shot him a suspicious glance. 'What have you been told?'

'They say–' Josse thought it better not to mention the queen – 'that there is a group of knights on the island and that they are

47

involved in foul practices. Devil worship, apparently, and the abuse of young boys.'

The man was rigid with tension. 'What else?' he demanded.

Josse hesitated. Then, for there seemed to be no choice, 'It is said the late king is involved.'

Now the man relaxed. Nodding, looking knowingly up at Josse with a sardonic smile, he said, 'And she's sent you to find out if it's true.' Josse did not reply. 'Oh, it's true all right.'

Josse said, 'Tell me.'

The man did not speak for some moments. He got up and stepped over to the door and, as Josse moved aside, opened it the merest crack and peered out. Satisfied, he shut it again, barred it and resumed his seat on the bench. Then, as if he had to get on with his tale before his resolve evaporated, he said in a low, swift mutter, 'There's this knight, Philippe de Loup. He's got a stronghold on the island, a castle that's more like a fortress, right up on the north-west tip, where the winds blow and the sea frets come up like will-o'-the-wisps and hide the evil that's done there. They call it World's End and I tell you, they're right. Nobody goes there unless they have to – it's haunted, it is, and we all avoid the place like it were the devil's own.'

'I was told there was a group of them,' Josse said. 'This de Loup's companions must go there.'

'Oh, *they* do,' the guard agreed. Leaning closer, he said, 'They call themselves the Knights of Arcturus, although other folk refer to them as the Thirteen Nobles. They keep themselves to themselves, I'll give them that, but it's the way of it that people who make a dead secret of their comings and goings are always the subject of far more gossip and speculation than those who live their lives in the open for all to see.'

'I've never heard of either title,' Josse said.

'No, well, they're secret, like I say,' the guard said testily. 'Few folk *have* heard of them, for all that they've been around for a hundred years or more.' His voice dropped to a dramatic whisper. 'They guard something too terrible to be spoken aloud.'

'I see.' Josse wondered exactly where accuracy stopped and fear-fuelled local folklore began. 'So how does all this involve ... er, involve the important person who is recently deceased?'

The guard frowned momentarily, as if working out what Josse meant. Then, the cynical smile back on his face, he said, 'Oh, him. Well, they were here, de Loup and his knights, back in March. Towards the beginning of March, as I recall.' A few weeks before King Richard died, Josse thought. 'They came by night and the weather was foul, with a westerly blowing hard and seas as high as they come around here. I'll give those knights credit for their seamanship and their courage, I'll tell you that – you wouldn't have caught me crossing the straits on a night like that. Anyway, they landed safely and set off at a fast pace out across the island to de Loup's fortress. Something terrible happened that night. Screams were heard coming from the tower, dreadful, horrifying, agonized screams, enough to make a man's blood freeze in his body, and through the arrow slits in the room above that great fortified entrance there poured a brilliant, unearthly blue light that suddenly changed to blood red.' He sat back with a nod, as if to say, what do you make of that?

Josse was thinking hard. *Screams were heard*, he repeated to himself. Who heard them? But perhaps now was not the moment to ask. 'Go on,' he said neutrally.

The guard blinked in surprise. Josse wondered if he had expected a more awed response to his tale. 'Later that night, three men were seen riding away,' he said. 'One was tall and thin, fairish, like; one was short and lightly built; the third was broad in the shoulder, a big man. All three wore dark cloaks and pulled their hoods forward to conceal their faces. They raced across to the lee side of the island, where a small boat was waiting, abandoned their horses and climbed in. The boat set out instantly and they were rowed out to a larger craft standing off in the sheltered waters at the northern end of the straits. As soon as they were safely aboard, she raised her anchor, set sail and swiftly disappeared off into the night.' He fixed Josse with intent dark eyes. 'The broad-shouldered man was King Richard.'

Dear God in heaven, Josse thought. For this man to state such a frightful thing with absolute certainty, he must be very sure of his facts. He said, 'You tell me that screams "were heard", and three men "were seen". Who heard? Who saw? Is this witness truthful?'

The guard grinned. 'I guessed you'd try that,' he said. 'I'll tell you who heard the screams and saw that dreadful, unnatural light: it was my brother. He gets supplies in for de Loup and he'd done so that day. He went to meet the knights when they crossed by night from the mainland and he followed them up to World's End.'

'Why?'

'He had his reasons.' The guard, it seemed, was not to be drawn.

'And your brother identified one of these fleeing men as King Richard?'

There was a pause. Then, as if he had not heard or was ignoring the question, the guard said, 'That little boat was scarcely up to riding the waves, you know. It took some-one who has known these waters man and boy to row her safely out to the ship. It was all very well at first, because close in to shore the bulk of the island kept off the worst of

51

the gale. Once we were out in the straits, it was a different matter and all three of them had to start bailing if they wanted to save their own skins.'

' "Once *we* were in the straits"?' Josse repeated, pouncing on the word.

The guard gave him a quizzical look. 'Paying attention, aren't you? I like that when I'm telling a tale.' Then, abruptly turning from sarcasm to fierce intensity, 'It was me who saw the king. It's not easy to bail and keep your face hidden, but he almost managed it. Then he straightened up – muscle pain, I guess, for he had a hand in the small of his back – and he'd got his foot on the hem of that great cloak. Just for an instant, the hood was pulled sideways and I saw his face as clear as I see yours.'

'I thought you said it was pitch dark and a storm was blowing?' Josse said. 'How was it that there was light to see by?'

'We were coming alongside the ship by then,' the guard said smugly. 'They were leaning down over the side with flaring torches so that I could see where the ladder had been lowered.'

Oh, God.

For some time there was silence in the cold, musty little room. Josse was struggling to absorb what he had just been told, wondering frantically if the man could be lying and then dismissing the idea; why on earth make up such a dangerous story? What

52

would be the point? Suddenly he thought he might have answered his own silent question.

'Where is your brother?' he asked.

'Hmm?' The guard started out of his reverie. Then, with a scowl, 'Dead.'

'Dead?'

The man was shaking his head. 'I *told* him not to!' he moaned. 'I said, "Don't you mess with the likes of Philippe de Loup, for there'll only be one outcome if you do," but he didn't listen.'

'So you mean,' Josse said slowly, thinking it out, 'that your brother followed de Loup and the knights to this fortress of his that night because he suspected they were up to no good? He spied on them in the expectation of seeing something he shouldn't and then attempted to make them pay for his silence?'

'That's about it, yes,' the guard agreed. 'For all the good it did him,' he added miserably. 'Now there's his rat-faced wife and his snot-nosed brats for me to care for, as if my own weren't enough.'

Josse hardly heard. 'But surely de Loup knows of your involvement?' he said. 'Why has he not ensured your permanent silence too?'

The guard gave a deep sigh. 'Because he doesn't know I was there. He thought my brother would see to the arrangements, just like he always did. It was only ever him.' Another sigh.

'Yet it was you, not him, who rowed the boat?' And you who saw the king's face, he added silently.

'Yes, well, I don't reckon old de Loup knew anything about that little boat.' His face creased in puzzlement. 'It was odd, come to think of it, for all the others went back the same way they came out. It was a private arrangement, I believe, between those three knights and my brother.'

'You don't know for sure?'

'No. See, my brother had cricked his neck that morning carrying a barrel of wine into de Loup's fortress. There was no possibility of him rowing a boat anywhere, never mind in the middle of the night in a gale.'

'So you acted as his substitute?'

'Yes, that I did. Weren't no need to tell anyone, so we didn't. I rowed the boat; I had the fee.'

'And de Loup never found out?'

'No, don't reckon he did. Like I just said, I'm not even certain he knew about it at all. As to who rowed it...' He shrugged.

After a while Josse said, 'I am sorry about your brother.' There was no reply except for an aggrieved sniff. Josse reached into the leather pouch at his belt and his hand closed on some of the coins within. Removing them, he said, 'You know, I believe, who sent me to you.'

'I do.'

'She commanded me to discover the

54

truth.'

The man's head shot up. 'I've told you the truth!'

'Aye, I believe you. This tale must not be told anywhere else.' He spoke with all the gravity and authority he could muster. 'Take these coins–' he held out a handful of gold and the guard instantly shot out his hands, palms up, to receive them – 'in compensation for your brother's death. What he did was both dangerous and wrong, but he has paid a terrible price, as have his wife, his children and you.'

'That we have,' the guard said heavily.

'But with this money I am also buying your silence,' Josse added softly. 'You have not told your story to anybody else?'

'*No!*' The denial shot out of him. 'Do you think I'm a fool? I dare not! Well, I told the queen of course. That secretary of hers admitted me to her presence, which is all but unheard of for a man like me, and we spoke alone. But I've not repeated my tale before this moment, I swear!'

'Why?' Josse asked suddenly.

The guard looked instantly suspicious. 'Why what?'

'Why tell anyone? Why bring this story to the queen's attention?'

'I would have thought that was obvious,' the guard said with a distinct sneer. 'Queen Eleanor's greatly loved here on the island. We may not see her very often but she's our special lady.' He sat up a little straighter. 'I thought it right that she should know what her precious son got up to.'

'I see.' It was an answer, of sorts, although Josse could not help but think that the gold now in the guard's hand was somehow more of a motive for having told what he knew than this alleged great love for the queen. 'Very well. So it's just the queen and you who know.'

'And you,' the guard pointed out.

Josse chose to ignore that. 'So,' he went on, 'if ever I hear rumours of the late king's presence here on the Île d'Oléron on a certain stormy night in March, I shall know who is spreading them. Yes?'

'Yes.' It was a croak.

'And I imagine you know full well what I shall do if that happens.'

'Yes,' the guard repeated. In the dim light his face looked pale and sweaty with fear.

Josse felt guilty; he was no Philippe de Loup, prepared to murder a man for spilling a secret, but this shivering, trembling man sitting before him did not know that. Which, for the sake of the late king's reputation and Queen Eleanor's peace of mind, was just as well.

Three

Josse and Brother Augustus were abroad very early the next morning. They made their quiet way to the stables, said to the grooms on duty that they were going to exercise their horses, and soon were riding down out of the castle. Josse had only the guard's vague description, but he could see the sun rising over the mainland behind him and, aware that the place known as World's End was on the north-west tip of Oléron, it was not difficult to find the right direction.

The May morning was bright but chilly, with a stiff breeze blowing out of the south-west bending the pine trees and setting the bright poppies in the grassy verges dancing. To begin with, there were a few huddled hamlets and solitary cottages dotted on either side of the rough track, but quite soon these dwindled, as did evidence that the islanders were using the land; within eight or ten miles of the settlement around the castle, cultivated fields were few and far between. The track grew steadily less distinct and it became clear that the dark guard had been quite right when he had said that nobody went up to World's End unless they had to.

The track curved westwards and all at once Josse and Gus were riding right by the shore. To their left, the land fell away in a low cliff, beyond which stretched a pebbly beach in which there were broad areas of sand, shining now as the surface water caught the early morning light. The wind had increased; it was easy to see why there were so few trees up here at the top end of the island. Those that survived the constant blast had sparse foliage, spindly branches and bent trunks. They looked, Josse reflected, like skinny old people distorted by long toil and endless hardship.

Now where, he wondered, had *that* miserable thought come from?

Without warning the strong wind grew still and straight away, as if it had been waiting its moment, a soft white mist crept up out of the rough ground. Looking out to sea, Josse was disturbed to see that a wide bank of fog was coming in towards them. The sun was quickly blotted out and suddenly it was very cold. He glanced across at Gus and was surprised to see that the lad's usually cheerful expression was quite absent; instead he was frowning, his normally smiling mouth drawn down into a scowl. Sensing Josse's eyes on him, he shivered and said, 'Not much of a place this, Sir Josse. Wish you'd left me to sleep in my warm bed.'

'Aye, Gussie, I agree, and I'm sorry I had

to bring you,' Josse replied. 'It's just that, as you see, it's a lonely spot and I wanted company.'

Instantly Gus's scowl melted. He looked faintly amazed, seemed to shrug, as if ridding himself of an unpleasant thought, and said, 'Well, Sir Josse, I reckon it's me who should say sorry, for moaning at you like that.' Slowly he shook his head. 'Can't think what came over me, but for a moment there it seemed as if all the light and joy in the world had been sucked away.'

Oh, dear Lord, Josse thought. He waited until he was sure he could speak normally and then said, 'All right now?'

'Yes,' Gus said stoutly. 'Let's ride on!'

They rode for another couple of miles along the shore. Presently they saw a large, dark shape looming up out of the swirling mist. Drawing closer, they made out a squat structure, its stark walls unbroken by any embrasure or window; it was in fact more like a fort or a guard tower than a human habitation. Perhaps, Josse thought, that was what it was. It must surely be Philippe de Loup's stronghold, and he was grateful now for the concealing fog. Were anyone up on those forbidding walls looking out, they would find it difficult to spot Josse and Gus.

They rode right up to the tower. It stood on a low rise, and all around it was a deep ditch filled with roughly hewn stone and stuck with poles whose ends had been sharpened into spikes. There did not appear to be any means of entry. Slowly Josse circled the walls and on the far side, facing inland, discovered a heavy, iron-bound oak door. It was fast shut and there seemed no way of getting across to it. Above the massive door, there was a series of three arrow slits; within, he realized, must be the room above the entrance of which the guard had spoken.

Gus had been going round the fortress in the opposite direction. Coming face to face with Josse, he said, 'There's the door, but how do they get to it?'

'They probably sprout big black wings and fly,' Josse said lightly.

Gus's face fell. 'Oh, don't, Sir Josse,' he whispered. 'Not here.'

Josse had to concede that the lad had a point.

Gus had leaped down from his horse and was kneeling down on the bank of the ditch. After a moment, he said, 'Sir, I think I can see how it's done.'

I'm blessed if I can, Josse thought. Sliding off Horace's back, he went to stand beside Gus. 'How?'

'See, there's a way down this side of the ditch and it winds along the bottom for a bit, then goes up there—' he pointed – 'to where there's a sort of platform of earth just under the wall.'

'But the wall's solid,' Josse observed. 'There is no way in there, Gussie.'

60

Gus straightened up, still staring at the wall. He raised his eyes to look up, then down again, and then he repeated the action. He smiled. 'Yes there is. They throw a rope with a hook up to the top of the wall and, when it bites, someone climbs up – it's not far, only perhaps four men's height – and they scramble over the battlements, down the steps, open the door and push out a plank bridge. Look, Sir Josse,' he added, his voice high with excitement, 'you can see where the planks have lain!'

He was right. The ground on the near side of the ditch opposite the door was beaten hard and flat. Now that Josse knew where to look, he could see what Gus had noticed: distinct marks and scratches up the wall above the little platform. Just the sort of marks that would result from someone climbing up repeatedly.

'Well done, Gussie,' Josse said with genuine admiration. 'What a sharp pair of eyes you have, lad!'

Gus said modestly, 'Oh, it was nothing.' Then, as if embarrassed by the praise, he hurried on to say, 'But why do they take such trouble, Sir Josse? D'you think there's something really terrible inside that has to stay hidden away?'

Josse had not shared the dark guard's revelations with his young companion; he simply said, 'Aye, Gussie, I'm afraid there probably is.'

Gus nodded sagely. Then, 'Reckon I could get us in there, providing there's an access on the top. If you want to, that is?'

'Oh, er, aye, I do want to, but it's quite a climb, Gussie. It could be dangerous.'

Gus smiled. 'I was a fairground entertainer before I was a lay brother,' he said. 'I can still tumble, turn somersaults and walk a tight-rope, although I'll admit there's not much call for such tricks at Hawkenlye and the habit gets in the way. That little old wall is no great challenge to me.'

Josse returned the grin. 'Pity we haven't got a rope. We'll have to—'

'Aha!' Gus got up, hurried over to his horse and drew down his saddlebags. Opening one, he said, 'Rope, plus a pretty pack of food I wheedled out of that serving maid with the fair hair and the dimple, and a small flagon of beer.'

'Now do you see why I didn't allow you to stay in your bed? Gus, you're a marvel!'

Gus was already swinging the long length of rope. 'It's not much use without a grap-pling hook,' he said dejectedly, 'and that was the one thing I didn't think to bring.'

Josse was quite determined not to be beaten. Standing back a few paces from the ditch, he stared up at the crenellated top of the tower wall. 'Can you swing a rope as well as climb one?' he demanded.

'Yes.'

'Then what about that?' He pointed.

62

'Above the door and then to the right for a couple of arms' length – see? There's a place where there are two gaps in the parapet close together, and the raised stonework between them is quite narrow. Could you circle it with the rope?'

Gus looked, for what seemed quite a long time. Then he said, 'Aye.' Swiftly he made a running knot in one end of the rope, threaded the other end through it and swung the loop over his head a few times. He stepped up to the edge of the ditch, took careful aim and let the loop fly. The first and second times, it missed and the rope came snaking back down again; the third time, he found his range and the loop popped over the slim upraised section of wall and held fast. Holding on to the other end of the rope, Gus slipped quickly down into the ditch and up the other side and, before Josse could say anything except 'Be careful!' he was shinning up the rope.

Josse was so carried away with the thrill of what Gus had just achieved that for a perilous moment he had forgotten that falling into a ditch full of sharp stones and pointed stakes was not the only danger. As this realization flashed its urgent warning in his head, he called out, 'Gussie! Come back!'

Gus paused, swung himself round so he could see Josse and said, 'Why? What's the matter?'

Trying to shout quietly, which was quite

impossible, Josse said slowly and deliberately, 'There may be people within.'

Gus paled. Instantly he slipped back down the rope and landed on soft feet on the little platform.

'Leave the rope,' Josse called, 'but come back over here – we'll watch for a while.'

Gus nodded his understanding and soon was back with Josse on the other side of the ditch. Quickly and quietly they fetched the horses, which had wandered away a short distance in search of grazing, and Gus replaced his saddlebags. Then they led their mounts over to where, inland from the fortress, three of the stunted, distorted trees huddled together. There were wind-blasted gorse bushes at their feet and they made as good a place of concealment as Josse and Gus were likely to find out there in the wilderness. They tethered the horses, then settled on the thin, spiky grass to begin their vigil.

As the morning wore on, the strengthening sun began to burn off the mist, helped by the returning south-westerly wind, but then, just as before, abruptly the wind fell and the mists rolled back again. No birds sang; all was eerily still, save for the constant swirling of the strange white fog. Beside him, Josse felt Gus shiver. Well, he thought, I know one sure cure for chilly flesh and low spirits. He stood up, fetched Gus's saddlebags and broke out the food and drink.

They watched for a long time. Nobody approached the tower; nobody emerged. Once or twice Josse went up to it and walked slowly round, calling out, 'Halloa! Halloa within!' but each time met with no response. If there was anyone inside, he or she was keeping very still and very quiet.

Finally Josse made up his mind. 'Come on,' he said, hauling Gus to his feet. 'Now or never.'

Gus grinned. 'Better make it now, then.'

They left the horses tethered by the trees and went back to the tower. As before, Gus descended into the ditch, clambered up to the platform and began to climb the rope. This time, he did not stop. Josse watched nervously as he reached the top of the wall and, with no apparent difficulty, slipped over it. Then he disappeared. Josse waited for a few unbearable moments. He was on the point of calling out when Gus's head reappeared.

'We were right!' Gus cried. 'There's a door up here and it's bolted on the outside but not locked. I'm going in.'

'Watch out! Be careful, Gus!' Josse called. Stupid, *stupid*, he told himself. The lad's creeping about unarmed inside the isolated tower of a man suspected of worshipping the devil, abusing and maybe killing young boys, and I tell him to be careful!

The next endless minutes were some of the worst in Josse's life. He tried to fight it but seemed powerless to prevent the frightful images flooding his mind. Gus at dagger point. Gus bound and imprisoned. Gus dead, that cheery young spirit snuffed out, and all my fault ... no. *Stop.*

Just as he knew he could not stay there doing nothing for another instant, there was the sound of bolts being shot back and the door to the tower opened. Gus looked out and said brightly, 'All clear! The place is empty and I've found the planks. I'll slide one across and you can come in.'

Weak with relief, Josse hurried to receive the end of the heavy plank as Gus pushed it out. Such was his state of mind that, although the plank was only a hand's span and it was a long fall to the bottom of the ditch, he barely noticed the peril of his own entry into de Loup's stronghold.

He stood with Gus inside the door. They were in a large stone room, quite bare, out of which a spiral stair ran up. There were no arrow slits here; the only light was that coming in through the door. The air was damp, dank and very cold, and the walls ran with moisture. Rings were set in the stones, as if for tethering animals. He glanced across at the stair and, indicating it with a jerk of his head, went over to it and began to climb.

He experienced the strangest sensation as his feet found each successive step; it was as if he were trying to climb up into some medium other than ordinary air, one that had a mass and a weight of its own and that did not want him coming up into it. He was having to make such an effort that he was soon panting from the exertion and it felt as if a vast force was pushing down on the top of his head. He heard Gus gasping for breath; it was quite a relief to realize that it was not only he who was affected.

He struggled to the top of the spiral stair and emerged into the room above, stepping aside to let Gus come out and stand beside him.

Gus looked frightened. 'What is it, Sir Josse?' he hissed. 'What's here that we can't see?'

'I don't know, Gussie.' Josse forced himself to speak aloud, in as normal a voice as he could manage. It would not help if both of them were too scared to do anything but whisper. 'Did you remark this ... this presence on your way down to open the door?'

Gus forced a smile. 'Reckon I was in so much of a hurry to let you in that I wouldn't have noticed a five-legged cow standing in my way. Wh–what d'you think it is?' Despite his best attempts, the boy's fears were gaining on him.

'I think,' Josse said forcefully, 'that evil deeds have been done here and that they have left their mark, but they were done by human men, Gussie. Not ghosts, not ghouls, not devils, but men. Remember that.'

'Human men,' Gus repeated. 'Right you

are, Sir Josse.' He did not sound altogether reassured.

Josse's heart filled with affection and pity for him. 'You know what would be really helpful, Gussie?'

Gus looked at him very apprehensively but he managed to say bravely, 'No, sir. What? Anything I can do, tell me.'

'Well,' Josse said, adopting a carefully anxious expression, 'the worst thing that could happen would be for someone to come along and surprise us here inside the fortress, so if you can find the courage, could you, do you think, go down again, cross over the plank and keep watch? Then you can give me warning if anyone approaches.'

Gus's relief was very obvious, but still he steeled himself to protest. 'Reckon that's giving me the easy job, Sir Josse,' he remarked. 'Me stay out there nice and safe while you prowl around here on your own? Oh, no.'

'Oh, yes,' Josse said firmly. 'And, dear old Gussie, that is an order.'

Gus paused for one more moment. Then he turned, raced down the stairs and Josse heard his footsteps thumping on the plank.

Now, he thought, I am alone.

He waited until his alarmed heartbeat had slowed a little, then began a careful pacing of the room above the entrance. Just as the dark guard had described, there was a row of arrow-slit windows right over the door, but

other than that the stone walls were unbroken. In the far corner of the room, Josse
could make out a ladder whose upper end
disappeared through a trapdoor in the roof;
it must lead to the battlements and perhaps
also to one or two chambers on the upper
floor. If de Loup and his knights made a
habit of coming here, they would have to
have somewhere to eat and sleep, and this
barren, evil room had no domestic facilities
of any kind.

What it did have, Josse saw as he began a
careful circling of it, was a long table made
of smooth, unembellished oak set a couple
of paces out from the wall opposite to the
arrow slits. Its shape called something to
mind, and after a moment's thought he
realized with a shiver of dread that it looked
like an altar. It stood up on a stone dais
reached by three wide, shallow steps, and at
either end there stood heavy iron candle-
sticks, man-height, each bearing three ex-
pensive beeswax candles. Pushed up against
the wall behind the altar was a large wooden
chest. Josse stepped round the altar – un-
thinkingly he gave it a wide berth – and
crouched down in front of the chest.

It too was made of oak, and bound with
bands of iron. It was fastened with a hasp,
which, to Josse's surprise, lifted to his tentative touch. He raised the lid of the chest and
peered inside. Because of the poor light, it
was difficult to see what was inside, but

straight away the smell hit him.

Instinctively he drew back and was about to bang down the lid of the chest. Then he thought, but I have to know. That is why we are doing all this. Steeling himself, he leaned forward again.

Moving aside slightly so that a little more light fell on the contents of the chest, he saw that it contained folded cloth. Picking up the top layer, he stood up and shook out the folds of the material. It was a robe, made of silvery-grey silk, its wide skirts stained with dark brown. Dried blood, Josse thought instantly. But the stench was not that of old blood; it was faecal. What in heaven's name had been going on here?

He put the robe aside and drew out the next folded item. This too was a robe; this time deep blue. He took out the rest of the chest's contents: thirteen robes, the ones at the bottom of the pile apparently older than the rest and with the air of not having been used in a long time, for they were dusty and the fabric was thin and spotted with age. Slowly Josse folded them all up again and stored them back in the chest.

As he tucked in the folds of the silver-grey robe, he noticed that there was a device embroidered on the left breast. He studied it and made out the figure of a woman in a strange horned headdress. She appeared to be standing in a boat shaped like the crescent moon. He rummaged back down the pile of robes and found that every one bore the same device.

It was with a huge sense of relief that finally he closed and fastened the chest. He stood up, his knees protesting, and straightened his back. He moved round to the front of the altar, staring at it and trying not to let the terrible images it seemed to transmit lodge in his mind. No. *No.*

He took a step back, then another. The heel of his boot caught against a slightly raised stone slab and hastily he looked down. He saw beneath his feet some marks: brown marks, dry now but, from the pattern of splashes, clearly once liquid. He bent down and took a cautious sniff. Very faintly came the metallic smell of old blood.

It was enough. Dear Lord, it was more than enough. He flew across the room, down the spiral stairs and came to a halt in the doorway. 'Gus! *Gussie!*'

Alarmed by his tone, Gus, who had been standing on guard across the ditch, spun round. 'Sir Josse? Are you all right?'

'Aye, my lad, aye, or at least I will be when we get away from this frightful place. Come over – it's time for you to repeat your entrance procedure in reverse.'

Gus hurried across the plank and, as soon as Josse was safely over on the far side, drew it back inside the fortress. Then he slammed the door, and Josse heard the bolts shoot home. He waited impatiently for Gus to climb the spiral staircase and the ladder and then, when Gus appeared on the battlements, called up to him, 'Is there a way you can climb down and bring the rope away with you?' It would be a mistake, he realized, to leave evidence that someone had been inside.

'Yes, I reckon so,' Gus called back. 'It's good and long, so I'll tie one end round my waist–' he did so – 'and loop the rope round the stone bastion, then lower myself down using the free end.'

It sounded highly dangerous. 'But you—' Josse began.

'Don't worry. Just watch, I'll be all right!'

In no time Gus was bouncing down the wall, fending himself away with his feet and feeding the rope hand over hand. He reached the bottom – Josse let out the breath he had been holding – and jerked the rope free of its support, catching it as it fell into his waiting arms. He looped it over his shoulder, then scrambled down into the ditch and up the other side.

Wordlessly Josse put his arms round the young man in a hard hug. 'Well done,' he muttered. Then, releasing him, added, 'Now, let's pray our luck holds while we make our escape.'

It did. Whatever Philippe de Loup was doing that May afternoon, he was doing it well away from the Île d'Oléron. Josse and Gus kicked their horses to a canter. Then, as if the animals were as affected as their riders by the brooding, lowering atmosphere of World's End, both broke into a furious gallop.

As the desolate north-west corner of the island was left behind, the mist cleared and the sun came out.

Part Two

The Shining City

Four

Although it was late in the afternoon by the time Josse and Gus were back in the vicinity of Eleanor's castle at the other end of the island, Josse was gripped by the desire to get away to the mainland. Despite the sunshine that had streamed down on them once they were out from that eerie, malevolent mist, he had gone on feeling cold and shivery. It was as if some malign influence that hung around Philippe de Loup's fortress had adhered to him like a deadly cloak, for there had been evil in that dreadful place: Josse had almost been able to taste it.

He made up his mind. 'We're not staying in the queen's castle tonight,' he announced to Gus. The relief that flooded Gus's face suggested he had been fighting the same sense of horror as Josse. 'There's no point,' he went on, 'since our business here is done.'

'Right, Sir Josse,' Gus said. Then, tentatively, 'D'you mean us to leave the island right now, then?'

'Aye.' Josse heard Gus mutter a fervent 'Thank God', which exactly echoed his own sentiments. Thinking that it was only fair to give the lad some sort of explanation, he said, 'I needed to look inside that place up at World's End, Gussie, and thanks to your ingenuity and your nimble hands and strong feet, we've managed to do so.' He glanced at his companion. The lad must be aching to ask why they'd had to break into de Loup's stronghold and what Josse had been looking for, but he was a lay brother, trained in the habit of obedience, and he didn't.

They rode on in silence for a while. Josse was thinking hard and eventually he came to the conclusion that if Gus were to share the perils of this mission, as indeed he already had, then it really was only fair to tell him just why he was being asked to risk his life. I need not tell him the whole story, Josse thought; the outline should suffice.

'Gussie,' he began, 'the queen has given me a job to do and it looks as if it's going to be dangerous.'

'I'll help you, Sir Josse,' the lad said gallantly. 'The lady abbess didn't want you going into peril by yourself and she said I was to watch out for you,' he added with a touching note of pride.

'And there's nobody I'd rather have,' Josse said sincerely. 'But the peril is real, lad.'

'I know, sir,' Gus said, his voice hushed. 'I saw inside that fort place.' He hesitated. 'Wh–what d'you think they get up to there?'

'I do not know for certain,' Josse said gravely. 'Rumour has it that they practise devil worship and—' No. There was surely no need to tell this innocent young man the rest. 'And other things,' he finished lamely.

'There was a smell like the slaughter house,' Gus said slowly. 'A smell of blood and of ... Well, terrified animals ... er ... well, they shit themselves, and there was that smell as well. Wasn't there?' The use of the coarse word had made him blush.

'Aye, Gussie, I noticed it too.' He thought again of the stains on the silver-grey robe.

'D'you reckon they sacrifice animals up there in that room, Sir Josse? Is that it?'

Well, humans were animals, of a sort.

'Aye, Gussie,' Josse said. 'I reckon they do.'

'Oh!' Gus looked aghast. Then he seemed to pull himself together. 'Is that the mission, then, sir? To find out what the men do up there in the fort and tell the queen so that she can stop it?'

'That's a part of it,' Josse acknowledged, 'but there's more, although I'm afraid I can't tell you the rest.'

Gus appeared to be ahead of him: 'There'll be grand and famous names involved, I'll bet,' he said perceptively. 'Some great lord or knight, I'll warrant, and the queen's worried because rich and powerful men ought not to behave like that, and she'll want to—'

'Aye, lad,' Josse said, interrupting hurriedly. Good Lord, if the lad were allowed to go on with that train of thought, before long he would have guessed the whole sordid, terrible tale. 'So our task is to find out who

79

is involved and discover all that we can about them. They're not at the tower, we know that, and I very much doubt if they're lodging anywhere near Queen Eleanor's castle. I think the best thing we can do is return to the mainland and try to pick up the trail.'

'Do we have any names, sir?' Gus asked. 'We'll have our work cut out if not.'

Josse grinned. 'Aye. We have the name of the man who owns that fortress. He's called Philippe de Loup.'

Gus's eyes widened in astonishment. 'I've heard that name! Not exactly like you just said it, but the "Loup" bit.'

'In what context?' Josse demanded.

'Saul and I were going to our quarters the first night we were here and there was a band of children playing tag out in the yard behind the kitchens. It was quite late and this big fat woman came out looking for them because it was their bedtime. Anyway, two of them were being really naughty and wouldn't come even when she kept on calling, and she said, "If you're not in by the time it's dark, the Loup will get you," and then they came scurrying in quick as you like.' He shook his head. 'I reckoned she was referring to some sort of local bogeyman. I never imagined he was *real*.'

'Perhaps he's both,' Josse said slowly. 'If fearsome rumours have built up about that tower out there on the point, then its master would indeed have become a figure with which to threaten naughty children.' Perhaps too, he added silently, for one or two local boys it became more than just a threat. That thought, though, was dreadful and he tried to put it out of his mind.

They were close to the queen's castle now and with great relief Josse turned his attention to practical matters. 'We'll leave the horses by the gate, Gussie, and slip in quickly to pick up our packs.'

'I have mine with me.' Gus indicated the two saddlebags slung across his horse's back.

'Even better,' Josse said, managing a laugh. 'Then you wait outside the gates with the horses while I fetch mine. I'll seek out the chamberlain and tell him we've been called away. The sooner we're away from here, the better.'

Gus suddenly looked fearful. 'He might come after us, this de Loup, if he finds out we've been nosing around his old tower, mightn't he?'

Josse was torn between honesty and the desire to reassure. Honesty won. 'Aye, Gussie, well he might. But,' he added hastily, 'even if he finds out we were there, which isn't very likely because I don't think we left any sign of our little visit, he'd have to discover who we were, where we came from and where we'd gone. All of which suggests to me that the sooner we get off Oléron and lose ourselves over on the mainland, the safer we shall be.'

By nightfall they were many miles from the
Île d'Oléron. An incurious ferryman had
taken them over the straits in company with
a group of others and, once on the mainland, they had ridden hard for several hours.
They had stopped at a tavern to eat a surprisingly tasty supper, and Josse had ordered
wine. Then they had gone back outside into
the warm evening and ridden for another
hour. When finally they stopped, it was on
the edge of a pine forest right away from any
human habitation: Josse was intent on
burying their trail.

Wrapped in cloaks and blankets, they
made themselves comfortable on their beds
of pine needles. Almost immediately, Josse
heard Gus's breathing deepen as he slipped
into sleep. It was a soothing sound, but Josse
was wakeful. As they had been riding along,
he had been working out a plan; now he
needed to go over it again to see if it was
sound.

King Richard and these mysterious
Knights of Arcturus had been at Philippe de
Loup's tower early in March. Was the late
king one of the Thirteen Nobles? Were the
two who had hastened away with him? It
seemed likely. For some reason, the trio had
left separately and been rowed out to a
waiting ship by the dark guard. The rest of
the knights might have left later that night,
or the next morning, or they might have

stayed on for a few days. For sure, they had not been there when Josse and Gus had gone into the tower, and there had been no sign of recent occupancy. Nevertheless, Josse had no way of knowing when Philippe de Loup last left his tower, or his present where-abouts. Not that it really mattered, because he did know the subsequent movements of one of the others. King Richard had gone from the Île d'Oléron to Châlus, where on the evening of 26 March he had been struck by the arrow that subsequently killed him.

In the absence of any other option, Josse made up his mind to follow in the late king's footsteps. There was really nothing else he could do. With that decided, he turned on his side and was soon asleep.

It was well over a hundred miles from Oléron to Châlus. Josse and Gus had cover-ed a good part of the journey in their fast ride the previous evening and now Josse reckoned they had less than eighty miles to go. They might make it in two more days if the weather stayed fair and no mishap occur-red.

On the morning of the third day, they climbed a low ridge and from its summit looked down on the devastation that had once been the peaceful land surrounding the castle of Châlus. The castle itself was still standing, although the gaping holes in its walls and the blasted, ruined entrance showed clear evidence of the besiegers' fury. Broken siege engines stood on the churned-up earth like the skeletons of some huge, nightmarish monsters. Some distance from the castle, under the eaves of an area of thin woodland, there was evidence that a long, deep pit had recently been dug and filled in. Beside it, there was a group of women kneeling in the mud. They were weeping. Whatever use might have once been intended for the fields around the castle must surely now have been abandoned, for the land was deeply scarred and every living thing upon it, from grass to tall trees, had been blasted away.

This, Josse reflected sadly, was what happened when a castle was besieged by a man like King Richard.

He and Gus rode on. Ahead of them on the track, two men were trying to get an ox cart out of a deep rut. One man was pushing at the right-hand wheel of the cart, the other dragging at the oxen's harness, calling out encouragement to the beasts and, when that failed, swirling his whip high in the air and bringing it cracking down on their pale backs.

Gus was off his horse and running to the man pushing at the wheel. 'I'll help!' he cried. 'No need to whip the oxen, master–' he turned to the other man – 'they're doing their best.'

Josse saw the man's frustration turn to

anger. He too dismounted and, hurrying over, said to the man with the whip, 'Forgive my young friend – he meant no criticism.'

'Hmm.' The man was still scowling.

Josse hurried to join Gus. 'We'll both help you,' he said firmly. 'With three of us heaving at this wheel, we ought to get it out of the rut.'

The man with the whip apparently saw the sense of that and reverted to pulling on the oxen's harness and reminding the animals what was in store for them back in their pen. Soon the combined efforts of Josse, Gus and the other carter got the wheel moving and the cart trundled on its way.

The man who had been pushing at the wheel hung back, sweating and panting, to thank his unexpected helpers. 'That's a rare act of Christian kindness,' he observed, wiping his face with a dirty scarf. 'And we haven't seen many of those around here of late, I can tell you.'

Nodding at Gus to see to the horses, Josse fell into step beside the man as he slowly followed behind the cart. 'Looks to have been a bad business,' he remarked, his gaze turning to the ruined castle. 'He was after treasure, or so I heard.'

'He was,' the man agreed. He seemed as reluctant as Josse to refer to the late king by name. 'Not that there was any. They say there was a pot of old coins, but I never saw hide nor hair of it. The rest of it – all that talk

85

of huge gold statues and the like – was just a wild story. I have no idea who or what began it,' he added piously.

I wonder, Josse thought. It seemed highly likely that something had started the rumour; people didn't normally invent such things totally out of the blue. Perhaps some man out ploughing with his ox team – *this* ox team? – had turned up something else besides the gold coins and, although he had tried to hide his discovery and keep his new-found riches to himself, word had leaked out and, in time, reached the ears of the king. It was possible, Josse thought.

'So the king ended up empty-handed,' he said.

'The king ended up dead,' the man corrected him. 'God save his soul,' he added, giving Josse a crafty glance.

'Amen,' Josse murmured.

'The aftermath was vicious,' the man said heavily. 'Oh, not straight away after he was shot – it all went quiet then, while everyone waited to see if— to see what would happen. The king, he sends for the archer who shot him and asks why, and the archer says, "Well, you killed my father and my brothers, and you were doing your best to kill me too, so do what you like with me and I'll gladly accept it if it means you'll be dead at the end of it, because it'll be worth it."'

'That was quite a speech,' Josse said, impressed.

'The king thought so too. He forgave the archer and said he was to be released.'

'Surely *that* was a Christian act?' Josse said.

The man gave a bitter laugh. 'It would have been, if the king's orders had been obeyed.'

'Oh. Weren't they?'

'No, of course not. Soon as he was dead, that captain of mercenaries of his got the archer back, flayed him alive and hanged him.'

Josse, who knew of the mercenary Mercadier and his reputation, said nothing.

'They stormed the castle the night the king died,' the man went on matter-of-factly. 'Those who didn't die in the fighting were hanged from the battlements.'

'Nobody was left alive?' Josse was hardly surprised; it was the usual way if a besieged castle refused to surrender and was ultimately defeated and, this time, the fury of the king's men would have been further fuelled by his death.

'Not a one, out of those caught inside.' The man sighed. 'They do say a few slipped out by night once it was certain what would happen, but who knows what's become of them?' He shrugged.

Who knows indeed? Josse thought.

They walked on in silence. Glancing round, Josse saw that Gus was pacing along behind, leading the horses. He said to the man beside him, 'I'm looking for a knight by the name of Philippe de Loup. Have you heard of him?' It was a long shot to suggest that if King Richard had come here to Châlus, then de Loup had come with him, but it was worth a try.

Immediately Josse was very glad he had made that try, for the man turned to spit in the ground and said, 'Him. Yes, I have.'

'I heard tell–' Josse lowered his voice to a murmur – 'that he belongs to some strange group called the Thirteen Knights, or something, and I—'

'I don't know nothing about the Thirteen Nobles,' the man said very firmly, although his unconscious correction of 'Thirteen Knights' to 'Thirteen Nobles' suggested quite the opposite.

'But you know of de Loup?'

After a pause, the man said, 'Yes.'

'He has lands around here?'

The man shook his head. 'Not that I know of. He came with the king, along with a few others including that light-eyed friend of his ... What's his name?' he added to himself, his brow creasing in concentration. There was a brief pause, and then he snapped his fingers and said, 'Ambrois de Quercy, that's the man.'

'Is de Loup still here?' It seemed too much to hope that he was.

'No, he's long gone,' the man replied.

Josse felt himself slump in dejection. It had seemed promising for a moment and now—

'De Quercy's not left, if that's any use to

you,' the man said.

'Where is he?' The question snapped out of Josse and he hoped his informant would not take offence and clam up.

Fortunately, the man did not seem to have noticed; he was pointing into the distance, where beyond the woodland and the grieving women Josse could make out a group of tents. 'That there's where they tend the wounded. You'll find de Quercy in the end tent.'

'He was wounded in the fighting?'

The man laughed hoarsely. 'No. He's tortured with the bellyache and his bowels have turned to water. With any luck,' he added viciously, 'the bugger'll die.'

A short while later, Josse and Gus drew up beside the tents and, dismounting, Josse handed over Horace's reins. He had given the carter a couple of coins and, hiding them under his tunic so fast that they appeared to vanish, the man had laid a finger to the side of his nose and given Josse a wink, as if to say, All that's our little secret, isn't it? If the man dying of dysentery could put Josse on to de Loup's trail, as he was fervently hoping he could, then those coins were a small price to pay.

He entered the tent. On both sides were rows of low cots and straw mattresses, each bearing a sick or wounded man. In attendance were black-clad nuns, vividly bringing to Josse's mind the Hawkenlye nursing sisters, and one of them approached him with a look of enquiry on her weary face.

'I seek Ambrois de Quercy,' Josse said without preamble. The sister, he was sure, was in no mood for small talk.

'Over there.' She gestured. 'Second cot down. He's very sick,' she added in a hiss. 'You'd better be quick.'

Josse walked across to the bed where de Quercy lay. He did indeed look near death. His face was as pale as the linen sheet drawn up to his neck, and his eyes had sunk in his skull. His hair was wet with sweat.

'Ambrois de Quercy?' Josse said softly.

The man's eyes flew open. They were pale and almost colourless. 'Who wants to know?' he rasped.

'Hugh de Villiers,' Josse said, making a name up out of the air.

'What do you want?' De Quercy's eyes closed again.

'I seek Philippe de Loup.'

The man smiled, the expression stretching his skin horribly. 'You do, do you? You and a hundred others.'

Josse stored that away to think about later. 'Is he here?'

'No.' Unconsciously echoing the carter's words, de Quercy added, 'Long gone.'

'Where?'

The dying man's eyes opened again. 'Get me some water,' he commanded, jerking his head towards a jug and a cup that stood on the floor beside his cot. Josse did as he was asked, holding the cup to de Quercy's lips. After a couple of sips he turned his head away. Then, 'Chartres.'

'*Chartres?*'

'Yes, he has gone to Chartres,' the man repeated, saying the words with insulting slowness and clarity as if addressing an idiot.

'Why?' Josse was still stunned by the news.

'They are building a new cathedral there. Have you not heard?' De Quercy persisted with the same insulting tone. 'De Loup wishes to make his own *special* contribution.' The cracked, bleeding lips spread in a cruelly sardonic smile.

Why, Josse wondered, the emphasis on the word 'special'? 'You mean—' he began.

But de Quercy had started coughing, so violently that his whole frame shook. Josse refilled the cup and offered it. De Quercy drank greedily, coughed some more and started to choke. One of the nuns hurried over, elbowed Josse out of the way and, putting one strong arm behind de Quercy's shoulders, raised him up off his pillow. She thumped his back and a lump of something bloody shot out of his mouth to land with a plop on the sheet. The coughing lessened and then stopped, and she laid him back on his mattress, pulling back the stained sheet and sponging at it with her apron.

Josse stared down at de Quercy's tunic,

uncovered now. On the left breast, over the heart, there was a small embroidered insignia of a woman in a horned headdress standing in a boat shaped like the crescent moon.

Josse slipped out of the tent before anyone could think to ask just what he thought he had been doing disturbing a sick man like that. He hurried over to where Gus stood with the horses, and said curtly, 'Mount up, Gus – we must get away from here.'

Gus instantly obeyed. As Josse set off up the track leading around the woodland and off to the north, kicking Horace to a canter and then, as people, animals and tents were quickly left behind, to a gallop, he could hear the hoofs of Gus's horse pounding along behind. When they had been riding fast for some time, he slowed, then stopped. Turning to Gus, he told him what de Quercy had said.

'Philippe de Loup's gone to Chartres!' Gus looked every bit as surprised as Josse had been. Then, surprise turning to apprehension, Gus whispered, 'That's where Abbess Helewise has gone.'

'Aye, lad, I know, but I doubt she'll be there yet,' Josse said reassuringly, 'and even if she is, de Loup doesn't know her, nor she him. There's no danger to her from him, I'm certain.' He wasn't quite as sure as he was making out, but there was no need to admit it. 'Come on, Gussie,' he added, quite sharply, for Gus was still shaking his head anxiously. 'I need you to think.'

'Sorry, Sir Josse. What am I to think about?'

Josse smiled, and Gus's tense expression eased. 'De Quercy told me that de Loup has gone to Chartres because they're building the new cathedral and de Loup wants to make some special contribution,' he explained. 'Now what, young Gussie, are we to make of that?'

Gus rested an elbow on his saddle-bow and leaned on it. 'Well,' he said after a moment, 'he could just have meant that, like most rich folk, de Loup is going to pay for a bit of glass, or a statue, or something.'

'De Loup?' Josse said disbelievingly. 'The man who owns that evil tower and puts it to unimaginably terrible use?'

'Maybe making a show of giving money for the new cathedral is intended to cover up how evil he is,' Gus said shrewdly.

'Perhaps.' Josse sighed. 'But it doesn't seem right...'

'On the other hand,' Gus went on slowly, 'maybe he's planning mischief. Maybe "special contribution" means he's going to do something destructive.'

'The cathedral has suffered more than its fair share of mysterious fires,' Josse murmured. 'Is it— Could it be that a man of Philippe de Loup's nature cannot bear to see something good and holy rising from the ashes, and so has gone to Chartres to make sure it doesn't?'

'They had a fire five years back.' Gus spoke eagerly now, his words tumbling out. 'One of the pilgrims back at Hawkenlye told me. Lightning struck the old cathedral and started the blaze and everyone feared that their precious relic had gone up in flames. At Chartres, they've got the Blessed Virgin's nightgown, you know, Sir Josse, the one she wore when she gave birth to Our Lord.'

Josse smiled. 'So I've heard, Gussie. I believe it's called the Sancta Camisia.'

'Anyway, it turned out that some of the old priests had managed to grab the nightie and they'd hidden in the crypt or something with it, and it was quite undamaged.' His face awestruck, he whispered, 'It was a miracle, wasn't it, Sir Josse?'

'Perhaps it was, Gussie, or—'

But Gus wasn't listening. 'What if someone like de Loup or one of his old knights started that fire and it wasn't the lightning at all?' he said. 'And, now that they're getting on with building the new cathedral, he's gone to Chartres to burn that one down too?'

'Why would he do that, Gussie?' Josse asked, although, remembering the palpable malevolence in the room in the tower, he thought he already knew.

'Because he's bad,' Gus said simply.

Josse had heard enough. He gathered his

reins, nudged Horace's sides with his knees and moved off. 'Come on,' he said. Gus, understanding, clicked to his horse and took up his place beside Josse.

By Josse's best calculations, the abbess and her party could hardly have reached Chartres before today, but he and Gus were still two hundred miles away. They had been riding hard since they left Oléron; both they and their horses needed a few lazy days, not another long journey.

But that was just too bad.

Five

In a well-concealed encampment close to the city of Chartres, Joanna sat on the fringe of a circle of her people thinking back over the past two years. This was her third visit to the city and the tension in the air was far more noticeable than ever before. Her people's habitual expression was one of serenity that changed readily and frequently to joy; now they moved through their daily round looking preoccupied and worried. What was more, as Joanna well knew, matters could only get worse.

The grave problem facing Joanna and all her kind was that the cathedral of Chartres had been built on one of their most sacred places. Beneath the hill where successive cathedrals had been sited there was an ancient sanctuary cave; within the cave, the Well of the Strong poured out its vital earth energy. To Joanna's people, this precious, holy spot was the dwelling place of the Mother Goddess and for countless generations they had honoured her there, setting up her image in the form of a beautiful dark-wood statue of the fecund, heavily pregnant goddess.

The original church, they had told Joanna, had been erected over the sanctuary centuries ago, when the new religion started to spread. Successive constructions had followed, each larger and more ornate than its predecessor, each steadily nudging out the ancient spirituality of the site and putting in its place the version that the new priests believed to be the only one. Ironically, Joanna's teacher said, the Virgin Mary, whom the new men worshipped, was not in fact very different in character and nature from the Mother Goddess. It was only the black-robed priests who insisted that it was heresy to say so.

For the people who still followed the old ways, this was the problem. To them, it did not matter in which guise the Great Mother was revered and they would have been perfectly happy to share their sacred place with the newcomers. To them, as the old teacher put it, all gods were one god and behind them was the truth. It was evident, as in the beginning they tried to explain to the new priests, that the power coming from the figure who now had to be called the Virgin Mary was the same dynamism that the people of the old religion had sensed so forcefully emanating from the Mother Goddess. As the decades and the centuries slowly passed, however, it became clear that the priests did not feel the same tolerance towards them.

The beginning of the end had come, the old teacher sadly told Joanna, when three hundred years ago Charles the Bald, grandson of Charlemagne, presented the cathedral with its most precious relic. Legend had it that this relic had been given to Charlemagne by the patriarch of Jerusalem while the great emperor was on a pilgrimage to the Holy City. It was, or so they said, the tunic worn by the Virgin Mary when she gave birth to her holy son.

'And is it?' Joanna had demanded.

The old man had sighed. 'Child, it makes no difference whether it is or it isn't. The pilgrims who come to the cathedral believe that it is and so to them that has become a truth. The garment itself has responded to the faith of the worshippers and, even were it not sacred to begin with, it has acquired sanctity now.'

Joanna had puzzled over this. 'But if it isn't

the Virgin's tunic–' and she could not find it in her to believe that it was, thinking it far more likely that a clever Jerusalem merchant had got hold of some old cloth and made several such garments to sell at great cost to gullible Crusaders – 'how can it acquire sanctity?'

The old man took her hand and held it in a hard grip. 'Because worship imbues a place, or indeed an object, with special powers,' he said. His grip tightened. 'That is why we are here, child! That is why we cannot give up our most sacred place without a struggle! It was holy from the start of time, which is why our forebears were first attracted to it. Over the centuries, our people have gone there to praise the Great Mother and take offerings to her, and they have poured out their love, their prayers, their hopes, joys, aspirations and sorrows into her receptive ears. She is there, she always was, and she always will be. But also we are there; she holds our past as a people.' He paused, then added softly, 'She holds our heart.'

Joanna understood as well as she believed she was going to. She understood quite enough, anyway, to pour her whole being into her people's final battle to protect what was theirs. They had taught her well, those revered men and women, and in the course of her earlier visits she had absorbed everything that they had tried to explain to her. It had been tough; the elders were not known for being gentle or patient teachers. The first time, Joanna had been at the secret encampment outside the city for the entire summer and she had been made to study for long periods every single day. Her second visit, the previous autumn, had been shorter and its purpose had been to assemble as many of the people as possible to attend the great Samhain celebration at the end of October. That night was burned into Joanna's heart, soul and mind; she knew she would never forget the moment when the elders had called to the people to add their power to the circle and the vast cone of power had risen up like a vortex from the depths of the ancient sanctuary to blast its light into the night sky. The good folk of Chartres had cowered in their beds and nervously reassured each other in the morning that it must have been a peculiar sort of lightning.

For Joanna, there was another difficult aspect besides the tough teaching programme and the perils of travelling to and fro across the water. Joanna had not been permitted to take Meggie with her to Chartres and the child had been left with her father. Not that Joanna objected to that, for Josse was a dedicated, responsible and very loving parent, and Joanna trusted him totally. No, what she found so hard to bear was that Meggie, too young to dissemble, had made it perfectly clear that she loved being with her father as much ('More?' whispered the voice

99

of doubt in Joanna's mind) as being with her mother. Each time that Joanna had returned to her little hut in the Great Forest and Josse had brought Meggie back to her, the child had seemed a little more Josse's and a little less Joanna's.

It *hurt*.

Joanna had been told about the fire that had destroyed the old cathedral on the night of 10 June five years ago. Lightning had struck the roof, they said, and the fire that had immediately blazed up had been ferocious, consuming everything except the south tower, the west front and the crypt. The crypt, Joanna had mused privately. The crypt, which is how they now refer to the sanctuary and the well; strange, how that should be quite undamaged. Nobody even hinted that the fire had been started by the people in their despair, but Joanna knew that some of the elders could summon the vast, dark clouds and bring down lightning out of them; she had seen it done. If the fire had been the work of her people, then the act had been misjudged, for the Christians had been greatly impressed at the miraculous survival of their holy relic and were moved to start pouring money, skill and labour into rebuilding the cathedral in what looked as if it would be record time.

Joanna's people were reconciled now to the fact that nothing they could do would stop the rebuilding. Their purpose had accordingly changed; now their sole aim was to ensure that something of their beliefs, their ancient faith and their precious deity of the female principle should be incorporated into the stones and the very fabric of the rich merchants' great new cathedral rising up on the hill.

Now, in the early summer of 1199, the workmen were about to begin laying the labyrinth that would stretch across the nave of the cathedral. It seemed strange to the people that the priests should have chosen to use this ancient symbol, since it was not of their own new religion but had come down out of the secretive, dark past. The people understood its power and its potential, although the elders doubted that the priests did. That was to their advantage, though; the labyrinth being one of their own symbols, it would be relatively easy to put their power into it. It was as if the priests had unwittingly given them a little door through which to pass, and the people fully intended to use it.

Joanna had no idea yet what role she would play in the ceremony. Whatever it was, she vowed she would ignore her fatigue and a persistent, nagging backache and throw her whole self into it. Since she had arrived in the secret encampment at the beginning of May she had done everything demanded of her, from taking her turn at the domestic chores, such as food preparation and clearing-up, to sitting in the meditative state for hours on end as she strove to join her consciousness and her power with that of her companions. Uniquely for Joanna among the specially selected of her people, there were extra complications. She had Meggie with her, and the demands of a six-year-old child did not always blend harmoniously with the sacred duty of a power figure of the people.

When Joanna received notification in the middle of April that she was to return to Chartres, she did what she had done twice before and sent word to Josse, asking him to come to the forest to collect Meggie and care for her while she was away. On the previous two occasions, Josse had arrived swiftly, willing and eager to accept his charge. This time, Joanna had sent her message via Thomas the tinker; two days later, it had not been Josse but Thomas who had turned up at the meeting place on the edge of the forest. Sir Josse was not at home, he told Joanna; what was more, the young couple who now lived with him at New Winnowlands said he had gone to France and they did not know when he would be back.

Joanna had managed to hide her reaction while Thomas was with her but, as soon as he and his squeaky handcart had trundled off down the track, she had collapsed on the fresh green grass and wondered what on earth she was going to do. Initially she had been furious with Josse – how *dare* he go off like that without telling me! I need him and he's not here! – but she had come to her senses and realized that since she frequently went away without informing Josse, it was not unreasonable for him to do the same. Besides, he'd have come to tell me if he'd had time, she thought, I know he would.

She realized that she had not seen him since the previous autumn equinox, when he had joined in with her people's great ceremony and afterwards stayed for several days with her and Meggie in the forest hut. The fact that she had not found the time for him since then made her feel guilty.

However, the fact remained that he had gone to France for some unknown purpose – perhaps to do with the old king's death or the new king's succession? – and he was not there to take care of Meggie. Over the next couple of days, Joanna thought up various alternatives. Ask the nuns at Hawkenlye to look after Meggie? Ask some of the many forest people who would not be making the journey to Chartres? Ask the pair at New Winnowlands – unlike Thomas the tinker, Joanna knew them to be the Abbess Helewise's son and his wife – if they will care for her? But there seemed to be a good reason why she could not adopt any of these ideas. In the end, she dismissed all the possibilities and went for the obvious solution: she would take Meggie with her. Here they were, then, she and her lively, laughing daughter, in their own neat and tidy quarters within the hidden encampment.

Tonight, Joanna would have to ask one of the other women to watch over Meggie, for she had been commanded to attend a meeting of the elders. They were going to explain to her about the labyrinth and how they intended to use it. Joanna was excited, resolved to do her very best and, she had to admit, decidedly nervous. The afternoon and evening crawled by and her agitation increased; she seemed to feel watchful eyes on her and sometimes they had an intensity that made her skin crawl.

At last night came. The sounds of the day gradually faded, and in the distance the lights of the town went out. In the encampment, those not attending the meeting settled in their beds. The woman who was looking after Meggie brought her bedroll and made herself comfortable in Joanna's usual place. Meggie, already fast asleep, did not stir.

The woman must have noticed Joanna staring down at her daughter. 'Don't worry,' she whispered, briefly touching Joanna's hand. 'No harm will come to her. Not here.'

Joanna nodded, forced a smile and then slipped out of the shelter and into the darkness. Someone was waiting for her; a cloaked figure moved out of the deeper shadows and said softly, 'You are Beith?'

It was the name that her people had

bestowed on her. 'Yes.'

'I am called Ruis. Come with me.'

She fell into step beside him and they set off at a swift pace out of the encampment. To Joanna's surprise, they did not go away from the city, as she had expected, but towards it. It seemed illogical to hold a secret meeting within the town but, as Ruis led her up a track that widened into a street and emerged between houses on Chartres's central square, she realized that this was what they were doing.

With a quick look to right and left, Ruis took her hand and they ran quickly from the shadow of the houses across to the walls of the new cathedral, already soaring high above their heads. This meeting of the elders of her people to which she had been summoned was to be held within the cathedral.

Ruis picked up her astonishment. He smiled, leaned down and said softly in her ear, 'They may possess it in the day but this place is ours too and by night we reclaim it.'

Yes, she thought as they slipped through a gap in the wall between the huge foundations of two buttresses. Yes, that is, after all, our right.

She and Ruis had to hide in the shadows while a pair of night watchmen paused on their rounds for a leisurely gossip. Then, when the men had gone, Ruis grabbed her wrist and raced across the bare floor, ducked through a doorway and led the way down a low, narrow spiral staircase whose treads were slippery with moisture. He was careful with her, making sure she did not miss her footing. They emerged into a dimly lit open space and, gazing around, Joanna saw that it was a vast crypt. She sensed rather than saw how far it stretched, for the single lantern only lit its immediate vicinity. It had been placed on the floor in front of a massive wall and it illuminated what appeared to be a well.

Ruis led her forward and said, 'This is our sacred place. The water wells up from deep in the earth, where the *wouivre* glides through the ground and brings the power and the blessing of the Great Mother up to her children.'

Wouivre. Joanna knew she had heard the word before … Yes. Her venerable teacher in Brittany had explained about the strange currents that snaked and wove their way deep within the earth, some of them harmful, some beneficial. Some, such as those that came to the surface at the holy places, were so strong and brought such open-handed munificence that even the uninitiated could sense them. She had been to many of her people's sanctuaries and she thought she had experienced the full range of the Mother's powers; standing there in the dark crypt, she realized how complacent she had been. She had never felt anything like this.

She closed her eyes, surrendered herself

and let the force surround her. After a time
– she had no idea how long – she became
aware of quiet humming. Was it chanting?
Were her people responding to the power,
honouring it by singing its praises? Or did
the unearthly sound emanate from the earth
itself? She did not know. It did not really
matter.

Presently she felt a touch on her arm.
Opening her eyes, she saw that a slim, grey-
clad figure stood beside her. Bowing low, not
in the least surprised to see the Domina here
so far from home – if, indeed, the Great
Wealden Forest *was* her home – she greeted
the revered elder.

The Domina, now holding Joanna's arm,
led her away from the well. Instantly she
sensed a diminution in the power that had
thrummed around her; it was a relief and
yet, oddly, as soon as it faded she missed it.
The Domina was walking purposefully
down the crypt into a far, dark corner.
There, as Joanna's eyes adjusted, she made
out a group of figures standing in a circle.
Two of them parted to make room, and the
Domina and Joanna took their places.

The man who then began to speak was tall
and broad-shouldered. Joanna had the impression that he was quite young for a Great
One of the people, but his face was shadowed by his deep hood and she could not see
whether her impression was accurate. His
voice was low-pitched and he spoke softly;

sometimes it sounded more like the wind in the trees than a human voice. Perhaps he wasn't human. Joanna arrested the fanciful thought. Of course he was human!

She made herself concentrate on what the man was saying. He was describing the labyrinth and, although some of what he said was familiar, he also spoke of matters so far beyond her knowledge or experience that she could only gape. He spoke of an island deep down in the purple southern sea where, hidden in a maze, a king imprisoned a creature that was half man and half bull; of how every nine years seven youths and seven maidens were sacrificed to this creature until at last one came with the courage to kill it; how this man, helped by a priestess of the Great Mother, made his way to the heart of the labyrinth, unravelling the priestess's ball of thread as he went; how he slew the monster and made his escape. The labyrinth was the priestess's dancing floor; there she danced along its winding path, ever circling and doubling back, until at last she reached the still centre and the great vortex of power that she raised was freed and blasted out into the upper air.

'The mystic dance brings on the trance state,' the soft, compelling voice continued, 'in which power is raised and manipulated.' The hooded face turned slowly and Joanna caught the sudden glint of bright eyes. 'Power from the earth, power from the Great

Goddess, power that we shall raise here as we dance the labyrinth that the priests have commanded to be laid down. With this power we shall imbue this place with the very essence of the spirit that we revere and it shall be marked so that it never fades.' He held up a circular object that, from the soft orange glow, Joanna thought must be copper. On it were two figures, one a man, one a strange hybrid with the massive head and shoulders of a bull and the lower body of a human male. 'This shall be placed at the heart of the labyrinth.' The voice waxed stronger now. 'This is our sign.'

But they'll see it and they'll take it away, Joanna thought, unable to suppress her doubt. They won't allow us to—

Another thought broke across hers; another's mind gently but firmly reassured her. *They will accept this rich gift and they will not think to question its origins*, he said, right into her mind. *Have faith, Beith, for it will be so.*

She looked straight at the hooded man. Now by some trick of the light she could make out his face. Not that she needed to see him, for she already knew him; his mind speaking to hers was unmistakeable. It was the Bear Man.

As the silent group of elders and their companions slipped like shadows away up the steps to disperse into the night, Joanna obeyed the unspoken summons and went to

109

stand in the black shadow of one of the massive pillars supporting the crypt's roof. When everyone else had gone, he came to claim her. He took her hand, led her up the steps and out across the vast floor of the skeletal cathedral – they passed quite close to one of the watchmen, but the Bear Man must have cast some sort of a glamour about them, for the man did not appear to see them – and then like shadows they passed out into the darkness.

He took her to a place apart from the secret encampment. She lay in his arms until she fell asleep, and in the morning he was gone.

Six

It had taken Helewise's party a week to travel from the Île d'Oléron to Chartres. They arrived late one sunny afternoon and Helewise was instantly struck by the sense of almost frantic activity. Rumour had spread of the townspeople's great efforts, which had begun almost immediately after the fire had destroyed their precious cathedral. The cardinal had told them that the miraculous preservation of the Sancta Camisia was a sign from the Virgin Mary that she wanted a new and more magnificent cathedral built in her honour, so the Chartres people had hastened to start hauling stone from their local quarries. Now, five years on, the massive buttressed walls of the nave rose high up into the blue summer sky. The air was hazed with stone dust and sawdust; all around the cathedral site stonemasons and carpenters worked as if possessed by a spirit of irresistible urgency. Huge carts arrived in a constant stream from roads leading down from the site, each laden with another load of building materials. The noise was deafening: mallets hit chisels into stone; saws bit into timber; horses snorted and struck sparks from the cobbles with their great hoofs; men shouted instructions and exchanged ribald comments.

For several moments, Helewise and her companions simply sat on their horses and stared. Then she turned to Sister Caliste and Brother Saul and said, 'I could go on watching this amazing scene, but evening approaches and we must find lodgings. Come, let's try down there.' She pointed towards a narrow street between rows of close-packed houses.

They had not gone far before a man and a woman stepped out in front of Helewise, who was riding at the front of the little procession. She drew up Honey and said warily, 'What is it? Can I help you?'

The man had swept off his cap and was

making her a clumsy bow. 'No, Sister, it's me as wants to help you,' he said. Glancing over his shoulder, he lowered his voice and said, 'I shouldn't go down this street. Down at the bottom, there's ... er ... I mean, it's not suitable, not for you.'

The woman with him elbowed him out of the way and said, 'What he means, Sister, is that down there's where the brothels are. If you and your companions want a nice, safe place to stay, there's a convent down that road.' She pointed across the square. 'Further out, there's the shanty town where most of the workmen put up, but the convent's not as far down as that so you'll be quite all right.' She beamed.

'Thank you,' Helewise said, privately wondering why people always imagined that those who wore the habit of religion had to be preserved from the rough side of life. 'We shall follow your advice.'

The three of them turned their horses and set off back up the street, across the square in front of the cathedral and down the road opposite. Presently they came to a stout stone house set slightly back from its neighbours with iron gates leading into a small courtyard and what appeared to be stabling beyond an arch on one side of the main building.

A nun came out through the open door of the house, saw them and with a smile unlocked the gates. 'Abbess Helewise?' she

112

enquired.

'Yes.'

'Please dismount and come in. I will send for someone to care for your horses. They have had a long ride, as indeed have you.'

For one bright moment Helewise thought Josse must be here and had notified the convent that she was on her way, but no, that was impossible, for he would surely have stayed on at Oléron for another day at least and could not have overtaken her.

A nun in a white veil had come hurrying to take the horses and now Helewise walked beside the sister who had admitted them, Brother Saul and Sister Caliste behind them. 'Queen Eleanor's messenger arrived yesterday evening,' the nun explained.

'He must have ridden hard to arrive a day before us!' Helewise exclaimed.

'Yes, indeed. They keep horses ready all along the roads between the main towns, you know. A man can ride very fast if he has a constant supply of fresh horses.' Turning, the nun took in Caliste and Saul, as dusty and travel-stained as Helewise. 'Your lay brother may lodge with the male convent servants,' she said, 'and your nun may attend you.'

'Thank you, Sister...?'

'I am Sister Marie-Agnès,' the nun replied. 'When you have refreshed yourself, I am ordered to take you to our Mother Superior, who has already made enquiries concerning your mission.'

As Sister Marie-Agnès led the way to a clean but unadorned guest room, Helewise reflected on the extraordinary qualities of the queen. She was not far short of eighty years old but still she kept a watchful eye on all that was important to her. Amid every other concern – including her grief – she had thought to prepare the way for Helewise.

It looked, Helewise thought hopefully as she sank down on to the narrow bed and watched Sister Caliste set about unpacking their bags, as if this business might be quite simply and speedily concluded. Then they could all go back to Hawkenlye – she swung her legs round and lay stretched out on the hard straw mattress – and what a relief that would be.

Over the next two days, Helewise threw herself into her mission. The convent's mother superior – an elderly nun with an aristocratic bearing who was called Mother Marie-Raphael – accompanied her out each morning and together they sought out men of every calling from master mason to muleteer. Their task was not easy, for it meant enticing men away from this vitally important job to another, lesser one, and in a foreign land. Had it not been for the queen's letters bearing her seal, Helewise realized that even with the formidable Mother Marie-Raphael beside her she would

114

have got precisely nowhere.

On the evening of the second day, she sat in the convent parlour with Mother Marie-Raphael going through the many names and notes that she had scribbled down on scraps of parchment. 'I think,' she said slowly, 'that we are doing well. The master mason has studied Queen Eleanor's design and has undertaken to begin on plans for the new chapel straight away, and he has said he will come to Hawkenlye as soon as he can. In the morning, I am to see a carpenter who knows of a team turned off here because at present there is no work for them. The men to whom I have spoken have all promised to spread the word and anyone interested in coming to England will seek me out here.'

Mother Marie-Raphael nodded. 'It is because it is for the queen.'

Helewise picked up her meaning. 'Yes. Even outside her own land of Aquitaine, she is much loved.'

The old nun made an eloquent gesture of contempt. 'Boundaries are not important for one such as she.'

Helewise was not sure the queen would entirely have agreed. 'The workforce who build the great cathedrals seem to be a law unto themselves,' Helewise said, 'with no strong allegiance to any except their own kind.'

'Yes, that is quite true. They give their devotion, their sweat and blood to those who inspire them. And–' she smiled wryly – 'to those who can pay. Now, Helewise, I shall send for food and wine, for you and I have been on our feet since early this morning and we have earned a little respite.'

She got up to summon a servant but just at that moment there was a tap on the door and Sister Marie-Agnès came into the parlour. 'Please, *ma mère*, there's someone outside asking for Abbess Helewise.'

Mother Marie-Raphael frowned. 'It may be the carpenter, although we did say tomorrow.'

'He's not a carpenter; he's a man of quality, even if he is very tired and extremely dirty,' Sister Marie-Agnès said. 'He's got a young monk with him.'

Helewise was on her feet. Her heart was singing but she managed to maintain a calm expression. 'It sounds as if they are Sir Josse d'Acquin and Brother Augustus, who accompanied me to the Île d'Oléron,' she said. 'There was a matter that they had to see to before coming on here to Chartres.'

Mother Marie-Raphael smiled. 'I was informed that this knight would join you here. I am relieved that he has arrived. Bring him in,' she said, turning to Sister Marie-Agnès.

Bobbing a curtsy, the nun hurried away down the passage, to return shortly afterwards with Josse striding behind her. Helewise looked at him; he was, as Sister Marie-

116

Agnès had said, filthy, his face, hands and garments stained with dust and sweat. In that quick glance she also detected that he was deeply worried.

'Sir Josse,' she said, 'it is good to see you.' Turning to Mother Marie-Raphael, she made the introductions.

'The lay brother who arrived with Abbess Helewise is lodging with the convent servants,' the old nun said, studying Josse intently. 'There is accommodation there fit for one of your rank, Sir Josse, if you will accept it.'

'Aye, I will, and I thank you,' he said.

'Go and refresh yourself,' Mother Marie-Raphael said in a tone that brooked no argument, 'and then return to us here.'

Helewise could not protest, much as she longed to speak to Josse alone. She would have to wait to find out what fearful discovery had put that look on his face; she just hoped the wait would not be too long.

They found their time for a private talk early the following morning when, as soon as the morning office had been said and breakfast eaten, Josse asked Helewise to show him around the cathedral site. It was some time before the carpenter was due to present himself and they set off immediately.

'What have you been up to?' she hissed as they walked. 'Something awful has happened – I can tell just by looking at you.'

117

He hesitated and she sensed conflict in him. 'I know that whatever the queen sent you to do was highly confidential,' she whispered, 'but if it's so bad, can't you tell me so that perhaps I can help?'

He gave a rueful smile. 'It is terrible and I don't think you can help, my lady.' He glanced at her. 'Nevertheless, I shall tell you, for the matter is not over and it is dangerous. I would not have the risks increased out of ignorance.'

She did not entirely follow, but the important thing was that he was going to confide in her. 'Go on, then,' she urged. 'What did the queen ask you to do and what did you find out?'

He told her.

It was all that she could do to keep up her steady pace, so deep was the shock. 'The *king* was there?' she said.

'Hush!' He glanced around but there was nobody close enough to have heard. 'Aye. Looks as if he was.'

'And you think some unspeakable crime was committed in that tower?'

He looked down. 'Er ... aye.'

Suddenly she knew without a doubt that he was keeping something back. 'Can you not tell me?'

'It is only a suspicion,' he said quickly. 'I dare not even reveal what I fear to you, my lady, until I know for certain.'

She was frowning in puzzlement. 'But why

have you come here, Sir Josse? If your purpose is to investigate this dreadful matter to its conclusion, then should you not be on the trail of this man de Loup?' She spoke the name so softly that it was more like mouthing the words.

They had come to a stop in the square and stood together staring up at the workmen swarming on and around the cathedral. 'I *am* on his trail,' Josse said quietly. 'The trail leads here.'

Josse escorted the abbess back to the convent, where, she told him, she was to meet a carpenter who might agree to go to Hawkenlye, and then he wandered off around the cathedral wondering how he was to find de Loup. Ask, he thought. And what will be my reason for seeking him? He frowned; with an evil man such as de Loup, it seemed best to prepare very carefully. It would not be wise to say he had come from Oléron, for that would instantly arouse the man's suspicion. I'll say I've brought word from Châlus, Josse decided, that his friend Ambrois de Quercy's dying. Unable to come up with anything better, he asked directions and set off for the workmen's quarters. If Philippe de Loup's 'special contribution' was in fact innocent and simply involved a commission for a window or a statue, then that was a good place to start.

The temporary village that housed the

huge workforce was sited a short distance beyond the last of the town dwellings and consisted of a variety of structures, some stoutly made and some flimsy. Most of the men were absent, but Josse heard women's voices and, following the sound, came to a wash house where three girls and two older women were busy doing laundry.

Greeting them, he said, 'I am looking for a man named Philippe de Loup. Do any of you know of him?'

The girls stared back blank-faced, but one of the women glanced nervously at her companion and said, 'I've heard the name, sir.'

And you don't much care for it, Josse thought, watching the woman. 'I am told he is making a contribution to the new cathedral,' he said pleasantly. 'Has he hired a craftsman?'

Again the woman looked at her companion, who shrugged. 'I don't know the details, sir,' she said eventually, 'but I did hear it said that he's getting Paul de Fleury to do a statue for him.'

'Paul de Fleury?'

'He's a mason, sir. He lodges down there – the house right at the end.' The woman pointed along a muddy path between two huddled rows of dwellings. 'He's not there now. He'll be up at the cathedral.'

'Thank you.' Josse turned and set off back towards the city, but, once out of sight of the wash house, he doubled back and circled round until he reckoned he was at the end of the path that the woman had indicated. The end house was a neat little dwelling and he tapped on the low door. There was no reply. He peered in through the tiny unglazed window and made out a bare room scantily furnished. A single cup and plate sat on a small table; de Fleury, it appeared, lived there alone. Also on the table were a sheet of precious vellum, a quill pen and a pot of ink.

He returned to the cathedral and asked several men but, although some of them recognized the name, nobody could tell him where de Fleury was. 'I'm told he is to carry out a commission for Philippe de Loup,' Josse said to one man.

The man sniffed, hawked and spat. 'Well, nobody else was going to.'

De Loup's evil reputation, it seemed, had spread far and wide.

First thing the next morning, Josse sought out Abbess Helewise, to tell her about Paul de Fleury and explain that he was hoping, by setting off so early, to catch him before he left for work. She was clearly preoccupied with her lists of carpenters and masons but still she looked at him and, with anxiety in her eyes, told him to take care.

At that hour, few people were about and it was strange to see the cathedral deserted save for the circling pigeons. Something seemed to have alarmed them and suddenly they flew up in a great cloud, leaving a sole carrion crow, which came to land by a huge gap in the wall and strutted away inside.

Josse hurried on. Striding through the workmen's village, he was increasingly optimistic that he would find Paul de Fleury at home, for in most of the dwellings he heard and smelled the signs that the artisans were eating breakfast. He reached de Fleury-door and confidently put up his hand to rap smartly on its warped panels. To his surprise, it opened.

There was nobody inside. The cup and plate were in a different position – clearly they had been used since yesterday – and the piece of vellum was rolled up and tied with cord. Without understanding what prompted him, Josse picked it up and slid it inside his tunic. He was filled with a sense of foreboding and, pausing only to look into the tiny back room, where there was a low cot and a heavy cloak hanging on a nail, he left the house and ran back to the cathedral.

He knew as he sprinted across the square that something was wrong. The cathedral site was not deserted now; dozens of people were milling around, most of them talking earnestly in raised voices to whoever would listen. Someone pulled at Josse's sleeve and a man's spotty face pushed up close to his. The man was saying something about evil curses and heretics who would stop at nothing to interrupt the Lord's work, but Josse shrugged him off and ran on inside the shell of the new cathedral.

In the middle of the nave, several black-clad priests huddled over something on the floor. Josse noticed vaguely that a pattern of some sort had been marked out; it seemed to be formed of concentric rings. He stepped carefully around the marker pegs and approached the kneeling priests. Two of them looked up as they heard his footsteps and then he could see what they had been concealing.

At the central point of the pattern, a man lay sprawled on the floor. He lay on his back and his wide-open eyes stared up at the wooden falsework scaffolding directly above, from which he must have fallen. He wore a tunic and hose that were stained greyish-white with powdered stone and, on top of them, a heavy leather apron. He had light brown hair, which was now spread around his head like a halo. It was stained dark with blood.

'He's dead,' one of the priests said. He muttered a prayer, made the sign of the cross over the body and, leaning down, gently closed the man's eyes.

'You're sure?' Josse demanded.

The priest turned a mild face to him. 'See for yourself,' he invited. 'He's stone-cold and there is no heartbeat.'

Josse put a hand to the man's cheek. It was chill to the touch. 'Who is he?'

'We don't yet know,' the priest said. 'He was found only a short while ago – the first workmen on the site noticed a trio of crows hopping around here in the nave and then they saw what had attracted them.' He shuddered. 'Fortunately, the men drove them off before they did any damage.'

'He was a stonemason,' Josse said, studying the dead man. 'His clothes are covered in stone dust.' He looked up. 'We should send for the master masons. They all know their own men.'

The priest hurried to obey and soon returned with three men dressed, like the dead man, in dusty tunics and leather aprons. They stared down at the corpse and one said, 'Aye, I know him.' He gave a heavy sigh and added something that sounded like, 'Might have known.'

'Who is he?' Josse asked.

The master mason met his eyes. 'Paul de Fleury.'

Seven

Others came hurrying to join the group around the dead man and Josse, who had seen and heard enough, melted away through the crowd. They would find out where Paul de Fleury lived, he thought, search his house and belongings for some clue as to who had employed him and what work he had been doing that had necessitated the fatal climb up to the beam high above the nave. Josse had found the house already; the only thing within of any possible relevance was now inside his tunic. He knew who had engaged de Fleury and he strongly suspected that the fall had been no accident. He needed to inspect the nave very carefully, preferably by himself, but that was quite impossible for now. He would just have to wait.

He went back to the convent and asked to speak to Abbess Helewise. He knew by her face that she had already heard the news. She waited until they were alone in the bare little parlour before speaking.

'He is the man you went looking for,' she whispered. 'I recognized the name.'

'Aye, he is.'

'You don't think...? Sir Josse, it can't be that he is dead because he found out you were asking about him?'

He realized what she meant. 'You think he might have been so frightened that he killed himself?'

Slowly she nodded.

It was a possibility that had not occurred to him. It was likely that some well-meaning person had slipped the word to de Fleury that Josse had been looking for him. If he were engaged in some evil or criminal work, then it was conceivable that Josse's sudden interest could have panicked him into suicide. Nevertheless, Josse was pretty sure that was not how it had happened.

'I do not think so, my lady,' he said firmly. 'I think it is far more likely that de Fleury somehow became a threat to his employer and that de Loup lured him to the cathedral last night and killed him.'

'You ... *Oh!*' Her eyes widened. Then, 'Is there any proof?'

'None that I have found yet, although I have not had the chance for a proper look. I'm going out this evening, when everyone has gone home.'

'Surely they're not working there today, in the very place where a man has just died?'

'No, indeed.' He gave her an ironic look. 'The cathedral's crawling with priests and busybodies and they'll be there until the very last scrap of drama and speculation has finally been extracted.'

She smiled sympathetically. 'And in the meantime you are forced to sit here kicking your heels and bursting with impatience.'

He returned her smile. 'That might be so, my lady, except that there is this.' He extracted de Fleury's piece of vellum and unrolled it, spreading it out so that they could both look at it. Seeing it for the first time in good light, Josse gave a sharp exclamation.

On the vellum, Paul de Fleury had drawn a picture – in all likelihood, the design for the commission from his employer. He must have been a skilled artist, for the picture was beautiful, with flowing lines and a vivid emotional life. It depicted a slim, graceful woman in a horned headdress and she stood in a narrow craft shaped like the crescent moon.

The abbess did not seem to be able to take her eyes off the drawing. She said in an urgent whisper, 'Who is she? Oh, Sir Josse, what in heaven's name was de Fleury *doing*?'

'I have seen this before,' he replied. 'It is the device worn by Philippe de Loup and the Knights of Arcturus.'

'And de Loup wishes to have it incorporated into the new cathedral?'

'So it appears,' he agreed, 'if indeed this picture represents the figure that de Fleury had been commissioned to craft.'

'But...' The abbess seemed lost for words.

127

'Sir Josse, is this not a pagan image?'

He tore his eyes away from the drawing – something that was surprisingly difficult, for the figure seemed to compel the attention – and looked at the abbess. 'I suppose so,' he agreed, 'although...' He did not know how to put his reservation into words.

Slowly she nodded. 'I know,' she murmured. 'My head tells me that she–' very gently the abbess touched the figure – 'is a pagan goddess and that I should have no truck with her, yet she appeals irresistibly to something so profound within me that I cannot begin to name it.'

For some time they went on staring down at Paul de Fleury's powerful image and neither spoke. Then Josse sighed deeply and said, 'Philippe de Loup knew what he was about, that's for sure. If de Fleury's finished sculpture ended up with a fraction of the force of his preliminary design, then it would indeed have been something to behold.'

'Yes,' the abbess breathed. 'Only now the poor man is dead, and his great gift gone.'

'Why?' Josse asked softly, as much to himself as to her. 'Why kill him before the commission is done? It makes no sense.'

'Perhaps the commission *is* done,' she suggested suddenly. 'Perhaps he gave it to de Loup last night and, having no further use for his craftsman, de Loup killed him.'

Josse considered it. 'It's possible,' he agreed. 'Although if it's true, then where's

128

the statue? It was intended for Chartres – remember how I told you what Ambrois de Quercy said about de Loup making a special contribution to the new cathedral? If you're right and de Loup waited until the work was done and then murdered the workman, then the finished object must be here somewhere. It makes no sense for de Loup to have taken it away.'

The abbess was shaking her head. 'I do not know, Sir Josse.'

Abruptly he stood up. 'I will ask among the masons,' he announced. 'One of them may know if Paul de Fleury had a workroom and if he did, I'll go and look.'

She too had risen. 'May I come with you?'

'Of course.' He was delighted. 'I would have suggested it, only I had imagined your day was already planned.'

'I can spare the time for a healthy walk out in the fresh air,' she said firmly. 'Come on, let's see if we can find this putative work-room before the priests and the busybodies.'

Helewise let Josse precede her along the narrow streets since he appeared to know his way. Soon they were in the artisans' quarters and, after asking questions of a couple of people, found themselves on a dusty and much-trodden track between rows of low buildings, many open-fronted. Inside were the tools of the craftsmen's various skills: carpenters, masons, glaziers, blacksmiths.

On any other day, the row would have been bustling with purposeful activity; today, it was silent and deserted.

It will not last long, Helewise thought. Such is the fervour here in Chartres that they'll all want to get back to work. Tomorrow, everything will return to normal. Men in the middle of particularly precise and demanding tasks may even creep back later today.

Paul de Fleury had shared his workroom, deserted now, for inside were two plinths each bearing slabs of marble. De Fleury's colleague was working on the statue of a saint – St John, Helewise noticed, for he bore the Agnus Dei in his arms. The marble on the other plinth was covered with a cloth. Josse twitched it aside.

De Fleury had made a start on his figure. Her outline could be detected emerging from the smooth stone, the head on its graceful neck bearing the strange horned headdress, but the work had a long way to go.

'Here is our answer,' Josse said quietly. 'We are left, as I feared we would be, with a mystery. For some reason, de Loup fell out with his craftsman and, abandoning the commission, killed him.'

Helewise stepped forward to help Josse replace the cloth over the figure. 'I still do not see why de Fleury could not simply have fallen from the beam,' she said. It had been worrying her since Josse had first announced with such conviction that the poor man had been murdered.

'There are two things to consider,' Josse said as they stepped over the debris in the workroom and set off back up the track. 'First, it is only an assumption that he fell; made, I think, because he was found directly beneath the beam. I intend to speak to those who are dealing with the body and I shall ask about the injuries and judge whether or not they are consistent with the theory. Second, if he did fall, then, my lady, what on earth was he doing up there?'

By nightfall, Josse had as clear a picture as could have been achieved in a day. He had spoken to the monks who were preparing Paul de Fleury's body for burial and they had assured him that no man sustained such frightful and extensive injuries except as a result of falling from a great height. 'We see all too many such wrecked bodies,' one of them told Josse sadly.

He had also talked to the master mason who had identified the body and who, in answer to Josse's question, said that de Fleury's statue was to have been placed in a niche to the east of the South Porch, between windows dedicated to the Virgin and the Zodiac. This information, Josse reflected, provided no reason whatsoever for de Fleury to have been crawling about high above the nave.

He joined Abbess Helewise and Sister Caliste for the evening meal in the convent's refectory, nodding across to Brother Saul and Brother Augustus, seated at the long table where the servants ate.

'Will you take the brethren with you tonight?' the abbess whispered. 'There may be danger.'

'That remained true while Philippe de Loup was in Chartres,' he murmured back, 'for it was always possible that news might have reached him that I had been on the Île d'Oléron nosing around his tower. But I believe, my lady, that he has gone.'

'If it is true that he killed de Fleury, then yes, I agree that he would not stay here,' she hissed. 'What if you are wrong?'

He shrugged. 'Then I'll just have to be careful,' he said lightly.

'Take one of our trusted lay brothers,' she persisted.

'No, my lady,' he said firmly. 'I shall have to slip in and out of the cathedral site without being spotted by the night watchmen, and that's going to be difficult enough for one man alone.'

She sat back in her chair and he sensed that she had conceded the argument. They finished the meal in a slightly chilly silence but, as he got up and bade her goodnight, she looked up at him with a worried expression. 'May God watch over you,' she whispered.

'Amen,' he muttered. Then, summoning a quick and, he hoped, reassuring smile, he hurried away.

The moon illuminated the square too brightly for a man with a clandestine purpose. Josse stood in the shadows of a large house at the corner of the square for some time, studying the night watchman walking to and fro. He appeared to be alone and not over-conscientious, for quite soon he walked over to where a brazier burned a short distance from the cathedral's west entrance and remained there rubbing his hands over the flames.

Josse took his chance and slipped down the side of the skeletal building, moving out from the shadows at the last moment and running up the steps and through the space where the South Porch was being put up. Inside, the cathedral was deserted. In the middle of the nave, there was a dark stain.

Josse went swiftly out into the open space and stared down at the mark left by Paul de Fleury's blood. Then he looked up, verifying that the body had lain directly beneath the beam stretching from the north to the south walls of the nave. It was so high that it made him dizzy just staring up at it. It was daunting, for he was going to have to climb up there.

He ran lightly over to the south side of the nave and made his way along to where a ladder led up to the first level of scaffolding, three men's height above. Working steadily, making very sure of his hand- and footholds and trying not to look down, slowly he ascended, past the top of the great arch at the side of the nave and on past a row of clerestory windows. Above them were spaces for more windows – at least two rows, he thought – and finally he was up at the point where the great ribs of the vaulted ceiling would spring out from the walls.

The beam from which de Fleury had fallen stretched out from where Josse now stood to the other side of the nave some twenty paces away and, in the moonlight streaming down into the roofless building, Josse could see it very clearly. Looking out, imagining a man walking confidently across – imagining a man falling – made him feel dizzy and sick. He shut his eyes tight. That was far worse, for suddenly he felt as if he were spinning through the air, out of control...

Hastily he opened his eyes. Get on with it, he commanded himself. Cautiously he moved forward until he stood just short of the point where someone would set off to walk along the beam if for some reason his craft demanded it. Men performed such feats, Josse well knew, and he could only imagine that long habit removed the terror. There were handholds, of a sort, offered by the falsework that would support the roof as it was constructed, although these were spaced quite far apart.

He looked down. There were footprints in the dust. He kneeled, taking the carefully wrapped pitch torch from where he had stored it inside the neck of his tunic and lighting it with his flint. Its light flared – surely too brightly! – but if the watchman spotted it, there was little Josse could do. He had to *see*.

There were two sets of footprints, one considerably larger than the other.

How had it happened? Josse wondered. Had the murderer enticed de Fleury up here on some pretext, got him walking out across the beam and then somehow dislodged him? But the body had been found in the middle of the nave – at the spot, Josse now realized as he looked down, that would be the very centre of the strange ringed pattern that had been laid out down there so far below.

Was that significant? What *was* that odd pattern, and why was it there? Josse did not know. So, he thought, forcing his concentration back to the present task, let's say that the killer says to de Fleury, 'I've thought of a better place for the statue of the goddess in the horned headdress, one where she can gaze out unseen on those below.' Or maybe, he thought eagerly, there has been some protest about her pagan origins and in order to put her here at all, de Loup had to find somewhere less obvious. 'We'll put her high up where the roof joins the walls,' he says to de Fleury, 'so we'd better shin up and find a place.' Then up they climb and when they reach this spot, de Loup asks his craftsman to check whether the opposite wall offers a better place. De Fleury sets out across the beam – something he must have done many times before, if not here then on other builds – and when he reaches the middle, de Loup...

What? he wondered. What could he have done to make de Fleury fall?

Slowly he bent down and put his hands either side of the beam. Straining, he tried to move it. To his surprise, it moved quite easily. It did not move far, but then it would not have had to. Even a hand's breadth would have been enough. He sat back on his heels and extinguished his torch; he could manage the climb down without it once his eyes had adjusted and it was better not to be seen.

I will not swear that's how it was done, he thought. Only that it's how it could have been done.

Then, doing his best to rid his mind of the vision of a man falling through the air, carefully he went back down the scaffolding to the safety of the solid ground far below.

He did not know it, but someone other than the oblivious night watchman had been observing him ever since he had entered the cathedral. The people in the secret encampment knew about the man who had fallen to his death in the centre of the labyrinth and they knew they must counteract the evil that had sullied this most precious spot. They had ordered the powerful figures among their number to stand vigil in the cathedral by night, calling down the powers of good and beseeching them to push back the threatening darkness. This first night, the sunset watch had fallen to one of the men. The second watch was Joanna's.

She had had no idea that Josse was here in Chartres; all she had been told was that he had gone to France. So great had been her surprise when she had identified the tall, broad-shouldered figure in the nave that she had all but cried out. She had restrained herself – whatever her private feelings, she was here to do a job and abandoning her post to run out to Josse was no part of it – and settled back to watch what he would do. She guessed his purpose as soon as she saw him crouch down by the dark stain at the heart of the labyrinth and, as she watched him clamber up the scaffolding to the beam across the vault of the roof, she knew her guess was right. With her eyes fixed on his distant figure, she prayed to the Great Mother to make sure he did not fall. So fierce was her concentration that she thought she saw a faint shimmering figure made of light put out its arms to him.

She waited until he came down and willed

him to leave the cathedral via the opening by which she was standing. As he came level, she drew her light cloak carefully around her and said softly, 'Josse.' As his shocked eyes met hers and he opened his mouth to cry out, she added urgently, *'Hush!'*

He grabbed her arm, pushed her back against the wall and hissed, 'What are *you* doing here?' Then, as understanding dawned, he said, 'This is the place you told me about, isn't it? The place where your people have to come to protect something that's under threat?'

'Yes,' she said. 'That's what I'm doing now. The death here has brought a shadow and, in addition to our original purpose, we have to try to disperse it.'

He stared intently into her eyes. 'It was murder, or so I believe.'

She hesitated, but as he seemed to know already there was surely no harm in telling him. 'Some of my people were here last night,' she said. 'I can't explain but it's to do with the labyrinth.' She pointed to the markers in the nave. 'They saw two men climb up to the roof and one went out to sit astride the beam. He was looking down as if he were trying to find the centre of the maze, and the other man was giving him instructions. The man on the beam said, "I'm over the centre now," and then the other man kicked the beam sideways with his foot. The man on the beam slipped off but managed to wrap his arms tightly round it, but then the other man kicked out hard again and again and in the end he let go.'

'So it *was* murder,' Josse breathed.

'Yes.'

After a moment, he said, 'Are you to stay here all night?'

Smiling in the darkness, she said, 'No. I will be relieved shortly.'

She made out his expression as the moonlight glittered in his eyes. 'Shall I wait for you?' he said tentatively.

She did not know how to answer. Three nights ago, she had shared the Bear Man's warm, snug bed. Here now was an older love but one who had as great if not a greater place in her heart. I cannot compare the two, she realized, for they are so different that I do not think of them in the same way at all. Would it matter? If my people – *he* – were to find out, would they be angry with me?

She thought, as she had thought before, that if there were any necessity to love no other than the strange being who was one of her own, then she would have been told of it. In the absence of any such command, it seemed to her that she was free to do as she wished. She wanted to spend some time with Josse, although for many reasons it could not be long. Even so they could walk out into the concealing darkness together and she could bask in his love. She wanted that; she needed it, for she was in turmoil.

He was looking down at her, in his beloved face anticipation as strong as her own mixed with a very touching tentativeness. She put her arms round his neck to draw him down towards her and whispered, 'Yes.'

In the morning, waking in his hard bed in the convent's guest quarters, he was not entirely sure whether she had really been there or if he had dreamed it. He pictured her standing before him, holding the folds of her cloak around her. He had made out the bulk of her leather satchel beneath it but otherwise the darkness had hidden her from him. He had seen only her dark, mysterious eyes, which glittered in the faint light, and her sweet face, illuminated by love. Aye, he thought, it could all have been a dream.

He got up, washed and dressed, then quietly went out. He walked all around the cathedral site but try as he might he could not remember in which direction she had set off when, far too soon, she left him. A long moment together, her head resting on his shoulder, and some precious, murmured words; not even the chance to loosen their garments and press flesh to flesh before she had said she must go. He walked some distance away from the city, following paths and faint tracks, searching in likely looking areas of woodland, but there was nothing. If he had really seen Joanna and if she and her people were encamped somewhere in the vicinity, they were far too good at concealing themselves for him to find them.

He was back in the square in front of the cathedral when he spotted the master mason who had identified Paul de Fleury coming towards him. 'Good morning,' Josse said. 'You're looking for me?'

'Yes,' the mason said. 'I want to have a word with you before those priests try to stop me.' He looked around as he spoke, but the square was deserted.

'Why should they do that?' Josse asked.

'Because they reckon the death of Paul de Fleury is for them and them alone to deal with,' the mason replied.

'You don't agree? It happened on church property, after all, so maybe they are right.'

'They may be right but they don't know what they're at.' The mason looked grim. 'They keep speaking of an accident but all I can say is that they don't know the nature of the man who Paul was working for.'

He had implied the same thing the previous morning, Josse recalled. 'And you do?'

'We all do. Philippe de Loup approached several of my team and none of the others would work for him. He's bad, sir knight, I'll tell you that.'

'I see.' Josse was thinking hard. 'Your men do not trust him?'

'No. I tried to tell Paul, but he didn't listen.'

Josse was framing his next question. 'In what way is de Loup bad?'

'There's too many rumours about him for them all to be false. Besides, he's been involved in more than one suspicious disappearance, although he's always managed to talk – or more likely buy – his way out of trouble.'

'Who has disappeared?' Josse felt obliged to ask, but he thought he already knew.

The mason leaned very close and muttered, 'Lads.' Then, straightening up, he laid a finger beside his nose and said, 'That's all I'll say,' and firmly closed his lips together.

'I see,' Josse said slowly. Then, 'Is he here in the city?'

The mason laughed, a harsh sound with no mirth in it. 'Not him. He's too closely attached to this business with poor Paul and he's fled. He left at first light yesterday, I'm told, and the two others he followed here to Chartres have also gone.'

Irrespective of the monopoly that the priests were trying to impose, the master mason had obviously been pursuing his own enquiries. Josse put that thought aside, for something far more important had caught his attention. Two others. Two more Knights of Arcturus?

'Do you know anything about this other pair?' he asked.

The mason shot him a shrewd look. 'Do you?'

'No! I'm just ... just—'

'Just nosy?' The mason grinned. 'Well, I like the look of you, sir knight, which is why I'm telling you all this. I'm stuck here – I have a job to do,' he added with a touch of self-importance, 'but you, well, I reckon you're not one to let murder go unremarked. I don't know the names of the men de Loup was after but I can describe them. One's tall with fair hair, and the other is shorter, slighter in build and wears a deep hood.'

One was tall and thin, fairish, like; one was short and lightly built. The words of the guard on the Île d'Oléron bounced in Josse's head. Was it possible that, with the king dead, these two men now rode with a different master? It was little enough to go on but it was all he had.

'I don't suppose you know where they were bound?' he asked.

The mason's smile broadened. 'Funny you should ask,' he murmured, 'because as it happens I do. I've got contacts, see, and people keep their eyes peeled for me.'

'So where has de Loup gone?'

'Ah, now, I can't speak for him. He's very secretive and I'd guess that nobody but him knows what he's up to. I'm referring to the other two. *They're* bound for England.'

It was not what Josse had expected to hear. 'Why?' he demanded.

'Because,' the mason said, drawing out the word and clearly enjoying the moment, 'they're going home.' As if he wanted to make quite sure Josse understood, he added, 'They're English.'

Part Three

The Abbey

Eight

The abbess and her party arrived back at Hawkenlye at the end of May. The journey from Chartres had been swift and uneventful, progress greatly aided by the calm, sunny weather, which had kept the roads mud-free and flattened the seas for the crossing from Boulogne to Hastings. No matter how swiftly they travelled, however, it had not been fast enough for Helewise. Once she had done all she could in Chartres, she had burned to be back at the abbey getting on with the hundreds of tasks pressing on her conscience. Not only had she been away from her normal duties for six weeks, which in itself meant a great deal of catching up, but in addition there was now the vast and daunting prospect of the new chapel.

When the excitement of being home again faded, she sat at the big table in her little room one morning and reviewed the situation. The master mason whom she had engaged was due to arrive any day now, together with his team; he had told her that his work on the cathedral at Chartres would be complete by the end of May at the latest and he would then make his way over to England. He had explained the rudiments of the system: how he prepared the templates for the stonemasons, setting the job in motion, and how, once a certain stage had been reached, his job was done and he was free to move on elsewhere. She had noticed that her master mason was skilled at speaking a great deal of words without actually telling her very much, verifying the oft-repeated rumour that masons were secretive types. Not that it mattered; provided the chapel was built well and swiftly – nervously she recalled Queen Eleanor's firm resolve that prayers would be said there within the year – she did not need to enquire into the methods.

While she waited, ploughing slowly but steadily through her backlog of work, a part of her mind dwelled constantly on an image of the new chapel. She saw it in her mind's eye: a simple little building, beautifully proportioned, with perhaps one glorious window depicting the martyrdom of St Edmund. She could still see the glorious Chartres glass and to have just one example of that inspirational work in their own chapel was a dream that she knew she would fight for as hard as she could.

With a sigh, she firmly put the thought from her mind and went back to her accounts.

★　★　★

148

Josse had said farewell to the abbess, Brothers Saul and Augustus and Sister Caliste at the place on the road from the coast where the track for New Winnowlands branched off. He knew he would not stay long at home, for his mission for Queen Eleanor lay heavy on him. *Investigate these rumours and find out if there is any truth in them*, she had commanded. Well, he had, and there was. Perhaps he should simply have returned to the queen and told her so, but something in him stubbornly refused to admit the king's guilt. Richard might have had his faults, but descending to the level of a devil-worshipper and child molester was surely too much to believe. A voice that could only be Josse's own kept saying that there had to be an explanation...

So he had picked up the only lead he had and followed de Loup's two companions back to England. All through the long miles from Chartres to Kent he had asked after them, but nobody could tell him anything of a tall man with fair hair accompanied by a smaller man with a deep hood. Not that he was surprised; it was hardly a precise description. He had no more luck with the name Philippe de Loup. As he reached New Winnowlands and gratefully surrendered his weary body to the various ministrations of his household, he concluded that the only thing to do now was head for London in the hope that pursuing his enquiries there among its swarming population might yield a new path to pursue. It was, he admitted, a faint hope.

It was sheer luxury to be home. Will took Horace away to feed him up and groom him till his coat shone like jet; Ella excelled herself by sending up from the kitchen such a splendid variety of dishes that Josse felt his waist expanding daily. Dominic and Paradisa, who since their marriage three years ago had shared New Winnowlands with him, adding two-year-old Ralf and the newborn Hugo to the household, spoiled him in every way and generally made him feel like a loved person returning to the heart of his family. Loving and delightful as they were, however, and despite the natural affection Josse felt for the abbess's son and his wife, they were of course not actually *his* family.

He had little appetite for the next phase of his task and, indeed, was starting to consider returning to France to tell Eleanor what he had discovered and leave it to her to dig further. He had so very little to go on; the proposed trip to London would probably be no more than a costly waste of time. He seemed all of a sudden to be bereft of resolve: he missed his daughter, he missed Joanna and, after so long on the road with the abbess and her companions, he missed them perhaps most of all. Dominic and Paradisa did their best to include him in their life, but his common sense told him they would be equally happy without him. What, he thought miserably, am I to do with myself?

He frittered away several days at New Winnowlands. Then, returning one evening from exercising Horace, he rode into the courtyard to be met by Dominic and Will, both looking worried.

He slipped out of the saddle and Will hurried to take Horace's reins. 'What's wrong?' Josse asked.

Will jerked his head in Dominic's direction and muttered, 'Best ask him, sir.' Then he led Horace away to the stables.

Fear bit deep into Josse's heart. He spun round to Dominic. 'What's happened? It's not—' He bit back the words. He had been going to say, it's not your mother?

Dominic seemed to sense it. 'She's fine,' he said quietly, 'as far as I know. No, Josse, it's something quite different. Something really puzzling.' He frowned.

'What?'

Dominic grabbed his arm and together they hurried up the steps into the hall. 'Come and see.'

Inside, Paradisa was sitting on the floor. Beside her, the baby slept in his crib and Ralf played with a set of wooden blocks. Next to Ralf, another child bent over the playthings, helping him to make tall stacks and then noisily push them over, a game that had the little boy squealing with delighted laughter.

The other child had long, curly brown hair. She appeared to be about six or seven. Sensing Josse behind her, she spun round and he looked into her brown eyes, which sparkled with golden lights. Her strained expression broke into a joyful smile and, leaping up, she ran to Josse and threw herself into his arms. He felt her firm little body shake with suppressed sobs and, gently stroking her hair, he said, 'It's all right, sweeting; you're safe with me. I'll look after you.'

It was Meggie.

Dominic and Paradisa managed to restrain their curiosity until later, when Josse had finally put his daughter to bed. The remainder of the evening had been occupied with supper, a bath for the little girl and a lengthy bedtime ritual during which her father demonstrated the advantages of her hastily arranged bedroom, snuggled her down in soft blankets and told her three stories.

Finally he sank down in his chair and, looking first at Dominic and then Paradisa, said wearily, 'So what happened?'

It was Paradisa who told him. 'I was here in the hall in the middle of the afternoon,' she began. 'Dominic was out with Will. I'd just fed Hugo and he was asleep; Ralf wanted to go outside and I said he could play on the steps but no further because I had to keep an eye on the baby. I was dozing – it was warm this afternoon, wasn't it? – but suddenly I heard Ralf laughing. I thought at first that Dominic must have come back, but then I heard a child's voice. I hurried outside and there she was, sitting on the bottom step beside Ralf and showing him how to do cat's cradles with a piece of string.' She paused, eyeing Josse anxiously.

'Go on,' he said.

'She seemed to be quite alone. I didn't want to scare her, so I stood in the doorway and said hello, then asked who was with her – I thought maybe she had run on ahead to the house, in which case whoever had brought her would not have been far behind. Anyway, she said she was looking for Josse and that *they* had brought her home from the big Shining City where the building was going up. I said, "Where are *they*?" and she said they'd gone.'

'Did you look for them?' he demanded. Then, hearing the echo of his voice, made sharp by anxiety, he said, 'I'm sorry, Paradisa. I did not mean to interrogate you.'

'It's all right, Josse.' She gave him an understanding smile. 'I hurried out to look up and down the road, but there was nobody about.' Her smooth brow creased into a frown. 'The trouble is that I don't know how long she'd been there. As I say, I was dozing, and she could have been there for some time, in which case whoever brought her could already have been some distance away. Oh, I'm so sorry, Josse!'

'No need to be,' he said hastily. 'You've done nothing wrong, dear Paradisa – quite the opposite, in fact, because I'm sure Meggie must have been afraid, left here by herself, and you managed to reassure her and make her feel welcome.'

'It wasn't difficult,' Paradisa said. 'She knows me, of course, from when she's visited here before, and she seemed quite happy as soon as I said you'd be coming home before long.'

'I'm grateful,' he said. 'You have a loving heart and a child like Meggie can recognize it instantly.' He saw by the puzzled expressions on Paradisa's and Dominic's faces that they did not understand, so hurriedly he changed the subject. 'But why is she here?' he said. And, he added silently, where is Joanna?

He barely slept that night. He knew he must ask Meggie to tell him much more about this mysterious trip and why she had ended up all alone at New Winnowlands, but so far all he knew was that she had been in Chartres. Well, that made sense, for had he not met Joanna there less than three weeks ago? He had wondered afterwards if that strange meeting in the haunted and deserted cathedral had been a dream but, now that Meggie claimed to have been there too, he must conclude that it had really taken place. So for some reason Joanna had not chosen to leave Meggie with him this time but taken the child with her ... Of course! She couldn't leave Meggie here with me, he thought, jubilant at having resolved at least a small part of the puzzle, because I'd already left for France.

But why bring Meggie now? Perhaps it was because Joanna had remained in Chartres. She had mentioned her people's desire to banish the dark shadow cast by Paul de Fleury's murder, and there was also the business that had taken her there in the first place. Maybe that task, whatever it was, had still to be completed and, knowing somehow that Josse was going back to New Winnowlands, Joanna had sent Meggie to him in the care of some trusted friend.

Why in heaven's name didn't she *tell* me? he thought crossly. She could have explained it to me that night I met her. I could have collected Meggie there and then, and she could have travelled home with me. Dear God, but Joanna was an unfathomable, *difficult* woman. His irritation spilled over into anger and, sitting up in bed, savagely he punched his pillows. Anger did no good; he tried to calm his mind and think about what he ought to do next.

Well, he decided after some time, he still had a job to do for the queen and he could hardly take a small child to London while he attempted to pick up the trail of de Loup and his companions. He could leave Meggie at New Winnowlands while he was away, for she already knew Dominic and Paradisa and seemed happy in their company; she loved playing with little Ralf and was obviously entranced by the baby. Josse would explain to her that he had to go away for a few days but he would promise faithfully to be back soon. If she accepted that serenely, he would leave her here. If not, well, he'd just have to take her with him. It was, he realized, an appealing prospect.

He dragged his mind away from visions of himself and Meggie riding down a sunny lane and returned to the present matter. Before setting off for London he would pay a visit to Hawkenlye and go into the forest. He would seek out Joanna's people and demand answers to a few questions, such as why is Joanna still in Chartres, what is she doing there and how long is she going to be there? Another pertinent question might be who brought Meggie home? He might ask that too.

With the immediate future decided, Josse turned on to his side and settled down to sleep.

The master mason and his team arrived at Hawkenlye and within hours Helewise found herself in the middle of a dispute. Since she had been informed of Queen Eleanor's plan to build the new chapel, Helewise had envisaged it within the abbey walls; the mason, however, said firmly that there was no room even for the modest building he had in mind, not unless existing structures were radically altered or demolished. 'Impossible,' said Helewise. 'There is nothing wrong with any building here and it would be sinfully wasteful to damage or even alter them in any way.' Besides, she reminded herself, had not Queen Eleanor expressed her reluctance to alter any of the existing abbey structures? The mason – whose name was Martin – proposed to site the new chapel on an apron of land projecting from the forest opposite the main gates. It was abbey land – Helewise had verified that – but for some reason she had not explored she found it quite inconceivable for the chapel to be constructed there, so close to the forest that it would be in the shadow of the trees.

It was stalemate and neither Helewise nor Martin saw any way to break it. Meanwhile the team of stonemasons sat idle in the camp they had erected down in the vale and, as everyone knew, the devil had a habit of finding mischief for men with time on their hands.

In due course mischief arrived. Two days after the arrival of the masons, a badly wounded man wrapped in a bloodstained cloak was found at the abbey gates by the porteress when she went to open up after the first office of the day. The cloak was wet with dew and the man's hands so icy to the touch that at first Sister Ursel thought he was dead. Sister Martha, hurrying over from the stables on hearing the porteress's cry, bent down, put her cheek to the man's lips and said, 'He's breathing. Come, Ursel, we must take him to the infirmary before he bleeds to death.'

Sister Euphemia, busy organizing the early morning round of patient care, told the two nuns to put the man in the curtained-off recess at the end of the long ward. Summoning Sister Caliste, she stripped him, washed off the blood and inspected his wounds. He had been savagely attacked; there were blows to the forehead and left cheek, cuts and bruises to the shoulders and chest, and a deep slashing wound across the throat. Although this had bled copiously, Sister Euphemia discovered that no major vessel had been damaged; she watched as Sister Caliste neatly stitched the wound and then she prepared a dressing soaked in comfrey and diluted lavender oil and covered it up.

The man remained unconscious for most of the day. As the sun set, his eyelids fluttered open and he gave a hoarse cry. While Sister Caliste tried to calm his extreme agitation, Sister Euphemia hurried to find the abbess.

'I am Abbess Helewise and you are safe in Hawkenlye Abbey,' Helewise said, bending over the man a few moments later. He was, she noticed in a quick assessment, in his middle years, lean-faced and wiry, with greying light brown hair and hazel eyes set in a face whose lines indicated that he was more inclined to happiness than misery.

He stared up at her. 'How long have I been here?'

'You were found outside the gates this morning. You were wounded but the infirmarer and her nurse have tended you and they believe you will live.' She smiled.

'My throat hurts,' he said. Raising a hand, his fingers encountered the soft dressing. His face crumpled and he whispered, 'I thought I was going to die!'

Sister Caliste gave him a few sips of a greenish-coloured drink and after a moment or two his eyes closed.

'I will leave him to sleep,' Helewise whispered, 'and not bother him with questions until—'

The man's hand shot out and he grasped her sleeve. 'No!' he croaked. 'I must tell you, my lady abbess, for there is such danger and I am so afraid!' He struggled as if trying to get up, but as soon as his head was off the flat pillow his face paled and he moaned, 'Oh, but I'm so dizzy!'

Sister Euphemia gently but firmly pushed him down again. 'You have lost a lot of blood,' she said. 'Lie flat and still, and let us heal you.'

He gave her an ironic smile. 'It seems I have little choice,' he said. 'But there are things I must tell you, my lady–' he turned his eyes to Helewise – 'terrible things, and the evil is right here...' His eyes closed.

Helewise looked enquiringly at the infirmarer. 'He's rambling,' Sister Euphemia whispered, 'probably doesn't know what he's saying. I dare say there's a bit of fever in his blood and he'll—'

The man's eyes were open once more. 'It is a secret, my lady,' he whispered, 'a black, dark secret that was discovered by the Thirteen Knights long ago and far away. They knew its vast importance and they swore an oath to protect it. Thirteen, you see – the magic number that is the sum of moons in the year. There must always be thirteen and each one nominates his successor, so that as one dies the next takes his place and the company of the Knights of Arcturus is always complete.' He stopped, for the effort of speaking had made him gasp for breath. Sister Caliste offered more of the drink but he pushed her hand away; perhaps, Helewise thought, he realizes that it is a sedative and will take no more until his tale is told, although the great effort hardly seemed worth it when he was talking such incomprehensible nonsense.

'I was summoned in my turn, my lady,' he went on, grasping her hand in a painful grip, 'but it was odd, for the call came not from my old uncle, to whom I was close, but from another of the thirteen. My uncle did send me a message, but it was not the summons I expected when I learned he was dying. I could not understand it – I do not understand it even now – for my uncle sent me a note that was encrypted in a code only he and I knew, and he told me to *stay away*. Now what, dear lady, am I to make of that?'

Perhaps nothing, Helewise thought compassionately, for you are sick and probably have no idea what you are saying. In the morning, all this will seem like a bad dream and we shall find out what really happened to you. 'Try not to distress yourself,' she said soothingly. 'Drink the medicine that Sister Caliste has prepared, for it will help you to sleep and ease your pain. Tomorrow we shall speak again and I—'

'Tomorrow may be too late!' the man cried, his voice breaking. 'I cannot ... I cannot...'

The strong herbs were having their effect at last. As the infirmarer, Sister Caliste and Helewise watched, his eyelids drooped, the desperate tension in his face relaxed, and he seemed to slump down in his bed.

Sister Euphemia said softly, 'That's more like it. He's stopped fighting now and he'll sleep till morning, which will give his body time to start healing itself.' She smoothed the crisp linen sheet over the man's chest, now rising and falling with the long, steady breaths of deep sleep. 'We'll look after him, my lady,' she added, 'and I'll send word when he's ready to talk to you.'

'Thank you, Sister Euphemia. Well done–' she addressed Sister Caliste – 'you have provided the rest that he so badly needed.'

Then she turned her back on the infirmary's worrying but intriguing new patient and went back to her room to return to the vexing question of the new chapel.

Nine

In the mid-morning something else happened to push the problem of the chapel from her attention: Josse arrived and before him on the big horse sat his daughter.

Helewise, who had been on her way to the infirmary to see if the new patient was awake, saw them ride in and hurried over.

'May I leave Horace here?' Josse said after the most perfunctory of greetings.

'Of course, but—'

Josse had slipped down from the saddle and was lowering Meggie to the ground. 'Meggie, take Horace over there to the stables,' he said to her, pointing. 'He knows the way and he won't be naughty.'

Meggie, Helewise observed, did not need

that assurance. She seemed to have no fear of the big horse but, on the contrary, treated him with such easy familiarity that he might have been a pet puppy, though her head, with its brown curls, barely reached Horace's broad chest.

Josse was whispering urgently and Helewise turned to listen. 'She turned up all by herself at New Winnowlands yesterday afternoon,' he said, 'and I need to find out who brought her and where her mother is.'

'Joanna is not in the forest?'

He hesitated. Then, 'No. I last saw her in Chartres.'

In Chartres! Oh, why had he not mentioned it? Watching his face, in which the profound anxiety was all too readable, she realized that now was not the time to ask. 'You're going to speak to the Domina?'

'I need to speak to one of them, but the Domina may be in Chartres too – they're up to something there, something to do with the new cathedral. *I* can't fathom it.' He sounded both distressed and angry.

'The important thing is that Meggie is safe with you,' she said, and instantly saw from the sudden lightening of his expression that it was exactly the right thing.

'Aye, so she is,' he murmured. Then, with a quick smile, he held out his hand to Meggie, trotting back from the stables, and the two of them set off for the forest.

Watching them, Helewise realized that she

163

hadn't had a chance to tell him about the wounded man in the infirmary. She would make sure to do so when they came back.

Josse and Meggie walked slowly down the forest tracks until they reached the clearing between the ancient, majestic oaks where Josse had encountered the forest people before. In the middle, standing quite still in a pool of sunlight as if she was waiting for him, was the Domina.

Meggie gave a cry of delight and ran up to her and the old woman's severe expression relaxed into a smile. She bent down, hugged Meggie and whispered something. Meggie nodded vigorously and said, 'Yes, yes, I am, thank you, lady.'

'I asked her,' the Domina said, straightening up as Josse approached, 'if she is well and happy, and you heard the answer.' She stared down at the child. 'Indeed, I did not need to ask,' she murmured, 'for it is plain to see.'

Angry at what he read as a suggestion that his child might not be properly cared for by her own father, Josse said coldly, 'She is my daughter and I love her. *I* would not leave her unattended in a courtyard and trust that no harm would come to her.'

'We knew she was safe,' the Domina replied mildly. 'The abbess's daughter-in-law was within; her own child was playing with Meggie.'

'Why is she here?' Josse demanded, in no

way mollified by the Domina's reasonable answer. 'Why did Joanna send her home to me? I was in Chartres – I *saw* Joanna–' or at least, he thought, I believe I did – 'and she could have handed Meggie over to me then!'

The Domina regarded him steadily for some moments, Meggie, bored by the grown-up talk, had wandered away and was struggling to get up on to the branch of a birch tree. When the Domina finally spoke, it was not in answer to Josse's question. 'The spirit that has nurtured the world since its creation is retreating, Josse,' she said. 'Have you not perceived this? Men think with their heads and not their hearts, and they value material things to the exclusion of almost everything else. They build higher and more magnificently and say it is to the glory of God, but is it not rather to the glory of those who pay? Their great constructions shout out, "We have wealth," not, "We believe," and such a sentiment is not prompted by true faith.'

'I...' Josse was unsure how to reply. 'Joanna said they – you – have to protect something at Chartres that is threatened. Is that what you mean?'

'Yes. The spot where the cathedral stands in the Shining City was sacred to us long before the new religion spread from the East. We are and have always been willing to share it, for we understand that the priests are also profoundly moved by its power.

They, however, seek to exclude us, and now it is only by acting furtively that we have any hope of adding our own contribution to this precious place. We will not be ignored, Josse; we also have something to offer.'

Rarely for the Domina, her emotion was showing on her face; Josse saw a definite flush spread over the pale cheeks. He gave her a chance to recover, then said, 'Joanna implied something of the sort. She ... I know she is powerful now, and I thought she meant that she and others of your people would...' He did not know how to express it. 'Well, that you'd leave something of your power there in the cathedral. There's that maze thing – I wondered maybe if that would be a sort of focus for you.'

The Domina nodded. 'Yes, it is an ancient symbol and the priests do not truly understand it. They are laying down the labyrinth because we have put it into their minds to do so, and they will accept our gift of the sacred plaque that is to be placed at the heart of the maze. They believe–' there was a trace of scorn in her voice – 'that the labyrinth is simply a symbol of the journey to their holy city. It is that, it's true, but the labyrinth exists also on other levels that are far more profound. But,' she added conclusively, 'there is no need for any except us to know it.'

'So Joanna is there adding her contribution,' Josse said, returning to things closer to his understanding, 'and when she has done so, she will come back.' The Domina did not reply. 'She'll be back?' Josse spoke louder and turned the words into a question.

Still the Domina did not at first reply. Then, chillingly, she said, 'Something of her will return. As for Joanna herself, perhaps.'

Fear clutched Josse's heart in a cold grip. 'What do you mean?' he whispered. 'She *must* come back – her life is here. Her child is here.' I am here, he might have added.

The Domina stared at him and he thought he saw sympathy in her deep eyes. 'You love her, Josse, even though you do not begin to comprehend what she is. She in her turn loves you, although at present the task before her is so great that there is room in her heart and her mind for little else.'

'But—'

She raised an imperious hand and stilled the protest. 'This is what she was born for,' she said. 'Her birth was predicted, for her mother saw the future with unusual clarity and did what was necessary to protect the Great Spirit who inspires we who follow the old ways. Her mother gave up her bodily existence to ensure Joanna's survival. Joanna herself may have to make the same sacrifice.'

'Give up her bodily existence?' he echoed in a horrified whisper. 'What does that mean? She'll *die*, like Mag Hobson did?'

The Domina sighed. 'It is hard to explain, for you do not see very far into our world,' she murmured. 'Joanna's mother – the woman you knew as Mag Hobson – is dead to the physical world, it is true, yet the elders of my people experience her in a different realm. It is this realm to which Joanna may progress if—' She stopped. Then, in a whisper, 'If it proves necessary.'

In that terrible moment Josse could only think of losing her. His mouth suddenly dry, he said, 'Will I see her again? Will I be able to enter this different realm of yours?'

Compassion flooded the Domina's old face. She said gently, 'You may, Josse. You may.'

'And Meggie?'

'Oh, don't worry about her.' The Domina glanced across at Meggie in her birch tree and her expression softened. 'Meggie is extraordinary. She can see and speak to her mother whenever she wishes to. Listen.'

Josse did so and presently he heard the sound of Meggie's light voice deep in conversation with an invisible companion. 'That's...? She's talking to Joanna?'

'Yes, I expect so,' agreed the Domina.

Josse edged closer to Meggie and listened. '...and Josse's house is really lovely because I have my own bed in my own room and, although I like our little hut in the forest too, I like being with Josse and I love the baby – he's so sweet – and sometimes I...'

Josse had heard enough. Reeling, he turned back to the Domina.

But she had gone.

It was not easy to bring himself under control after such a succession of shocks, but Josse knew that for Meggie's sake he must act normally and not show his dreadful fear. Swinging her down from her birch tree, he said brightly, 'Come on, little one, the Domina's gone now and it's time to go back to the abbey.'

Meggie took his hand and they set off down the track. 'She's gone to find the others,' Meggie said. 'They're all a bit worried because of what's happening in the big new building and they need to reassure each other that it'll be all right.'

God's boots, Josse thought. Only six years old and she has the understanding of an adult. They walked along, Meggie now chattering happily about squirrels' dreys and deer tracks, and Josse marvelled all over again at this extraordinary daughter of his. They always said she'd be one of their Great Ones, he thought. What he had learned in that brief time in the clearing indicated they were right.

They emerged from the forest just above the abbey, behind the spot where, had they known, Martin the mason wanted to build the new chapel. Suddenly Meggie gave a surprised cry and, pulling her hand from Josse's, ran off to stand at the base of an oak tree. She was jumping up and down, trying to reach its lowest branch. 'Josse, help me!' she called, turning to look at him. 'I can't get up by myself.'

He hurried over to her. It was a huge tree and he was not at all sure that it would be safe for her to climb. She was fearless and would go right to the top if nobody stopped her. 'It's a very big tree, sweetheart,' he said. 'Why not try a smaller one?'

'*Oh!*' she exclaimed, becoming frustrated. 'I don't want to go *high* – only up to there.' She pointed.

He followed the line of her finger and, resting at the place where a branch about two men's height from the ground left the trunk, he saw a small bundle. 'I'll get it,' he said.

'I saw it first!' Meggie protested.

'I'll get it,' he repeated more firmly.

Meggie stuck out her lower lip. He swung up to the lowest branch, hauled himself up and put his foot on the branch above. Standing up and stretching, he got his fingers round the object. For a startled, disbelieving moment, he almost thought it sent a shock wave through him. Don't be fanciful, he ordered himself. The object was wrapped in soft cloth. It felt hard and it was about the length of his forearm and the width of his two fists. Clutching it, he climbed carefully down again.

He kneeled and placed the object on the ground in front of him. Meggie was right beside him; he could feel her warm breath on his neck. 'What is it, Daddy?' she asked excitedly.

Daddy. His heart gave a great lurch.

The moment had taken on huge dimensions. Before him was a strange object that even his limited powers knew was so far out of the everyday and the ordinary that it was all but incredible, and his beloved daughter had for the very first time called him by the name to which he had always been entitled.

Slowly, reverently, he unfolded the cloth. He and Meggie, both shocked into awed silence, sat back and stared. It was a statue of a woman seated on a low, simple throne. She wore a mysterious headdress like a pair of horns, or perhaps the crescent moon on its side. Her eyes were closed, and her blissful, beautiful face wore an expression that was at the same time serene and powerful.

'She is the Virgin Mary,' Josse whispered, but something told him he was wrong.

'No she's not,' Meggie whispered back. She put out her grubby little hand and gently touched the figure's belly. Then she picked it up and put it in Josse's hands.

Just then he realized what had troubled him. Meggie was right; this woman was not the Virgin. For one thing, unlike every representation of the mother of God that he had ever seen, this woman was heavily pregnant. In addition, whatever smooth, shining wood she was made from was also like nothing he had seen before.

It was black.

He had been holding his breath and now, noticing that his discomfort was rapidly growing, he let it out and tried to breathe in.

He couldn't.

He tried again, but it was as if he were under a sudden enchantment. His ribs felt as if they were encased in steel and, panicking, he turned wide, horrified eyes on to his child. Perceiving his distress, she smiled and calmly took the black figure from him. Immediately air whooshed into his lungs and he gulped and gasped, his eyes watering. Then the dreadful thought struck him: dear God, if it – *she* – can do that to me, a strong man, what will she do to a little girl? He lunged towards Meggie, ready to strike the black figure from her hand, but Meggie, muttering softly under her breath and with a happy smile on her face, was nursing the statue as if it were nothing more dangerous than a doll.

Walking back to the abbey, Josse suggested to Meggie that they leave the figure in the safety of the abbess's room. 'People come and go freely at Hawkenlye,' he explained, 'and we would not want such a wonderful object to go missing, would we?'

His daughter turned her bright brown eyes up to him. 'Nobody will steal her,' she said confidently. 'You know what she did to you.'

He did; it was all too vivid a memory. She must have seen the distress that briefly crossed his face, for she grasped his hand, gave it a quick squeeze and said, 'You can hold her now and nothing will happen.' She pushed the wrapped statue into his hands and reluctantly he took it, waiting for that paralyzing grip on his chest.

But it did not come.

'She didn't know who you were,' Meggie said. 'When you took her out of the tree and then when you held her, she did not know if you were all right or not. Now she does.'

Josse grinned. 'She did not appear to have that dilemma with you,' he remarked.

And Meggie said simply, 'Of course not.'

They went in through the gates and Josse led the way to the abbess's room. The door was ajar and, looking up, she smiled and beckoned them in.

Josse took a deep breath and, unwrapping the figure, prepared to explain to her what Meggie had found.

That evening, Josse went off to the vale to settle Meggie for the night in a cosy little bed beside his habitual place down in the monks' quarters. He had asked Helewise if he might return when he had done so and she had instantly agreed. She could tell by his face that something had happened; something that he did not wish to discuss in front of his child.

He came into her room, closed the door,

leaned back against it and then said, 'The Domina says Joanna had to stay in Chartres. She—' His face crumpled and tears filled his eyes. Brushing them away, he cleared his throat and went on. 'I don't understand, but the Domina seemed to be implying that what Joanna has to do may remove her into some other sort of existence and ... and I may never see her again.' Briefly he put his hand up to cover his eyes.

Helewise longed to rush over and comfort him. Longed to take this big, tough, brave man with the tender heart in her arms and pour out words of reassurance. Longed to say, I'm still here Josse and *I* love you!

But she was abbess of Hawkenlye. She stayed where she was in her chair.

When she felt she had given him enough time to control the emotion that threatened him, she said, 'Is it certain that this will happen?'

His red-rimmed eyes met hers. 'No. You know the Domina – like all her kind, she talks in riddles. All I could make out is that Joanna and the others have to give some of their own power so that what they are – what her people are – and what they believe in becomes fixed in the new cathedral. *I* don't know. It sounded like a lot of nonsense.'

Helewise said after a moment, 'I believe I perceive a little of what they are trying to do.'

'I wish you'd explain it to me,' he said, his grief making his voice harsh and cruel.

'I'll try.' She swallowed nervously, for she knew how crucial this moment was. 'Josse, did you not feel that the magnificent cathedral at Chartres is ... well, just a little brash? It's as if the rich people who are paying for it are determined to show off their wealth and their power, as if they want a permanent memorial – in the form of a window or a beautiful carving – so that, for all the years the building will stand, people will know their identity and how rich they were.'

He stared at her. 'That's what *she* said. She said–' he frowned as he tried to remember – 'that the spirit had gone from the world.'

'Yes. Yes, that's it!' Helewise said eagerly. 'And – don't you see, dear Josse? – her people recognize the spirit so clearly, for they are so close to the earth and to nature. Why, they don't have any permanent buildings, do they?'

'No,' he agreed.

But she noticed that, after the brief period of animation, his face had fallen into sorrow once more. It was time for some bracing encouragement; she prayed for the strength to provide it. 'Sir Josse,' she said firmly, 'we don't know what will happen for certain over there in Chartres and, from what you have told me, it sounds as if the Domina was just preparing you for one possible outcome.' He looked at her dubiously. 'It may not come to pass.'

He shrugged. 'I'll have to wait and see,' he

said heavily.

'Yes. Yes, you will.' She searched frantically for something positive with which to encourage him. Then she had it. 'You must keep your optimism,' she said, 'for Meggie's sake if not your own.'

'Meggie.' He repeated the name in a whisper and it worked. His face lightened and, giving her a look that was almost shy, he said, 'Today, she called me Daddy.'

Helewise was not sure she could trust her voice. She said softly, 'That's what you are, Josse.'

He stood mutely staring at her for a few moments. Then, shaking his head as if ridding himself of some thought that was unwelcome, he said, 'What about that statue, then? Did you feel its force?'

She was very grateful for the change of subject. 'Yes, indeed. Only when I first touched her, however. When I put my hand back on her a second time, it was as if ... Oh, it sounds silly, but I felt she knew who I was and accepted me.'

'Aye, I reckon that's the way of it,' he agreed. 'Meggie says–' his face softened – 'the figure has to decide if you're all right or not.'

'And presumably we are?' Helewise suggested.

'Aye.'

Well, that was good to know. 'The statue is surely very valuable, Sir Josse. Would you like me to find a safe place for it?'

'Aye, I would.'

She considered. 'I've put it for the time being in the back of my book cupboard.' She pointed to the recess let into the stone wall. 'It's wrapped in the cloth and hidden behind some account rolls.'

'That sounds as safe a place as any,' he said. 'Does anyone come in when you're not here?'

'Hardly ever.'

'Then let's leave it there.' He yawned, so overcome by all that had happened that he forgot to put his hand to his mouth.

'Go to bed, Sir Josse,' she said. 'Things may seem brighter in the morning.'

He looked at her and she almost heard his thought: Will they? Then he gave her a cursory bow and left.

She allowed a few moments for him to go out of the rear gate. Then she got up, made her way over to the deserted church and, sinking to her knees in front of the altar, began to pray for him.

Ten

The next morning, Helewise's master mason finally lost patience and announced that if they could not agree a site for the new chapel, he was going home. Helewise, ragged after a virtually sleepless night worrying about Josse, very nearly lost her temper.

'You have been engaged by Queen Eleanor and you will do no such thing,' she said, controlling herself. 'I will tell you where to build when I have decided. For now, you will just have to–' *what?* Dear Lord, what could this man and his team do while she made up her mind? – 'get on with your preparations,' she finished feebly. 'There is stone to cart, wood to select and purchase. Do that,' she ordered.

The flash of steel seemed to do the trick for Martin the mason, standing open-mouthed in amazement, put his cap back on his head, turned on his heel and said, 'Right you are, my lady.'

And that, for the time being, appeared to be that.

Nevertheless, Helewise knew she must make a decision. For one thing, that was no

178

way to treat a man with the standing of a master mason. She took a slow walk around her beloved abbey, trying to see it with new eyes and asking herself yet again which building could be sacrificed to make room for the new chapel. As before, she came up with the same answer: none of them. She walked on through the main gates, nodding a greeting to the porteress, and on up the slope to the forest fringe until she stood upon the flat piece of grass where Martin wanted to site Queen Eleanor's chapel.

Why not here? Helewise asked herself. Would it be so bad to have it outside the abbey walls? This is our land, after all. She had checked again, and the relevant document stated that the abbey owned the land right up to the first of the trees. She walked around the perimeter of the area, trying to visualize a small, simple chapel set there against the forest ... and she saw that, in the oak tree that stood out from its fellows like the prow of a vast ship, there was something lodged in the branches.

A chill seemed to creep over her, for she knew without a doubt what it was.

She hurried back to the abbey and sent word to Josse. When he arrived, she said tersely, 'Someone's been in my room overnight. They've taken the statue and—'

He muttered an oath. 'It's been stolen?'

'No, Sir Josse. It's back in the oak tree.'

'Who could have put it there?'

'I have no idea. Only you, I and Meggie knew where it came from. Only we, indeed, know anything about it at all.'

'Neither Meggie nor I put it back,' he said.

'No, Sir Josse, I did not imagine that you did,' she replied, calm in the face of his agitation. 'There is, of course, one other possibility.'

'That it flew there all by itself?' he suggested with a faint grin. 'My lady, you are getting carried away. It is not like you to be so fanciful.'

'I meant,' she said patiently, 'that one other person at least knows where the statue was: the person who put it in the tree in the first place.'

'And you propose that this mystery man observed that Meggie and I brought her back here; then late last night, when we'd all gone to bed, he crept into your room, managed to find the figure in her hiding place and took her back to the tree?'

It did not, she had to admit, sound very likely, but then it was more credible than a solid wooden statue flying through the darkness of its own volition. 'Well, it's one explanation,' she said lamely.

He smiled at her, a true, warm smile prompted by genuine amusement. Was it a sign that he was feeling more optimistic this morning? Had her lengthy, fervent prayer been answered? Oh, she hoped so! 'And a reasonable one, my lady,' he was saying.

'Still, however she got back into her tree, I'd better go and fetch her.'

'Yes, please do, Sir Josse. Meanwhile I will sit here and think of a more secure place of concealment.'

Josse hurried out to the edge of the forest, anxious to complete his mission before Meggie came to find him. He was not sure why but he knew he did not want to involve her in this small mystery. It was ... He could not explain it, but he was all too aware that there were undercurrents to this matter that he could not understand. He had left Meggie helping old Brother Firmin fill up the jugs of holy water that were prepared every morning for visiting pilgrims. Meggie had taken to the gentle old monk as if to a beloved grandfather and as for Brother Firmin, Josse had rarely seen him so happy.

He clambered up into the oak tree, got hold of the statue, which, he observed, had been put back in exactly the same place, and then hurriedly returned to the abbey. The abbess was waiting for him in the doorway of her room and, seeing her now in the bright sunlight, he realized how pale and strained she was looking. I don't reckon she had much sleep last night, he thought. She works too hard, bless her.

'Here's the figure,' he said, thrusting it at her. 'Have you thought of another place for it?'

'No, Sir Josse.' She took the figure and quickly bundled it away in the book cupboard. 'It will have to stay there for the time being, for there is another matter I have to attend to.'

'What? May I help?'

She gave him a grateful smile. 'Yes, in fact I believe you can. Two days ago, we found a badly wounded man at the gates and he's been in the infirmary ever since. I know nothing about him – he's delirious, and I'm afraid he's been rambling, telling us some weird tale of ancient secrets. Anyway, Sister Caliste has just come to tell me that he's awake and I'm going to see him to hear if he makes any more sense today.'

'And you'd like me to come with you?'

'Yes, Sir Josse. Two of us together will do better than one alone in shedding light on whatever trouble he is in, and perhaps we shall be able to help him out of it.' Without further explanation and looking slightly sheepish – he smiled, guessing that her real reason was to keep his mind off his anxiety – she turned and set off determinedly for the infirmary.

The infirmarer was waiting for them and led them to the recess at the end of the ward. The abbess preceded him through the gap in the curtains and stood at the head of the bed, so that to begin with all that Josse saw of the patient was his torso and his long legs.

'You are feeling better today?' the abbess

enquired.

'Aye, my lady. I have slept for hours, I believe, and it has been a healing sleep, for—'

I know that voice! Josse stepped to one side so that he could see the man's face, but he needed no verification. The man in the bed looked up, saw him and exclaimed, 'Josse!'

Josse, looking from him to the abbess, said, 'My lady, why did you not tell me his name?'

'I do not know it!' she protested.

Josse grinned. 'He is Sir Piers of Essendon,' he said, 'and he has a manor up on the high forest ridges to the west of here. We have known each other,' he added, 'for years.'

The wounded man was struggling to sit up but Sister Caliste, watching him anxiously, eased him back on to his pillows. 'He is still very weak,' she explained.

'Weak I may be, but I am no addled fool whose wandering wits cannot tell a true tale!' Piers said crossly. Then, fixing Josse with a hard stare, 'Josse, they think I'm delirious, for all that I have no fever and when I try to tell them what happened to me, they look at me pityingly as if I were an over-imaginative *child*!' He all but spat out the last word, wincing in pain as the violent movement tugged at his wounds.

'We thought you were dreaming,' Sister Caliste said apologetically, 'and if we urged you to rest and not tire yourself by trying to talk, it was because we truly believed it best for you.'

Piers's face softened at her gentle voice and he looked up at her. 'I know, lass,' he said. 'Forgive me, for I'm worried out of my wits and if I yell at you, it's only from frustration.'

'Yes, I know,' Sister Caliste said serenely.

'What's worrying you?' Josse asked. 'We can help, perhaps?'

'Josse, it's an extraordinary tale and I'm not sure I'd believe it if another man related it to me,' Piers exclaimed. 'Nevertheless, I'll try.' He paused, breathing deeply. 'A very long time ago, a group of thirteen knights came across something amazing out in Outremer. It did not originate there – it came from an even more distant, darker land. It represents ... No, I cannot yet reveal that.' A shadow crossed his face and again he winced in pain.

'The knights were permitted to know what this precious object was and they swore to protect it,' he went on. 'They formed themselves into a secret brotherhood, which they named the Knights of Arcturus; as you may know, in the heavens Arcturus lies in the constellation of Boötes, which we observe to have thirteen stars, and it is the guardian of the two bears, Ursa Major and Ursa Minor. The object that was found in Outremer represented something of vast importance and the Knights of Arcturus swore to protect it, for they understood that it was under

184

grave threat and that with time this threat could only increase. They further comprehended – or perhaps they were made to comprehend – that if this important thing were to be lost to the world, it would be gravely, unimaginably to the world's detriment.'

'What was it?' the abbess whispered. Her eyes, like those of Sister Caliste, Josse noticed, were wide with wonder.

'I may not tell you. Yet,' Piers added with an apologetic smile. 'But listen to the rest of my tale. One of the original thirteen knights was my own forefather, back through many generations, and, as is our custom, his place among the Knights of Arcturus was taken at his death by a nominated member of his own family. Thus the secret is kept within the same clans and, in time, it was my uncle's turn to join the thirteen. Now, I knew nothing of any of this until very recently when, knowing he did not have long to live, my uncle summoned me and told me of my strange inheritance. He warned me to prepare for the summons and told me that I must obey it. I had no choice.' He sighed.

'You said before–' the abbess spoke tentatively into the small silence – 'that your uncle sent a note commanding you to stay away.'

'Aye, my lady, indeed I did, and I could not fathom it because I had received a contradictory message from another of the thirteen. I did not know what to do – why should I be called by one of the knights, yet told in no uncertain terms by my own kinsman to stay away? Fool that I was, I told myself that my uncle was old and perhaps his wits had unravelled. Then I made my preparations and set off for France, where the knights had convened.'

'You were curious, I don't doubt, to discover what lay at the heart of this mystery,' Josse suggested. 'And, besides, your uncle had impressed upon you its importance.'

'It is generous to ascribe such a noble motive,' Piers said with a small smile, 'but I fear simple curiosity is nearer the mark. So I announced my plans to my household and gave orders for my best horse and my new tunic to be prepared. I told my young squire that he was going to attend me on an exciting journey and set him to readying my gear. But then the poor lad fell down the courtyard steps and broke his ankle and, since I couldn't present myself to the knights without a suitably trained attendant, I borrowed a lad from my neighbour. He was a good boy, bright, presentable and well mannered. He knew his stuff, and the two of us got on fine. We had an easy journey and reached the rendezvous on time, and a godforsaken spot it was too.' His eyes clouded. 'Dear Lord, but if only I'd obeyed my instincts and turned back,' he muttered. 'Well, I didn't, and now I'm dealing with the terrible consequences.'

'What did you discover?' the abbess asked, in what Josse thought was commendably close to her usual tone.

'Whatever pure motive may once have prompted the Knights of Arcturus,' Piers said solemnly, 'it and they have changed out of all recognition. But then they are now extremely powerful and wealthy, and that is very often a dangerous combination. They believe themselves to be above the law, for among their number are men from the very highest levels of authority. I mean that,' he added forcefully. 'You would not believe ... But I must tell you what happened.' He closed his eyes briefly as if steeling himself for some ordeal. 'My lad and I went in all innocence to that dreadful place and, far too late, I found out why my uncle had tried to warn me off. I believe they killed the poor old man,' he added. 'I know he was ill, perhaps already dying, but I am almost certain that they found out what he had done and hastened his end.' He looked sad. 'It was cruel, for he was a good man, perhaps the last true Knight of Arcturus that there will ever be.'

'Yet they did not kill you too?' Josse said. It was surprising, since if the knights had found out that Piers was no more corruptible than his uncle, why had they allowed him to live?

Piers gave a hollow laugh. 'Oh, they tried,'

he said bitterly, 'and I've been on the run from them ever since. Don't let them find me,' he said desperately, his eyes going rapidly from Josse to the abbess and back. 'You must not, for they ... they are an abomination.' The last word was barely a whisper.

'We will guard you to the best of our ability,' the abbess said. 'You will never be left alone here in the infirmary, where nuns are on duty day and night. The gates are locked at sunset,' she added.

'Do they know you've come to England?' Josse asked. He thought he already knew the answer.

'One, the worst of them, yes, *he* knows.' Piers gave a shudder. 'As for the others, I cannot say for sure. They have spies everywhere, though, so I expect word has been sent to summon them.'

'And they know where your home is?'

'They do.' Piers exchanged a glance with him. 'Which is why I have no intention of going there.' He twisted in his bed and gave a cry of pain; Josse saw a line of bloody patches suddenly bloom out along the bandage round his throat.

Sister Caliste sprang forward. 'Keep still!' she ordered, already picking at the edge of the pad that the bandage held in place. 'The stitches are pulling – you must rest, Sir Piers.' Glancing up at the abbess, she said, 'Please, my lady, he does himself harm when he becomes agitated.'

'We will return later,' the abbess said and, with a glance at Josse, led the way out of the recess. 'Someone tried to cut his throat,' she said very quietly as they walked back to her room. 'He has not told us anything of the attack, but he was badly beaten, so perhaps he has no memory of it.'

'Aye, that's likely,' Josse agreed. 'My lady, I am concerned about this lad that he took with him to the rendezvous. He has not spoken of the boy's fate.'

'I noticed that too,' she said. 'I pray that he is safe.'

Josse had been thinking very hard ever since he had heard Piers's story. What if it was to the Île d'Oléron that Piers of Essendon had gone for this rendezvous? What if the Knights of Arcturus had decided that his young squire would make a suitable victim for their abhorrent practices? Supposing Piers had fiercely objected both the terrible deed they were about to do and their choice of victim and somehow had managed to get his squire safely away. Then, when the rest of the knights discovered that they had fled, two of them – perhaps including Philippe de Loup himself – had, together with the late king, set out after them, the three of them rowed out by the dark Oléron guard to the waiting boat. They must have been desperate to catch Piers; once they realized that he was not going to join them, the decision must surely have been made to kill him. He knew far too much about them to be allowed to live. He knew too – he *must* do – that King Richard was either of their number or at the least an eager witness to their foul practices.

But had Piers been telling the truth when he claimed to have had no knowledge of the knights' foul reputation, or was the truth rather that he *had* known, had gone eagerly to the island with a victim to offer up and then something had gone wrong? Perhaps now, to cover his tracks, he was only pretending to be horrified...

Josse dragged his mind back from that unpleasant thought. What he had been trying to decide, all the time Piers was speaking, was if he should now tell the abbess the full story of the horror that had happened on Oléron. It was all very well for the queen to swear him to secrecy; now that this ghastly business had surfaced in England – right here in Hawkenlye Abbey – he was convinced that secrecy was no longer of prime importance.

Interrupting the abbess, who was still speculating anxiously about the fate of Piers's young squire, he said, 'My lady, there are more things I must tell you.'

Then, once they were safely behind the closed door of her room, at last he revealed to her the full account of what Queen Eleanor had commanded him to do and what he had discovered since.

When he finished, her face was ashen.

Josse could not settle. It had been a relief to unburden himself to the abbess, but since finishing his long discussion with her – which, comforting though it was, had not really offered any answers – he had been distracted from anything he had tried to do. Not wanting to distress Meggie, who picked up his moods with uncanny accuracy, he left her helping Sister Tiphaine pick herbs and took himself off for a walk.

He found that he had gone straight into the forest. Not thinking, letting whatever force that was acting on him guide his steps, he went slowly on and, as he had thought he would, in time he came to the clearing where Joanna lived in her little hut.

The open space around it was neat and tidy, just as presumably she had left it, although he noticed that the herb beds badly needed weeding and many of the shrubs were showing riotous growth. He went over to the door of the hut, unfastened the complicated knot in the rope that kept it closed and went inside. He was instantly hit with her presence, for the little room was redolent with the scent of sweet herbs and hay.

It was warm; the sun outside was hot. Feeling drowsy, he climbed up on to the sleeping platform and closed his eyes. It was as if she were beside him. He could smell the delicate floral scent that seemed to cloud around her; he could feel her cool, firm flesh. 'Joanna,' he whispered, 'where are you?'

There was no answer.

He must have slipped into a light sleep for suddenly she was there with him, lying behind him and cuddled up against his back; she felt so solid that he knew she was real. But I'm dreaming, he thought, confused. Then he stopped trying to work it out and simply relaxed against her. 'Joanna,' he said again, and he thought he heard her say, 'I love you, Josse. I always will.'

He awoke to darkness and he was shivering with cold. Hurrying out of the hut – without her, it was not a place he wanted to be – he realized that in fact the sun had not yet quite set. He carefully closed the door and retied the rope. Then, still under the influence of his vivid dream, he made his stumbling, bemused way back to the abbey.

He was not sure when he first knew he was being followed; in his present condition, he realized that his senses were very far from their usual sharp state and it proved quite difficult to make himself attentive. He moved on, trying to be quiet, and the unseen shadow came after him.

It was a huge relief at last to see the open space beyond the last of the trees. He emerged from the forest on to the patch of ground beneath Meggie's oak tree and automatically looked up at the place where the figure had been. It was back there once more.

From the darkness behind him he thought he heard someone take a soft breath. There was the faint crack of a snapped twig and a whistling sound that could have been a sword stealthily drawn from its scabbard.

It was too much. Josse broke out of whatever spell held him there and ran as fast as he could for the abbey gates.

Eleven

The abbey was no longer the calm refuge that it was designed to be. Several times a day, ox carts came slowly down the track, heavily laden with sandstone blocks from small local quarries and huge loads of timber. The stonemasons had set up their workplace close to the apron where Martin wished to site the new chapel, and within the abbey walls the air was full of dust and noise.

Helewise recognized that Martin had chosen a sensible place for his masons to prepare the stone, but a petulant voice in her head kept demanding, 'Why is he working just there, as if he would emphasize that it is the only place for the queen's chapel?'

She would have liked to talk it over with Josse, but the poor man had worries enough. He had come running to find her yesterday evening, red in the face, out of breath and, unusually for him, frightened. 'It's back in that damned tree!' he said, instantly apologizing for the profanity. She had not believed him – it was twilight, after all, and his eyes could be playing tricks – but the figure was gone from the cupboard in the wall.

This morning, just before the midday office, Helewise went out to look once more at the site on the forest fringe. She tried to ignore the stonemasons, the carters and the shouts of the men engaged in unloading the carts, and looked beyond them to the small area of flat land in front of the trees. Would it be so very bad to have the chapel outside the walls? There was one important advantage to siting it there: when the abbey gates were locked at nightfall, having the chapel outside them meant that those in need of solace would still have somewhere to pray.

There was also the strange matter of the statue. Something – no, she corrected herself firmly, some*body* – seemed quite determined that the figure belonged not in the book cupboard within the abbey but out there in the tree. Josse had claimed that the beautiful woman in the horned headdress was not the Virgin, for she was pregnant and made of black wood, indicating, he said, a black skin.

Helewise was not so sure. The Virgin Mary had been pregnant, hadn't she? The conception of her precious child might have been unorthodox but she had carried the baby and delivered him just like every other mother. Who could say what colour her skin had been? She was a woman of the hot southern lands, so might she not have been considerably darker than her usual depiction in paintings and statuary?

There was no doubting the power of the figure. Helewise was not entirely sure if she was right, but some very deep instinct told her that this power, although alarming, was good. Perhaps the statue was some earlier artist's vision of the Mother of God. Perhaps he – or she – had been inspired by the Virgin in some earlier guise.

Helewise, quite shocked at the thought, dismissed it. Goodness, it was surely heretical! Somehow, though, standing there so close to the Great Forest, she could not make herself believe this. Without realizing it, she seemed to have walked up close to the tree where the statue had been found. It was now back in her room – Josse had fetched it first thing this morning – but she knew that it would soon return to the tree. That is where she wants to be, Helewise thought dreamily. Perhaps we should do as she wants and let her stay in her chosen spot. Perhaps we should build the chapel there and make a special place within it for her. As the concept waxed in her mind, she seemed to hear a voice saying, 'Do it.'

Josse spent the first part of the morning with Meggie. Brother Erse the carpenter was busy making a series of carvings of the Apostles for the new chapel, and Meggie, intrigued at the way people came out of the wood, as she put it, wanted to try. She sat with Erse, and Josse watched as the monk solemnly handed her an offcut of oak, put a chisel and a light hammer in her hand and showed her how to make the first incisions.

It gave Josse pleasure to observe that his daughter seemed to have skill in her small hands. Her figure had none of the stylized grace and power of Erse's saints, but then it was her first attempt and it was a very lifelike hound.

As the morning wore on, he knew he could no longer postpone the task that was waiting for him. If he was right and Piers had gone to the tower at World's End with his young squire and then escaped, it seemed likely that two of the three men whom the Oléron guard had rowed away from the island that March night were Philippe de Loup and King Richard. All three men were hard on Piers's trail. Which one was de Loup, the tall, fair one or the one described as short and lightly built? Josse had no way of knowing. The Chartres mason had referred to de Loup having followed two others to the city;

had one of the men been Piers, in the company of some fellow traveller he had met on the long road from the Île d'Oléron? Oh, but it all seemed to fit! De Loup and perhaps other Knights of Arcturus must have lost Piers's trail after leaving Oléron and gone with the king to besiege Châlus, where the lure of treasure had proved more powerful for Richard than the prospect of trying to find Piers, but then the king had met his death, the treasure had vanished, and the Knights of Arcturus had returned to the urgent matter of finding and silencing the renegade.

I must speak to Piers again, Josse resolved. I need to ask him if I'm right. I must make him confirm – if, indeed, he knows – whether the king, de Loup and a third man followed him as he fled from Oléron.

Against his volition something else that the Oléron guard had said kept echoing over and over again in Josse's head: *Screams were heard coming from the tower, dreadful, horrifying, agonized screams ... and through the arrow slits ... there poured a brilliant, unearthly blue light that suddenly changed to blood red.*

What were they doing up there? Did they snatch Piers's young squire, bind him, tie him face down to the altar and then make Piers watch as de Loup stepped up to the dais? He recalled the splattered blood and the stained silver robe and his mind turned in horrified disgust from the irrevocable conclusion. Was it the lad whose screams rang out into the night? Was it his sacrificial death that turned the blue light blood red? Dear God, if so, then what a frightful end to a young life.

Abruptly he stood up, and wood shavings tumbled from his lap. Meggie looked enquiringly at him. 'I have to go and speak to someone, sweetheart,' he said, forcing a smile.

'But I haven't finished my fox!'

'I thought it was a hound.'

'It was but its tail's too bushy so it's a fox.'

Brother Erse grinned. 'I've done the same myself, Sir Josse, when a face I was carving turned out more like one saint than another. I'll watch over her,' he added quietly. 'If you're not back by noon, I'll take her along with me and get her something to eat.'

'Thank you, Brother Erse. See you soon, Meggie.'

In the infirmary, he asked to see Piers but Sister Euphemia, hurrying to intercept him, said it was impossible. 'He has a fever,' she said. 'We have done everything we can to cleanse that wound in his throat but still it has become foul.'

'Will he live?' Josse muttered.

'I hope so.' The infirmarer glanced over at the curtained recess where Piers lay. Her tone, Josse thought, did not sound very optimistic.

'I have to speak to him,' Josse said. 'It's very important.'

'You'll get no sense out of him today,' Sister Euphemia said firmly. 'He's raving again. Something about some boy who died and he was to blame. It's the fever, Sir Josse. Either that or a guilty conscience.'

'Then I *must*—'

'Not till I say so! Go away and leave us alone. If your man recovers, I'll send for you.'

And with that Josse knew he had to be content.

He decided to go back into the forest. If he had been in his right mind last evening – and he was not sure he had been – then there had been someone following him as he returned from Joanna's hut. Could it have been de Loup? Having tried and failed to kill Piers, was he hanging around waiting for the opportunity to try again? Why? Because, he answered himself, Piers is horrified by the Knights of Arcturus and, far from becoming one of the thirteen, he may well betray them. Perhaps he had already done so.

Josse diverted from his path and, going up to the little room by the gate where the porteress kept watch, he collected his sword and his dagger. If he was going to come face to face with the sinister Philippe de Loup, he did not wish to do so unarmed.

He stepped warily along the tracks between the trees. Now, in early summer, they

199

were in full leaf and he could not see far. He held his knife in his hand; within these narrow confines, it was a handier weapon than his sword.

He walked on. There were no sounds other than the songs of a thousand birds and the soft rustling of the leaves. The forest felt unusually peaceful. Perhaps he was wrong about having been followed.

Presently he found himself outside Joanna's hut. As he had done the previous day, he let himself in. Everything was just as he had left it and again he climbed the ladder up to the sleeping platform. Answering some strong unspoken summons, he lay down and closed his eyes.

It seemed to him that suddenly night fell; he knew in a part of his mind that he must be dreaming, for outside it was midday, the sun high in the clear sky. He surrendered to the vision that was overcoming him.

She was there with him, lying in his arms, her body pushing against his. He held her close, so close, as if his dreaming self tried to meld her firm flesh with his. She was murmuring to him, sweet loving words, and her face was wet with tears. He thought he heard her say that she had come to bid him farewell. 'Are you dead, my love?' he whispered, lips against her soft, clean hair, tears running down his cheeks and into his mouth.

She said, 'I am altered, dearest Josse. I am

200

here but not here – I can see you, and my child, and I shall always be with you, loving you, protecting you, calling down blessings on you. But...' She did not go on. Could not, he thought, grief burning through him, for her own sorrow prevented the words.

Deeper sleep followed and when at last he awoke, his memory of the dream was fudged and already fading. Was it true? Had she managed somehow to reach him and tell him that he would never see her again? Oh, but she had seemed so very real – he could have sworn that the place beside him in the bed was warm from her body.

Slowly he sat up, dazed, bemused, not understanding where reality ended and dream began. He would feel the pain of loss very soon now. He knew, in some fundamental part of himself, that the woman as he had experienced her was no more, but he kept remembering her soft voice speaking those precious words: *I shall always be with you.*

Out of habit, for she always kept the hut so neat and tidy, he reached round to plump the pillows and straighten the covers. Beneath the pillow where in his dream she had laid her head, he found something.

He picked it up and, wonderingly, stared at it. It swung on its silver chain and it was heavier than he had imagined. It was the bear claw that she always wore round her neck.

Slowly, not knowing if he was doing the right thing, he slipped the chain over his head and tucked the claw inside his tunic.

He was barely aware of closing up the hut and setting out back to the abbey. His senses were full of her and it was as if she walked beside him. She was ... *in* him, he realized. In some strange way far beyond his comprehension, she seemed to have slipped inside his consciousness.

Inside his soul.

Stay, sweeting, he implored her. Stay with me.

He paced on, so deep within himself that it was some time before he registered the soft but regular sound of someone following him. Suddenly alert, he dragged his attention away from the sweet ways where he had walked with Joanna and back to the perilous present.

Listen. *Listen!* There – and there again. Someone was creeping along behind him, carefully matching their footfall to his so that it was barely audible. He went on, trying not to give away the fact that he was aware of his pursuer. Keep the element of surprise, he thought. Act naturally and then when the opportunity arises, grab it.

He waited until he had passed a dense thicket of bramble and holly, then, without breaking his stride, swung off the path and crouched down behind it. The footsteps came on and after a moment a cloaked, hooded figure slipped past. Silently Josse stood up and with a great leap was on the path behind the man – who was slight and considerably shorter than Josse – throwing one arm round his neck and pressing the point of his knife to his throat. The hooded figure stopped dead.

Josse said, 'Do not move a muscle.' Holding the knifepoint steady, with his left hand he caught the edge of the hood and pulled it back, revealing a head of smooth brown hair, neatly trimmed. Stepping back a pace, withdrawing the knife a little but still pointing it firmly at the man, Josse said, 'Turn round.'

He was hit with a series of surprises. First, the man facing him was not a man but a boy of no more than fourteen or fifteen, the tanned skin of his chin innocent of even the fluff that would precede his beard. The lad was slightly built and, although perhaps tall for his age, still nowhere near the height of an adult. The second surprise was that he was smiling broadly, the expression of joyful relief revealing clean, even teeth and crinkling the skin around the brilliant blue eyes. The third surprise was that Josse knew who he was. He sheathed his knife, threw out his arms and, embracing the boy, cried, 'Ninian! What in God's name are *you* doing here?'

And Joanna's son said happily, 'Looking for you.'

They found a clearing into which the sun

shone down, and Ninian took off his heavy cloak and spread it on the grass. He and Josse sat down side by side, Josse twisting round to stare at him, for he could hardly believe his eyes and kept wondering if this was still part of his dream.

But the boy had come here to find him and it was no time to sit gaping like a stranded fish. 'What has happened, Ninian?' he asked. 'Why were you looking for me?'

'I knew you'd be at the abbey or here in the forest,' the boy replied. 'I've been watching them down at the abbey and I saw you several times, often with that little girl.'

That little girl, Josse thought. I'll have to tell him who she is.

'Then yesterday when I was up here I saw you and followed you.'

'I know,' Josse said gently.

'Do you? Oh, I thought you hadn't noticed me!'

'Most people would not have,' Josse said. 'I was a bit scared and on the lookout for anything out of the ordinary.'

'I get scared here too,' Ninian admitted. 'It's quite awesome, isn't it? The trees are so ... *old*.'

'Aye, they are.' Then, 'Ninian, what's the matter?'

The boy's composure broke. His voice shaking, he began to speak, the words tumbling out of him. 'I went to France with Sir Piers of Essendon. I was sort of lent to him, for his own squire broke his ankle and couldn't go. We ... we went to this island where the wind blew such a gale that you couldn't see for sea spray and we battled our way the whole length of it to a place where there were no dwellings and no people about, not even fishermen, and just this horrible tower. They said it belonged to someone called Philippe de Loup and he was a lord, or something, and everyone had to do what he said. There were other knights waiting for us and all of them put on long, slippery robes embroidered with the same picture. There was another boy there too – his name was Stephen and he was a bit older than me. The two of us were left in a dark, dank space just inside the entrance and all the men went up into the room above. There was a lot of singing – well, chanting, really – and we saw this weird blue light flickering on the stairs. I've never seen anything like it before.' He shuddered. 'Then they came for Stephen. They put a manacle on my wrist and fastened the other end to a ring in the wall, so I knew something bad was going to happen. Not that I could have got away – the door was bolted and I couldn't reach the bolt.'

Oh, Ninian! Josse cried silently, but he did not speak; it was clear that the boy was only just managing to keep his composure and tell his tale and sympathy might make him break down and be unable to continue.

'They— I heard more chanting, and then Stephen screamed and it was cut off suddenly, as if they'd stuffed something in his mouth. I could still hear him, though – a sort of terrified moan that suddenly went really high-pitched, as if he was hurting badly. Then there was a crash and a sudden brilliant flare of red light. All the knights started to cheer. I heard them stamping their feet up there, making a sort of rhythmic pattern; then one of them started to come down the stairs and I knew he was coming for me.'

Josse could only begin to imagine the lad's terror. De Loup, you shall answer for this, he thought grimly. Whatever it takes, you'll die for what you did.

'But then all at once lots of things happened very quickly,' Ninian said. He shot a quick glance at Josse and then lowered his eyes. 'It was all a bit of a muddle and I'm not quite sure about the details. Anyway, before I knew it I was wrapped up in a big cloak. *This* cloak.' He pointed to the one they were sitting on. 'Someone – it must have been Sir Piers – took the manacle off my wrist and carried me outside. I heard him shouting something about the horses and then I was thrown up on to a huge horse and he got up behind me. I pushed the hood aside and we were galloping as fast as the wind, racing across to the lee side of the island where a little boat was waiting with a man beside it. They – he and Sir Piers – pushed the boat through the surf into the sea and we all leaped in. The man rowed us out to a ship that was standing offshore. The ship set sail as soon as we were on board – well, not the man who rowed the boat – and in the evening of the next day it dropped us at La Rochelle.'

'Then what happened?'

'Sir Piers and I set off for Chartres. Sir Piers had something with him that he said had to be left there. It was meant to go in the new cathedral.'

'Meant to?' Josse repeated.

'Yes.' Ninian gave him a slightly guilty smile. 'Only Sir Piers said we mustn't leave it there because everything was different now. I didn't understand what he meant, although something had really upset him and I was worried, because I like him. He's a kind man and I was happy to serve him. Anyway, because I wanted to help him, if he said we had to bring the thing safely back to England, then that was good enough for me and I did what I could to help.'

'And where exactly is this thing now?'

Ninian was watching him closely. A smile began to form on his lips. 'You already know, don't you?' he said. 'You found it – or rather, that pretty girl did. You keep putting it away in the abbess's room, but that's *wrong*, Sir Josse. She's meant to be out here in the forest. She's much too powerful to be shut up in a cupboard.'

After a while, Josse said, 'What do you want me to do, Ninian? If Philippe de Loup has, as I suspect, followed you and Sir Piers back to England—'

'Oh, he has,' Ninian said. 'Although it's not so much us he's after as what we brought with us.' Then his face fell and he said, 'He attacked Sir Piers and tried to cut his throat. I hit him with a big, heavy stick and he sort of collapsed, but I'm afraid I didn't hit him hard enough because he managed to get up and ride off. I think he thought Sir Piers was dead. I got him on to his horse – Sir Piers, I mean – and left him at the abbey gates.' He eyed Josse anxiously. 'Is he still alive?' he whispered.

'Aye, lad, or he was when I set out this morning.' Josse tried to sound reassuring. 'But why did you not come in? They're good people at the abbey and they would have helped you. They'd have hidden you from de Loup.'

'Yes, I know.' Ninian smiled slightly. 'The nuns hid me once before, remember?'

Josse smiled too, for the image was irresistible; the resourceful Sister Caliste had dressed the young Ninian up as a nun and pretended to be teaching him how to sew. 'Aye,' he said softly.

'I couldn't come in,' Ninian said. 'I had *her* to look after, and she wants to be in the forest.'

'Her...?' With a slight shock, Josse realized

that he meant the figure. 'She doesn't want to be within the abbey walls?'

'No! I keep telling you!'

'Very well,' Josse said soothingly. He grinned. 'I'd better stop returning her to the abbess's cupboard, then.' Ninian grinned fleetingly in response. 'Shall I take you to the abbey now? It's safe there and—'

'No, Sir Josse.' Ninian spoke with a firm and undeniable authority and suddenly Josse remembered who had fathered him. Good grief, and didn't it show? Fleetingly he wondered if Ninian knew. 'I cannot go to Hawkenlye because I have to stay in the forest. It's ... it's sort of where I belong and I feel secure out here.'

'Where do you sleep?' Josse asked. A thought struck him: perhaps he wasn't the only one visiting Joanna's clearing. 'In the little hut?' he asked gently.

'No.' Ninian stared down at his boots. 'It's my mother's place. I know that. But she isn't there any more. I've looked and looked and I can't find her, and I ... well, I don't want to be there without her.'

'I know, lad,' Josse murmured.

'I've been using the house,' the boy went on, and Josse could hear the effort it took to move away from the emotional subject of his mother. 'You know, the house in the woods where we were all together, her and you and me. It belonged to her and so I suppose that it now belongs to me.'

209

Belonged. Oh, dear God. 'Do you think...? Ninian, what's happened to your mother? Do you know?'

Ninian's blue eyes were wet with tears. Staring at Josse, he said, 'I think she's dead.'

Twelve

It was only with grave misgivings that Josse left the boy out in the forest. He walked some of the way back to the house with him, and then Ninian said he preferred to go on alone. 'I'd better be quick,' he said. 'It's past the time I usually see to my horse.'

Trying to mask his fear for the lad, Josse said lightly, 'You used to have a pony called Minstrel.'

Ninian's face lit up. 'Fancy you remembering that! Minstrel came with me when I went to Sir Walter's, but I'm much too big for him now.' It was said with a touching note of pride. 'The youngest pages ride him. He's old and a bit slow, and they can't come to any harm.'

'Aye,' Josse said absently. Sir Walter. That would be Sir Walter Asham, the knight with whom Josse had placed Ninian when Joanna had abandoned the outside world and gone to live in the forest. It was, as she had said at the time, no life for a boy like Ninian, who had such rare and noble blood in his veins.

'And *then* I got the horse I have now, and he's called Garnet because his coat is reddish chestnut, and— Josse, you're not listening!'

'I am!' Josse protested. Then, for the piercing blue eyes gave the impression that they saw all too clearly, 'Well, I heard the last bit. I was thinking about Sir Walter. Ninian, why did you not go to him for help when Sir Piers was attacked? His manor is only some twenty miles from here. Did you not know the way?'

'Of course I did! Josse, I couldn't – it would have been like abandoning Sir Piers and I had been commanded to serve him, so that wouldn't have been right at all.'

Josse was thinking ahead. 'But you will go back to Sir Walter when ... er, when this matter has been settled?'

Ninian stared at him for a long moment. Then his eyes slid away. 'I don't know,' he muttered.

'But you're in the middle of your training! Your mother intended you to have the upbringing that prepares a man for the life of a knight and she—'

'My mother is no longer here,' Ninian said coldly. 'It is now up to me to decide the course of my life.' His hard gaze softened. 'I'm sorry, Josse. I did not mean to be rude. I have to protect the statue, you see, and I can't really look beyond that at the moment.'

'Aye, I understand.' Josse looked down into the intent face. You won't go back to your old life, lad, he thought in a sudden flash of insight. I can't see clearly what you'll do instead, but it won't be what your mother believed was right for you.

'Josse?' Ninian was looking anxiously at him. 'Is something the matter?'

'No, of course not.' Josse forced a laugh.

They were now quite close to the house in the woods where Ninian was living. 'Go back to the abbey,' Ninian said. 'I'm quite all right. I like it here,' he added.

Despite his misgivings, Josse saw that it was true. 'Shall I come and see you tomorrow?' he suggested. He very much wanted to tell the boy about his little half-sister.

'No, I'll come to you,' Ninian replied. 'I'll wait behind the big oak where I put the statue.'

'Very well. Until tomorrow, then.' And with a cheerful wave, he turned and paced away.

Helewise had been summoned to the infirmary, where Piers was anxiously asking to speak to Josse. 'He is not here just now,' she said to the sick man, standing by his bed and taking his hot hand in hers. 'Can I help?'

'Oh, my dear lady, I would speak of matters not fit for your ears!' Piers protested.

'You refer to the activities that went on in the tower on the Île d'Oléron?' she asked

212

softly.

His face, already flushed with fever, burned a deeper red. 'I am ashamed that you should have had to hear such things,' he muttered. 'But no – the matter that lies so heavily on my mind is something very different.' He paused, studying her intently. 'My lady, I have spoken of the dark secret that the Knights of Arcturus were formed to protect.'

'Yes,' she agreed. She sat down on the edge of his bed, for now they both spoke very quietly.

'It did not originate in Outremer but in Egypt, during an early age of the world when men worshipped strange deities who bore the heads of animals,' Piers whispered. 'There was Horus the falcon-headed, Thoth with the head of an ibis, Hathor the helper of women, in the image of the divine cow.'

The poor man must be suffering dreadfully, Helewise thought, to see such frightening, febrile visions. But she did not interrupt.

'Above them all there were Isis and Osiris,' Piers went on, 'husband and wife but also twin brother and sister, who fell in love in the womb and who did not desert each other, even through death and beyond, for when Osiris was murdered and dismembered by Seth, Isis reassembled his body and by her magic restored him to life. She was the life-giver, loved and worshipped all over the

213

old world and she—' As if he suddenly remembered where he was and to whom he was speaking, Piers abruptly stopped and said anxiously, 'My lady, I beg your pardon, that I speak of such things within this holy place.'

'It's all right,' she said soothingly. 'Go on.'

He was fretful now, turning his head on the pillow, and she felt his fingers grasp hers convulsively. 'They had answered Pope Urban's great call to arms and most of them went out to Outremer with Robert of Normandy or his cousin, the duke of Flanders.' She realized he was now speaking of the Knights of Arcturus. 'I don't know which of them discovered it – their camp was some distance away from Jerusalem and it is said that a group of them came across their find by purest accident.' He sighed heavily. 'There were learned men among the original thirteen, men with unorthodox views, and since arriving in the East they had been distressed at the war they saw waged for a holy purpose. The world was changing and the sounds of steel clashing against steel and the screams of wounded men dying in agony drove out the quiet voice of the spirit. To find what they found was somehow *meant*, for it possessed within it an older, simpler power and it spoke with a voice of ancient wisdom.' He closed his eyes. 'Or that is what they say.'

'So they hid their discovery,' she said slowly, 'and in time brought it back to the

West and formed themselves into a guardian group, and the eternal task that was theirs and that of their descendants was to keep it safe.' She thought she had a good idea what the nature of this discovery might be.

'It began with such a pure and noble motive.' His voice was infinitely sad. 'But there is a seductive appeal in secrecy, is there not? The power affected the descendants of those first honourable men and, in only a hundred years, they have fallen from the heights of honour to the depths of depravity. Dear sweet Lord, no wonder my poor old uncle tried to warn me off.' He closed his eyes, his face crumpling in distress.

'Were they...? Is it their intention to guard this secret for ever?' she asked.

He opened his eyes, agitated again. 'No! They were meant to judge when the moment was right to reveal what they knew,' he said urgently. 'That was why Philippe had to go to Chartres – the knights had considered concealing their treasure within the new cathedral, so that the power would always be there for those who knew to go looking for it, only ... only...' A tear rolled down his cheek. She waited, and slowly he recovered his control. 'That proposal was outvoted,' he said flatly. 'Instead Philippe was to take funds from the knights' coffers and commission a special statue. He found a talented mason and gave his orders, but the mason, de Fleury, found out something – I do not know what – and tried to make Philippe pay for his silence. He might have picked up some unpleasant little details about Philippe but the poor soul did not know nearly enough; no man threatens Philippe de Loup, not if he wants to live.'

'And so you—' she began, but then she stopped. She thought she understood now. Many things that had deeply troubled her all at once began to clarify, and the heavy burden she had been carrying for the past two days no longer weighed her down. 'Sir Piers?' She spoke very gently, for she thought he had slipped into sleep.

His eyelids fluttered open. 'My lady abbess!' He seemed surprised to see her. 'Did you wish to speak to me?' His expression clouded. 'Oh, but I have to speak to Sir Josse,' he whispered anxiously. 'Is he here?'

And, aching for him – he seemed to have totally forgotten their intense, disturbing conversation – she repeated what she had said a few minutes ago. 'He is not here, I'm afraid. I will ask him to come and see you when he returns,' she added. 'Sleep now, Sir Piers.' Then she got up and tiptoed out of the recess.

Helewise's footsteps led her automatically to the church but, as its shadow fell over her, unnaturally long in the light of the setting sun, she realized that it was not where she needed to be. She muttered a quick prayer to the loving spirit whom she knew kept it in

216

his protection. Nothing, she thought fiercely, nothing could change her love for he who gave up his life to save the world, but another voice was calling to her and it was not to be found within the abbey's walls.

She walked out through the gates and up the grassy slope until she reached the edge of the forest. Then, taking a deep breath, she went in under the trees. She glided slowly, as if in a dream, and, as she moved beneath the leafy branches, dapples of rosy sunset light patterned her black habit.

Sunshine, shadow. Light, dark.

The play of light was hypnotic and soon she felt that she had entered a trance-like state. Her mind, which was always so busy, overflowing with all that each day demanded of her, gradually grew calm. It was, she thought, stopping to give it her full attention, like a child's bouncing ball, which, as the initial impetus dies, bounces lower and lower until it is still.

Alone out in the quiet of the forest, Helewise stood with her eyes closed and she thought she understood. That strange moment of epiphany when she had speculated about the black statue had penetrated deep within her. Now she knew what it meant and, as realization flowered, it was as if she had always known, as if all her life there had been two Helewises. There was the one who loved the Lord and had for most of her adult life served Him within Hawkenlye Abbey –

217

for the past fifteen years as its abbess –but there was also the Helewise in whom ran an understanding and a full acceptance that other ways also led to the divine.

With the realization came so much more and, as the tumult of thoughts exploded, she understood that the effort of suppressing them had been enormous, and that she had been making it for some time.

She sank down on to the short grass beside the track, her mind leaping back. There had been the business of the heretics and that sweet-natured woman whom Helewise ought to have denounced; she vividly recalled the night when she had kneeled before the altar, to see after hours of anguish the tender face of Christ. Aurelia – yes, the woman's name had been Aurelia. Helewise had let her go. Then there was the abiding presence of the forest people and, indeed, dear old Sister Tiphaine, at least still half pagan. There was Joanna, whom Josse loved...

She turned her mind from that. This, she told herself firmly, is not about Josse.

She was a nun – an abbess – and it was exactly what she wanted to be, for her love of and faith in the Lord was profound and sincere. But her role meant that she must serve another master, whose nature was no longer what she had believed it to be. She was bound by that great, powerful, impersonal and increasingly furtive body, the

Church, and sometimes she barely recognized this master at all.

She drew up her knees, rested her folded arms on top of them and put her head down on her crossed wrists. She closed her eyes. She sat there for a long time.

Then slowly she came back to herself, got up, stretched her stiff limbs and set out in the twilight to find Martin and tell him he could start building the chapel in the morning.

Very early the next day, Josse left Meggie in the care of Sister Tiphaine and set off for Tonbridge. He might not be able to persuade Ninian to accept a more secure lodging but at least he could make the place where the lad was a little safer. Philippe de Loup was after him and Piers – or, as Ninian had said, after the statue; well, Josse would do all that he could to stop Philippe in his tracks. Ninian had wounded him, perhaps gravely. He had not come to Hawkenlye for aid, but it was possible he had gone to the canons at Tonbridge. Josse would go and see and, before he did so, visit Gervase de Gifford and alert him to the danger in their midst.

He rode into the sheriff's courtyard while the family were still at breakfast. Gervase ushered him inside and offered him food and drink; both were very welcome, for Josse had ridden out from Hawkenlye with no more than a cup of water and a hard heel of bread inside him. As he wolfed down the food – it was delicious but he was in a hurry – he did his best to answer Sabin de Gifford's cheerful remarks. She sat beside her two-year-old son, Simond, and the child quickly overcame his awe at having Josse at the breakfast table and threw a lump of soggy rusk, which scored a hit on Josse's hand. For a few precious moments, Josse relaxed; Sabin and Gervase's home was welcoming and always had been and, now that Sabin was over her grief for her old grandfather, who had died the previous Christmas, it was once more a happy place.

Josse finished his food and Gervase, drawing his chair closer, said, 'Now, Josse, to what do we owe this very early visit?'

'Aye, I'm sorry to disturb you at breakfast, but my errand could not wait.' Briefly he told Gervase and Sabin about Philippe de Loup. Only when he had finished his tale did he add quietly, 'The young squire is Joanna's son.'

Sabin gasped. 'The one who—' She stopped. Then in a whisper, 'Joanna told me about him when we all stayed in the inn at Dinan.'

Josse stared at her. 'Did she tell you *all* about him?'

'Yes.' Sabin's eyes were wide. 'But I have told nobody, not even Gervase. I promised, you see,' she said, turning to look at her husband.

'There is some secret concerning this boy?' Gervase demanded.

'Aye,' Josse admitted, 'but it is Joanna's secret, Gervase.'

The sheriff frowned but then shrugged and said, 'Very well. So, Josse, Ninian prefers to hide out in the house in the woods and will not accept the shelter of Hawkenlye, and you wish me to help him by hunting down the man who tried to murder his master. Have I got it right?'

'You make him sound like a petulant child,' Josse protested. 'He has very good reasons for staying out in the forest. One, he is of the forest people's blood and they will guard him. Two, he has what he sees as a sacred mission to guard this statue that Piers has brought to England and keep it from de Loup's hands. Three—' three was more difficult; it was something that had occurred to him in the small hours and he was not sure if he could speak of it in a level voice – 'three is that Ninian fears some harm has come to his mother and he prefers to remain out there in her territory.' He cleared his throat. 'He is staying in the house, as I told you, but my guess is that he visits her hut regularly.'

There was silence. He could sense Sabin's huge sympathy and even Gervase seemed affected. After a moment, the sheriff said gently, 'And you, Josse? Do you too fear for

221

Joanna's safety?'

Abruptly Josse stood up, pushing his chair back so violently that it fell with a loud crash on to the stone floor. The little boy gave a cry of distress and hastily Sabin took him in her arms, soothing him. Josse barely noticed. I have to get out, he thought wildly. I cannot bear to think about my fears.

'Josse?' Gervase hurried along beside him as he strode out. 'What is it? What's happened?'

Josse spun round to face him and saw in the sheriff's face nothing but kindness and concern. He brushed a hand over his face. 'I do not know, Gervase. I never *do* with her!' he added, his grief and anger spilling over. 'But I am told that ... I believe she may not come back.'

'Oh, Josse,' Gervase said very quietly. Then, briefly patting Josse on the back, he added, 'Keep us informed. You know you are always welcome here. And I will put word around of your Philippe de Loup. A knight from Aquitaine wearing a unique device on his breast is unlikely to go unnoticed. If he passes this way, my men will find him.'

As Josse nodded his thanks and hurried away to his horse, Gervase turned and went back inside the house.

Josse got his emotions under control during the short ride from the de Gifford house to the priory down on the marshy land close to the river. As he approached, he looked at the guest wing, rebuilt since the fatal fire two and a half years ago and now the scene of busy activity. He rode over to the stables, left Horace to be watered and went in search of Canon Mark.

The round-faced, bustling monk greeted him warmly and, after asking about Josse's health and the Hawkenlye community – Josse's allegiances were well known – said, 'What can I do for you?'

'I'm looking for a wounded man,' Josse said. 'He was hit hard over the head about–' how long ago? Ninian had left Piers at Hawkenlye four days ago, and that was presumably soon after the attack – 'about four days ago. I understand that he was able to crawl away following the injury but it is likely he needed medical care. He is not at Hawkenlye and I wondered if he might have made his way here.'

Already Canon Mark was shaking his head. 'Sir Josse, everyone hereabouts knows that Hawkenlye Abbey is the place to go if you have need of a healer,' he said. 'We have our Sabin de Gifford, whose skills as an apothecary are excellent and who treats all and sundry, both those who can pay and those who can't, but a hurt such as you describe would surely take a man to the abbey.' He was frowning and, as he finished speaking, his eyes seemed to focus on something in the distance. 'Unless...' His glance flicking back to Josse, he said, 'Was this man a knight?'

'Aye. I have not seen him, but I would judge that he would be well mounted and richly dressed. He probably wears an insignia on his breast depicting a horned woman standing in a boat like the crescent moon.'

'He's a foreigner?' Canon Mark demanded.

'Aye, from an island off the west coast of France.'

Canon Mark was nodding vigorously. 'He *was* here! He slept in our guest wing for a night, a day and another night, and we judged that he had ridden far and needed sleep. Other than leaving food and drink for him, we left him alone. Oh, Sir Josse, why did he not tell us he was injured? We would have sent for a healer to tend him! Sabin lives close by and she—'

'I believe he had his reasons for keeping his wound to himself,' Josse interrupted. 'I am sorry, Canon Mark, that I cannot tell you more, but for now I must know where he is. You said he *was* here; when did he leave?'

'But—'

'*Please.*'

Picking up Josse's urgency, Canon Mark put aside his curiosity and his distress at having unwittingly failed a guest who was in need and said, 'He left us yesterday evening. He set off up the road that climbs the hill to

224

the south.'

The road that led to Hawkenlye. And to the forest.

Hastily thanking the canon, Josse ran for the stables, dragged Horace's nose out of the water trough and, swinging up into the saddle, rode furiously away.

He wanted more than anything to find Ninian, but of the two of them he was the safer, for his hiding place was deep in the forest and he was under its protection. Piers, on the other hand, was known to be wounded and lay helpless in a place where anyone who asked a couple of questions could find him.

Josse handed the blowing, sweating Horace to Sister Martha and raced to the infirmary. He knew even before he had the chance to ask, for the curtains around Piers's recess were drawn back and the bed was empty.

Sister Caliste and a young nun in the white veil of a novice had stripped the sheets and were wiping down the straw mattress. Both looked deeply upset, and the younger nun had tears on her face. Seeing Josse, Sister Caliste spoke a quiet word to her companion and then came over to Josse, taking his arm and guiding him out of the infirmary.

'He's dead, then,' Josse said.

She nodded. 'We found him this morning.'

It was callous in the face of her distress, but he had to ask. 'His injury overcame him at last?'

'No, Sir Josse.' She spoke very quietly. 'He was much improved, for the infection in the wound was retreating and his fever was down.' She met his eyes. 'Sister Euphemia found tiny feathers in his nostrils. She thinks someone put his pillow over his face and held it there until he died.'

Thirteen

There was nothing more that Josse could do for Piers, but Ninian was out in the forest and Josse certainly could – *must* – help him. First he had to speak to the abbess.

'Where is Abbess Helewise?' he demanded of Sister Caliste.

'Oh, she and Sister Euphemia have gone to the church with Piers's body. They'll be in the crypt.'

He hurried away, slowing to a decorous walk as he crossed the floor of the church but then descending the stone steps into the crypt so quickly that he slipped and almost fell. Bursting into the low chamber with the huge pillars holding up the vaulted roof, he saw the two black-clad figures standing either side of the dead man.

He approached the abbess. 'Sister Caliste tells me that he was smothered,' he said, keeping his voice low.

'He was,' Sister Euphemia said grimly. Then, tears welling in her eyes, she muttered, 'And he was on the mend! We'd have had him on his feet inside a week.'

The abbess looked at him. 'You will no doubt be able to identify the hand of his murderer, Sir Josse?'

'Aye. Philippe de Loup.'

'Why should anyone want to kill a man like Piers?' the infirmarer asked sadly. 'There was no harm in him – he bore his suffering bravely and we all liked him so much.'

'Aye, he was a good man and he is dead because of it,' Josse said slowly, the realization firming in his mind as he spoke. 'Sister,' he said to the infirmarer, 'he was invited to join in an activity that was both a crime and a sin, and he refused. He took away something that was precious from the hands of men who were no longer worthy of it, and for that he had to die.'

The infirmarer was staring at him. 'He was a hero, then?'

Josse hesitated briefly and then said, 'Aye. He was.'

And Sister Euphemia said, with the ghost of a smile, 'I knew it all the time.'

He nodded to the abbess and, picking up his signal, they left the infirmarer praying over the body of Sir Piers of Essendon. Once outside the church, he turned to the abbess and said, 'My lady, now I must—'

'Go and find the boy. Yes, Sir Josse, I know. You fear that ... You believe de Loup will now hunt for him?'

'I know it.'

He turned to leave her but she called him back. 'Oh, Sir Josse?' She must have read the impatience in his expression for, with an apologetic smile, she said, 'I won't keep you long. Two things: first, I have given orders to my master mason that he may begin work on the chapel.'

Despite his urgency, her momentous announcement stopped him dead. 'Where is it to be?'

It seemed to him that there was an instant of perfect stillness. Then, with a broad smile, she said, 'On the forest fringe.'

'That is the right place,' he said.

Her eyes were suddenly glistening with tears. 'I know,' she said softly.

'The—' he cleared his throat – 'the other thing?'

'Oh ... Yes. I think young Ninian has been in my room again, for the statue is gone. No doubt you'll find her returned to her tree. Would you bring her back, please? Until she has a secure and fitting place in the new chapel, I really think she is safer in my cupboard.'

'I agree, my lady.' He did not entirely understand Ninian's insistence that the figure must be in the oak tree. If, indeed, it was the lad who kept putting her there. It

228

was the only explanation although, Josse realized now, Ninian hadn't actually admitted that he was responsible. 'I'll have a word with him,' he said, deliberately turning his mind from that worrying thought. Then, as he hurried off, he looked back at her and said, 'Good luck with your chapel.'

He thought he heard her gentle protest – 'It is not *my* chapel!' – and, smiling, he headed out through the gates and off towards the forest.

He had arranged to meet Ninian today, although the lad had not said when. As Josse hurried up the slope to the forest, he prayed silently that Ninian would be waiting for him. It was still early and the boy might not expect Josse to be there yet. He stopped to stand for a moment on the apron of flat ground projecting out from the trees where, soon now, a chapel would stand. Slowly he turned in a circle, envisaging the walls of the little building stretching and extending up into a roof that soared over his head. A plain altar, he thought, a beautiful cloth and a simple wooden cross. Aye, it ought to be simple, for although he had been a king, St Edmund was no cosseted weakling but a fighting man who had died leading his troops against the invading Danes. He would not have wanted luxury and pomp any more than King Richard. Well, both of them, saint and sinner, would have their wish.

Sinner.

Amid all his other concerns, Josse remembered his mission for Queen Eleanor. When he had found his answers, he would seek her out and tell her in person. Standing there on the site of the new chapel, silently he made a vow that he would not call this matter closed until he had summoned the courage to tell her to her face the truth about her son and the March night in the tower at World's End.

He crossed the space that would soon be the chapel's nave and ducked down beneath the branches of the oak tree. Recalling his undertaking to the abbess, he looked up, fully expecting to see the statue back in her usual place.

There was nothing there.

He bit down the flare of panic. Ninian's taken her to the house in the woods, he thought. Perhaps he sensed danger – he might even have seen de Loup lurking while he waited for the right moment to climb over the abbey wall and slip into the infirmary – and he's hidden her somewhere more secure. Perhaps she's safe with him at the house.

Fighting the fear that scorched through him, Josse briefly put his hand on his sword hilt and then set off towards the forest house. He had not gone far when he saw Ninian coming towards him. The boy looked worried.

'Josse, I did not expect to see you here yet,'

he greeted him. Relief was plain to see on the young face.

'What's wrong?' Josse demanded, clutching the boy by the upper arms.

'I saw a horseman on the track that runs close by the house,' Ninian said in a rush. 'I can't swear to it but I believe it was Philippe de Loup. The horse was a beautiful long-maned grey, and he rides such a mount.'

'When was this?'

'Very early – the sun wasn't up. I was awake and I'd gone out to watch a stoat with her young. She's worried because I'm living in the house and I'm too close to where she was bringing up her offspring. She moved her kits to a place under a hollow tree not far from the road that runs round the forest. I wanted to make sure they're all right.' Josse suppressed a smile; Ninian had inherited his mother's love of wild creatures. 'I heard a horse, hard-ridden, and crept close to the track to look.' He was studying Josse's face intently. 'What's wrong?' His tone had changed and now he sounded deeply anxious.

'Ninian, I have bad news. Sir Piers was found dead this morning.'

Ninian's face crumpled and Josse was sharply reminded that he was still little more than a boy. 'But ... Oh, Josse, I thought he was getting better.' Then, in a cry of grief, 'I thought I'd *saved* him!'

'You did, lad! He did not die of his

wounds. He was smothered.'

'De Loup.' Ninian's voice was cold and biting.

'Aye. So it seems.'

'Who else would murder him?' Ninian demanded, blue eyes alight, his grief spilling out as furious anger. 'He was decent and good, and nobody but a wicked, evil-hearted devil like de Loup would wish to see him dead!' He paused, panting, then said more quietly, 'It's because of what happened on Oléron, Josse. He wouldn't join in and because what they were doing was so foul, he took the statue. He said they were not worthy of her.'

'You mean the two of you had the figure with you all the way from the island?'

Ninian smiled faintly. 'Yes.'

'But I thought ... Piers implied the knights had the statue then. He said they had considered putting her in a place of honour at Chartres, only the proposal was outvoted and de Loup was to commission a new carving instead.'

'Did he? Well, don't be offended, Josse – Sir Piers would not have told you a lie without very good reason.' He paused briefly to think and said, 'The figure is what's important. Sir Piers would have been careful, I think, to remain vague about her. I do not entirely understand, but I was happy to obey Sir Piers because he was good and I liked him.' Ninian lowered his head so that Josse

232

could not see his face. 'I've always done what he told me,' he added quietly, 'even when it meant telling lies.'

Josse gave him a moment. Then he said gently, 'Have you got her?'

Ninian's head shot up. 'The statue?' He had gone white. Filled with dread, Josse nodded, and in a horrified whisper Ninian breathed, 'No.'

No wonder de Loup was racing away as dawn came up, Josse thought. Not only had he just killed Piers, he had stolen the statue. He had achieved his business in England and now without a doubt he would be making for France.

'Come on.' He gave Ninian a shake. 'Get your horse and your gear and meet me on the track by the forest house.' Ninian met his glance and Josse saw his own excitement reflected in the bright blue eyes. 'I'll hurry back and fetch Horace and we'll be on our way. We're going after him.'

As he sprinted back to Hawkenlye, Josse wondered if he had been right in saying he and Ninian together would go after de Loup. The boy's young, he thought as he ran, and de Loup is dangerous. Just then in his mind's eye he saw again those fierce blue eyes, so full of his determination to avenge the master he had served only briefly but come to like and admire; perhaps, even, to love. If any lad was in need of a father figure, then,

God knew, it was Ninian.

No, Josse concluded, panting as he trotted down the last slope to the abbey. I did right, for if I hadn't suggested he and I go after our prey together, he'd have gone on his own and we'll be safer hunting together.

He collected his horse and his gear in record time, pressed as he was and desperate to get on to de Loup's trail. He sought out the abbess and stilled her protests with a raised hand. 'I am sorry, my lady, but I have no choice.' He knew there were many things she wished to say but, smiling his apology, he said, 'I cannot take Meggie with me, for we shall ride hard and probably far and the mission is no place for a little child. Will you—?'

She did not need to hear the rest. 'Yes, of course. Meggie seems happy with us and we, for our part, love to have her here.'

Josse struggled with the sudden pain that the thought of being parted from his daughter brought so swiftly in its wake. He tried to smile. 'You all spoil her dreadfully.'

'Yes, we do,' the abbess agreed.

He did not know what else to say. 'Wish us luck,' he muttered.

And she, bless her, simply said, 'I shall pray for you, Sir Josse. Both of you.'

Then he was off.

He and Ninian picked up the hoof prints of the fast-moving grey, which went for some distance along the track that bent round the forest. But then the path met other, busier roads. The combination of a sunny morning and a time of intense activity on the land meant that many people were about and they lost the grey's trail in the hectic mix of cart tracks, horse, mule, ox and human footprints.

'Which port did he sail into?' Josse asked. They had drawn up at a place where the road divided, branching off due south or south-east.

'Pevensey, I think,' Ninian replied. 'That's where Sir Piers and I landed, and I believe he was hard on our trail.'

'Then my guess is that he'll go back.' Josse spoke with a confidence he did not entirely feel. 'He's a stranger here and, although he'll be aware there are many other ports, he's in a hurry so he'll probably do the easiest thing, which is return to the port he already knows.'

Ninian grinned. 'Good enough for me. Come on!'

Side by side they kicked their horses to a canter and plunged off down the road that led south.

They asked repeatedly after a well-dressed man on a white horse. One or two people said they had seen such a man and confirmed that he had been riding fast in the Pevensey direction. Eager now, Josse and Ninian urged their tired horses to a last effort. They pulled up on the quayside and, leaving Ninian to tend the horses, Josse hurried to speak to the captains of the variety of craft tied up there.

Quite quickly he returned to Ninian. 'He's gone,' he reported. 'Sailed about two hours ago.' Ninian muttered a curse. 'But it's not all bad,' Josse added, 'because we now know he's landing at Dieppe, which I would say confirms that he's making for—'

'Chartres,' Ninian supplied.

'Aye. He's murdered the man who was making the carving for the cathedral so he's going to put the goddess figure there instead. Do you agree?'

'He must not do so,' Ninian said vehemently. 'The Knights of Arcturus are bad men and any deed they do – especially de Loup – cannot help but be tainted. Besides,' he added with utter confidence, 'she belongs at Hawkenlye. She wants to be there by the oak tree.'

It was not the moment, Josse thought, to go into why the boy was so sure; even less to ask him just how the figure had communicated her wish. Josse was not sure there was ever going to be a time to ask that.

'...another ship sailing for Dieppe?' Ninian was saying.

'Hmm? Oh, aye – we can sail this afternoon. Small craft down there–' he pointed – 'will set us down in Dieppe late tonight.' He saw Ninian's very evident frustration at the delay and, with a brief touch on his arm, added, 'The wind's changing, lad. Hadn't you noticed? It was blowing out of the south-west all morning but it's gone round to the north. And since Dieppe is virtually due south, we'll have it filling our sails all the way and we'll make landfall not long after de Loup.'

As Josse had predicted, the crossing was swift, the sea made choppy by the strengthening wind. Ninian checked frequently on the horses, slung in hammocks under their bellies that kept them level as the ship pitched. Josse was impressed with the boy; whoever had taught him the duties of a squire had done a good job. They made themselves comfortable in a sheltered place amidships, where the motion was less violent, and both of them dozed. Josse had procured food and drink before they sailed and they ate a generous supper before they landed. It would be a long night.

They rode through the night, the north wind that had hastened their crossing at their backs hurrying them on. They stopped before dawn and found a sheltered place in a pine wood, where they slept for several hours. Ninian fed and watered the horses and then they set off again.

They approached Chartres at twilight the following day. For the last few miles of the journey Josse's senses seemed to have become almost painfully alert. He told himself that it was because they were closing in on Philippe de Loup and what was happening was simply a soldier's reaction to the approaching fight, but he did not entirely convince himself. Chartres was where he had last seen Joanna. Other than in his dreams and his imagination, she had not returned to the Hawkenlye forest – it appeared that she might never do so – and that suggested that she was still here. He had no idea if she was alive or dead – silently, angrily, he cursed the Domina, who would not or could not explain – but the singing in his blood told him that, in whatever body or form she now inhabited, Joanna was close.

He looked across at Ninian. The boy's face was grey with exhaustion, although he had not uttered a word of complaint. His determination is strong, Josse thought; he has a precious object to rescue and a death to avenge. I would not, he added silently, wish to be in Philippe de Loup's shoes.

Did the lad know that his mother had been in Chartres? Josse thought back. Speaking of the forest hut, Ninian had said, *She isn't there any more. I've looked and looked and I can't find her.* He had also said he thought she was dead, but swiftly Josse turned his mind away from that. So the boy knew she wasn't in the forest. It was, however, a long jump to assume he knew she had gone to Chartres. It was a difficult decision, and Josse wondered if he had any right to make it, but in the end he made up his mind. I shall not tell him, he told himself. The lad has enough to worry about in this pursuit of de Loup and what he carries. It would be unfair to burden him with the information that his mother may be close.

Did *she* know? he wondered suddenly. She had been in the habit of watching her precious, lost son in her scrying ball, even though she had once told Josse ruefully that it gave her a sick, blinding headache that at first had left her fit for nothing for at least a day. So had she done that now? Had she sensed that Ninian was on his way to Chartres, and was she looking out for him? What a reunion it would be, for she had not seen him in the flesh for ... Good Lord, it was seven years since she had asked Josse to help her find a place for her son and he had taken the boy to train as a page in Sir Walter Asham's household.

Without his volition, Josse's mind wandered back to that time. He too was tired and it seemed that he entered a dreamlike, half-asleep state in which the present faded away, to be replaced by the vivid past. Joanna had conceived Meggie in that cold, hard February. Josse had not known it – he did not meet his child until she was well over a year old – but Joanna had taken up a place in his heart that, whether or not he would ever see her again, would be hers for ever.

'Josse, we're coming up to the city walls.' Ninian's voice broke into his reverie.

With a disturbing mixture of regret and relief, Josse brought himself back to the present and turned his thoughts to finding somewhere out of the way where he and Ninian could stay.

Fourteen

In the morning, Josse set about enquiring after Philippe de Loup. Again, several men had heard the name and their faces registered varying levels of disapproval and disgust, but nobody had seen him recently.

'He's here for a secret purpose,' Ninian said as he and Josse ate a hasty lunch, 'so it's not very likely he'll be strolling around openly advertising his presence.'

'You are quite convinced he's got the figure and intends to place her in the new cathedral?' Josse asked through a mouthful of bread and dry spiced sausage.

'*Yes*,' said Ninian firmly.

Josse chewed thoughtfully. Then he said, 'Well, he won't do it in broad daylight. We'd better rest now, lad, so that we'll be fresh for later.'

Ninian watched him. 'What are we going to do?' The excitement in his face suggested that he already knew.

Josse wiped his eating knife and stuck it back in its sheath. 'We're going to find a nice little hiding place behind one of those huge pillars and keep watch.'

He heard Ninian's quiet exclamation. Then the boy said softly, 'Yes!'

They had found a place to stay in a humble establishment in an area of lodgings huddled out by the town walls. Josse had selected it because it was unobtrusive; he did not want word of his presence reaching de Loup's ears. To pass the remaining hours of daylight, they returned to their lodgings and Ninian, restless with pent-up energy, set about giving the horses and their gear a thorough refurbishment. Josse found a shady place in the small courtyard and, leaning back comfortably against a hay bale, watched Ninian work until his eyes became heavy and he went to sleep.

They found a tavern and ate supper, then, both wearing dark cloaks, made their careful way to the cathedral. As he had done before, Josse ducked into the shadows and studied the movements of the night watchmen – three of them tonight – until he had recognized a pattern. Then he whispered in Ninian's ear, 'Next time the one with the cudgel passes, we slip out behind him and go in there.' He pointed to the wide space between two buttresses. Ninian nodded. His tension was palpable.

They waited for what seemed like a very long time, but the watchman did not re-appear. Neither did either of his colleagues; with a shiver of alarm, Josse wondered why. Had they decided it was a quiet night and, seeing no necessity to maintain their patrol-ling, retired to huddle around their brazier? Or was it something else...?

The important thing was that they were no longer keeping watch. Josse nudged Ninian and together they raced from the shadowy street, across the open space and into the huge cathedral.

Josse looked around him. Torches blazed in several places, giving sufficient light to illuminate the long nave. He noticed immediately that much work had been done in the time that he had been away. He realized that the gap through which they had just entered was in fact one of the doorways, only as yet there was nothing but a gaping space. Apart from the other entrance, the encircling walls were now complete and in many places already stretched high above his head. In some places the rib stones of the vaults had already begun to creep out along the falsework supporting them. Looking up, Josse was awestruck all over again at the sheer scale of the construction. It was going to be utterly magnificent.

Ninian nudged him. 'Where does that lead to?' He indicated a low arched doorway deep in the shadows.

'I don't know. Why?' Josse whispered back.

'There's someone hiding there. I'm sure I saw movement.'

'Come on. We'll creep round, keeping our backs to the wall, and see who it is.'

It seemed to take a long time to make their slow and careful way to the doorway. As they approached, Josse drew out his long knife. They slowed their progress to a crawl, and Josse stared into the darkness behind each pillar before drawing level with it. They reached the arch and went on past it, investigating for some way on the far side. They found nothing.

'He's probably gone through the doorway,' Josse murmured softly. 'We'll follow.' Ninian nodded.

Josse went through the doorway and found himself at the top of a spiral staircase. The light from the nave behind him did not reach far and soon he was descending in pitch darkness. A light would have helped, for the steps were slippery and in places uneven, but it would also have alerted anyone beneath to their approach. He crept on, his right hand clutched on the hilt of his knife and his left maintaining a steadying contact with the wall. Ninian was right behind him. The boy's presence was both reassuring and something else to worry about.

They reached the bottom of the stairs. Edging forward, Josse peered out. There was a glow of light and by it he saw that they were in a crypt. Slowly, silently, they moved forward towards the light. Presently Josse made out the sound of soft chanting.

They emerged from the aisle that led from the entrance – it appeared that the layout of the vast crypt followed that of the cathedral above – and a dimly lit space opened out before them. There was a well and, beyond it, a dark opening leading to a further chamber. The source of both the light and the chanting appeared to be within. They crept on.

The further chamber, although lit only by a circle of lanterns about five paces in diameter, gave the appearance of being enormous. The vaulted ceiling arched over their heads, supported on massive pillars spaced at regular intervals. The circle of light appeared to surround a depression whose surface was bumpy and uneven, like the floor of a cave. A subterranean cave, Josse thought with a shudder, for now they must be deep under the ground, in the very womb of the earth.

One voice was chanting and it came from a figure that stood with its back to Josse and Ninian. It was tall, and the broad shoulders were hunched over a bent back. It was clad in a black cloak or robe whose folds swept down to the floor; it was bareheaded, the lantern light catching glints from the snow-white hair that flowed down to the shoulders. It – he – was intent on what he was doing. Before him on the rough floor was an object made of dark wood. The goddess had returned to her proper medium, but the wrong hand had brought her here.

Ninian gave a sharp, quickly suppressed intake of breath and said in Josse's ear, so softly that it was as if he mouthed the words, 'Philippe de Loup.'

The crooked back and the white hair suggested someone old, and Josse had imagined a man still in his full vigour. 'You are sure?' he murmured.

'*Yes.*' Ninian spoke with impatience. Then, 'Josse, we must stop him! She is not his to position or even to worship, for he has forfeited his rights.' Then, vehemently, he added, 'The guardianship of the Knights of Arcturus is *over.*'

Slowly Josse nodded. Then cautiously he began to move forward. Ninian was right beside him. They were ten paces from de Loup. Eight. Five. Josse raised his knife. Ninian had a dagger in his hand.

Josse was about to announce their presence and demand the figure when, very slowly, de Loup turned round to face them. 'Ninian de Courtenay,' he said in a low, strangely beautiful voice.

Even in that moment of extreme tension, a jolt went through Josse; Ninian used his mother's name, not that of his stepfather. Suddenly it seemed to him that Joanna was there beside him, her spirit standing guard beside her lover and her son.

Ninian pointed at the figure. 'You cannot have her,' he said, his voice high with strain and making him sound even younger than he was.

De Loup laughed. 'But I do have her,' he remarked. 'I have brought her to a fitting resting place.'

'It is not for you to decide what is fitting!' Ninian cried.

Now de Loup looked angry. 'Is it not?' he said coldly. 'It is for a stripling of a lad to decide, is it? A callow boy who thinks he knows everything is to dictate to grown men whose ancestors found her, worshipped her and guarded her for a hundred years?'

'You are not worthy of those ancestors!' Ninian shouted. 'She gave you power but you have abused the gift. You have descended into vice so vile that it is not to be spoken of in this sacred place, and it is only your wealth and the presence in your number of the rich and influential that keeps you immune from the laws of the Church and the State!'

If de Loup was angry, then Ninian was incandescent with rage. He stood straight and slim beside Josse, blue eyes catching the light and blazing like the heart of a flame. In a strange moment of detachment, Josse

246

thought, I wish his parents could see him. In very different ways, they would both be so proud.

Incredibly, Philippe de Loup was laughing. 'So, lad, what are you going to do?'

Ninian stepped over the circle of lanterns and up to de Loup. 'I am going to take her to the place where she wishes to be.' He put his dagger in his belt and, bending down, swiftly picked up the black figure, cradling her in both hands. Josse, moving forward with him, raised his knife and pointed it at de Loup's heart.

'You have another protector, I see,' de Loup said, regarding Josse out of dark, hooded eyes. 'You, sir, are going to see the boy and his treasure safe back to this new place?' He made the suggestion sound risible.

'Aye,' Josse said firmly. 'I am.' He kept the knifepoint up and Ninian stepped back outside the circle. Backing away, still facing de Loup, he moved with Ninian towards the stairs.

Just then a group of dark figures appeared out of the shadows, quickly crossing the floor until they formed a circle that echoed the circle of lanterns. But there were spaces among the figures; there were thirteen lanterns and only eight men. They had trapped Josse and Ninian in the space between them and the lights.

De Loup said pleasantly, 'Let me present

the remaining Knights of Arcturus. We are but nine now, I fear; one betrayed us, two died at Châlus and—'

'One of those was King Richard!' Josse burst out. They were trapped; there was nothing to lose. Perhaps if he revealed what he knew and told de Loup that others were in on the secret, he might at least buy them some time. At most, make a bargain. 'He was seen leaving the Île d'Oléron,' he hurried on. 'He was careless, for he let the boatman who ferried the three of you out to the ship see his face. The boatman is a loyal subject of Queen Eleanor and he told her what he saw.'

De Loup was chuckling quietly. 'And I suppose she has sent you, sir knight, to ensure that the secret never emerges?' Then, his face darkening, he spat out, 'Fool! Fool of a man, to believe the word of a peasant!' He winced suddenly as if in severe pain, putting a hand to his head. Then, dark eyes on Ninian, he said, 'You all but killed me, boy. You cracked my skull and something has happened to me—' He broke off. 'But, as you see, I still stand.' Then he made a movement with his right hand and as one body the eight knights stepped forward. One pace, two, three and then Josse and Ninian were face to face with their adversaries.

Josse tried to take in the quality of their opponents. Many of them were old and in a separate part of his mind he thought, the Knights of Arcturus are doomed, for no young men are rising up to replace them. He reckoned he could take on several of them and, switching his knife to his left hand, he drew his sword.

He heard Ninian cry out in the same split second that de Loup rushed him. He swung up his sword but de Loup leaped to one side. He wrested the figure out of Ninian's hand – the boy could not hold on to her one-handed and he held his knife in his right hand – and, leaping through the circle of knights, de Loup flew across the floor and away up the stairs.

The knights closed in. Josse and Ninian fought back to back. Horribly aware that Ninian had only one weapon, Josse swung his sword in wide circles in front of them both, trying to keep the knights back. One went down, crying out and clutching at a slash across his chest from which there instantly welled a line of blood. Another leaned forward to stab at Ninian and Josse caught him a heavy blow on the back of the head with his sword hilt. He too went down. Ninian was suddenly fighting hand to hand with another, and Josse caught the flash of white teeth as Ninian bit into the knight's hand and the knife he had been holding fell with a clatter to the floor. Then the knight's cry changed to an agonized grunt as Ninian's knee drove into his testicles. In addition to the courtly pursuits, then, squires were still taught to fight dirty. His blood singing from the thrill of the fight, Josse laughed aloud. A knight leaped on him from his left and a blade flashed up towards his throat; with a curse, Josse elbowed him away and drove his sword into the man's chest.

Four down, four to go. Josse wiped the sweat out of his eyes with his wrist and assessed his remaining assailants. He and Ninian had made some progress towards the stairs and now they managed to edge round so that the four knights still on their feet were on the far side of them. Now, backing steadily away, they could keep the quartet covered with their three weapons.

Two of the four knights were very old and already lagging back. One was breathless, blue around the lips and clutching his chest. The man beside him, equally old and bald-headed, round-bellied and limping, stopped to help him. Josse raised his sword and lunged towards the last two. One stepped hastily back; the other dodged and, his own sword raised, ran straight at Josse. Ninian's dagger flew through the air and landed at the base of the knight's throat. With a cry that quickly turned to a gurgle as the blood spouted out of him, his sword fell from his hand and he fell to his knees.

'*Come on!*' Josse shouted, grasping Ninian's shoulder; the boy was standing transfixed, horrified eyes wide as he stared at what he had done. Then, for still he did not move,

'De Loup's got the figure!'

That was enough. Ninian, white-faced and looking sick, bent to retrieve his dagger from the dying man's throat, wiped it on the cloak that pooled on the ground and ran after Josse up the steps.

As they emerged into the nave, the sight that met their eyes was so unexpected, so amazing, that they skidded to a halt. It appeared that the lanterns arranged below in the crypt had, by some extraordinary magical means, risen up through the solid floor to rest here on the ground above. Now, though, the circle of light was much bigger, stretching right across the wide nave, and instead of thirteen points of light there were now perhaps a hundred.

As Josse stared, he realized something: the light encircled the labyrinth.

There were dark-clad figures round the circle's perimeter – thirty or forty. He cursed himself for his stupidity: the Knights of Arcturus must have followers, adherents, perhaps, and had brought them to form a guard up here while they placed the figure down below. He and Ninian had fought off a group out of which more than half were so old and doddery that they barely counted; this was a different matter entirely.

One of the figures turned away from the light and, facing Josse, walked towards the place where he and Ninian stood against the wall. Josse raised his sword and stepped

251

forward. His mouth was dry and he was filled with dread, but his arm was quite steady. Then he saw that the man approaching him was unarmed. From within the circle behind him, white light had started to pulse.

The man said, 'We know why you are here and what you have just done. We are grateful, for without your intervention we would have had to deal with the intrusion into the sacred place beneath. They were an abomination and neither they nor any deed done by their corrupted hands could be allowed to remain here.'

'Aye,' Josse said, unable to look away from the circle of light and the white mist that seemed to be rising up within it, forming itself even as he stared into a cone shape. 'What is it?' he whispered, and the man smiled briefly.

'Power,' he said simply. 'This is our most holy place. We know now that we must share it with the men of the new religion, for they are stronger than us and far, far more numerous. We have had our time; now we must retreat into the shadows. But we will not go without honouring she who we hold most sacred. She was worshipped down there in the cave that hollowed out the earth where the crypt now lies. She was there from the beginning, she is there now, and she always will be. Our last great act of homage now begins and with it we leave the very best of ourselves to remain here in this holy spot for as long as the world lasts.' He paused, staring intently first at Josse then, with a start of recognition, at Ninian. He added softly, 'You may stay. But keep back!' He gave them a low bow, then, turning, went back to his place in the circle.

The cone of light was soaring high above their heads and its fast spinning was accompanied by a noise like the wind blowing across harp strings. The combination of light and sound was hypnotic and Josse felt himself rapidly detaching from the real world and entering some strange place that he neither recognized nor even began to understand ... until he saw Joanna.

Her face was pale and there were greyish circles round her dark eyes, as if she had just undergone some ordeal. She looked thin, although her face seemed fuller than he remembered and her breasts pushed against the fabric of her deep blue robe. He thought she had stars in her hair.

She was intent on what she was doing. In the way of dreams, he was suddenly right beside her. She turned, gave him a tired smile and said softly, 'Dear, lovely Josse.'

'Why are you here?' he asked through his tears. He thought he knew.

'It is time,' she murmured. 'This is what they have been preparing me for – they tell me this is what I was born to do, for Mag Hobson, my mother, was one of the greatest of my people and she conceived and bore me for this purpose.'

'Do you want to go, sweetheart?' It was so important to know! If she gave just one little hint of hesitation, he would ... he would...

What would he do? What *could* he do?

But her face was serene and the smile had spread, illuminating her face. 'Oh, yes, Josse,' she whispered. 'I have to – it is the only way.' Tears filled her eyes. 'It is not without reluctance, for I love you deeply and I shall miss you and the children – it is only because I know you will look after them so well that I can leave them.' She raised her hand and wiped her face.

'Will we ever see you again?' He was weeping openly now.

'Perhaps.' She tried to smile. 'Meggie and ... my daughter already sees me and speaks to me; this may be the gift that I leave to those of my blood. I hope so.'

'And me?' He could not stop himself asking, although he feared the answer.

'Josse, I don't know.' She leaned against him as she always did and he put up his hands and stroked the length of her smooth brown hair. 'I have asked my people the same thing but they cannot tell me. It is the first time that it has happened, for one such as I to love someone who is bound entirely by the limits of the earth.'

'I love you,' he said.

'And I you.' She managed to smile. 'And love doesn't die – that is the one rule of the universe that cannot change.'

'Find me, if you can,' he whispered.

'I will.' She stretched up and kissed him, long and deeply.

Then she was gone.

Now the vision was different. He knew he was back in the cathedral but it was subtly altered, as if his dreaming mind accepted that what he was seeing could not occur in a real place. He saw the figures standing like statues round the circle of light, every head raised, all eyes staring at the central point, every voice singing a chant of praise. Beyond them, the cone reached up, up to the high ribs where soon now the ceiling would soar up there above the wide nave, enclosing the space beneath and closing out the elements, the heavens and the stars. For now, though, the cathedral was still open to the night sky.

The vortex of white mist swayed and flowed, and within it could be glimpsed the central void. But all at once it was not empty; there were *people* in it. Josse stared at the figures. Sometimes they seemed to be a woman and a huge bear; sometimes it was a man who supported the woman as they twisted and turned, driven upwards, always upwards, by the power of the vortex. There was a flash of white light – so dazzling that it seemed to force its way right through Josse's eyes and inside his head, momentarily blinding him – and he thought he saw within his mind the image of a huge swirling tower of luminous brilliance that stretched from the zenith of the heavens above down, down through the space where one day the cathedral roof would be, down through the very centre of the labyrinth, down through the solid stone floor to the crypt below, into the heart of that strange cave-like depression, to bury itself at last in the earth far, far below.

Within the light danced the figures of Joanna and the Bear Man. They were a part of it now, as he knew they would always be. Other images flowed alongside them, forming, dissolving and forming again: a black woman in a horned headdress who rode on the crescent moon; the same woman, eyes closed in bliss and long, graceful hands clasped in the age-old symbol of protection across her pregnant belly; a child, as dark as his mother, sitting on her lap with a star in his hand.

All at once the voices of the people soared up into a paean of praise that rose to an unbelievable, deafening climax and then fell away. The cone of light flared like a bursting star and then went out. Josse, his head spinning and sick with vertigo, fell senseless to the ground.

When he came to, the great cathedral was

empty except for Ninian, curled up by his side. He kept quite still – his head ached agonizingly and he felt dizzy even lying down – and slowly let his eyes roam around.

His face was still wet with tears. Slowly he raised a hand and wiped them away. Did I dream it? he wondered. I must have done, for what I saw is impossible. The vision was, he decided, the product of his fears for Joanna and the aftermath of the fight, perhaps augmented by some herbal concoction that the people had been brewing and that made the white mist. He closed his eyes again. Is that what I believe has happened to her? he asked himself. Do I want to think she's gone far beyond my reach and I may never see her again?

No.

But he was afraid – very afraid – that she had indeed gone, and perhaps his dream version of her fate was the only one that he could find at all acceptable. If so, it was scant consolation.

Beside him, Ninian stirred. Very carefully Josse turned his head to look at the boy. His face too was drenched in tears.

Did he see what I saw? Josse wondered. Did he too witness his mother in that huge cone of power and understand, in part at least, that this was her destiny?

He had no idea. It was much too soon to ask, if, indeed, he ever could. Instead he put out his hand and clasped Ninian's. 'Are you all right?' he asked softly.

After a moment, Ninian said, 'Yes.'

Without another word they cautiously got up and, leaning on each other for support, slowly walked through the deserted cathedral and out into the dawn.

Fifteen

As they crept out of the cathedral, Ninian gave a gasp and pointed to where three bodies lay in the corner between a buttress and the wall. He and Josse hurried over and, carefully turning the men over to see their faces, recognized the night watchmen.

'Are they dead?' Ninian asked softly.

Josse inspected each one. 'No,' he replied. 'All three are breathing.' He had been feeling around the head of the third man. 'They've been knocked unconscious. De Loup's work, or one of his knights, to ensure they were not disturbed down there in the crypt.'

'Not de Loup, then,' Ninian said in a hard voice. 'He would have killed them.'

'We ought to take them somewhere they can receive care,' Josse began, 'and—'

'We can't, Josse!' Ninian exclaimed. 'There is a crypt full of dead and wounded knights behind us and we did the damage! Yes, I know we were defending ourselves and seriously outnumbered, but it'll take ages to prove that, even assuming we can, and in the meantime de Loup is running away.'

The boy was right. Josse looked down at the watchmen, one of whom was already stirring. If he and Ninian fled now, nobody need know they had ever been there. They could return to their anonymous lodging house, collect their horses and be away in next to no time.

He stood up. 'All right.'

Both Josse and Ninian guessed that de Loup would run for home. Denied his aim of placing the black figure beneath the cathedral, surely his only alternative would be to return her to the tower at World's End. It was only a guess, though, and, as they urged their horses on down the smooth, flat road that ran south-east beside the River Eure, Josse prayed that it was the right one.

As the sun came up across the water to their left, they saw ahead of them a long-maned white horse, head down as it grazed the lush grass beside the river. Beneath a willow tree, leaning back against its trunk with his knees drawn up and his head in his hands, sat Philippe de Loup.

He looked up at Josse and Ninian, wry resignation on his lined, chalk-white face. 'So you have found me once more,' he remarked. 'You are persistent; I will say that for you.' He closed his eyes.

'What ails you?' Josse asked.

De Loup opened his eyes and glared up at him. 'As I said last night, the boy has a heavy hand with a bolt of wood,' he said. He put up a hand and touched the back of his head. 'I believe he cracked my skull.'

Josse slipped off Horace's back. 'Let me look,' he said. 'Perhaps we can assist, or help you to where you can receive treatment.'

De Loup began to laugh. 'I said you were a fool,' he observed, 'and I was right. Do you not recognize an enemy when he stares you in the face?' Before Josse could reply, he added, 'Besides, it is too late.' He took a breath and squared the slumped shoulders. 'I can no longer feel the left side of my body.'

Josse thought rapidly. He had seen men take a blow to the head, get up and appear to be all right and then some time later, just like de Loup, take sick and die. It was as if the brain refused at first to admit it was fatally damaged.

Ninian had also dismounted. 'I will take her,' he announced, advancing on de Loup.

Something was wrong; it was only the swiftest of impressions but it registered in Josse's mind. Even as he yelled to Ninian, 'Watch out!' de Loup uncurled himself, his short, lethal knife an extension of his right hand, and with the full impulsive power of

260

his push off the ground, hurled himself on Ninian.

Terror turning him icy-cold, Josse thought it was all over in that first savage attack, but Ninian fought like a street urchin and by some trick he wriggled free of the stabbing knife, twisting round so that he kept his slim body out of reach. But de Loup, despite his injury, was stronger; soon he had Ninian's arm up behind his back, the knife to the boy's throat.

'Now I finish what I tried to do at World's End,' he panted. 'We needed two victims that night and we only offered up one, and the boy squealed like a girl while we dispatched him. He was not worthy of us or our great ceremony.'

Ninian struggled, his face contorted with rage. 'You had no right to take his life!' he cried. 'You tortured and shamed him, and his last moments on earth were polluted by your foul desires!'

De Loup wrenched up the boy's captive hands and Ninian bit down a scream of pain. 'As would yours have been, my pretty lad, but for the interruption! Make no mistake – what you heard us do to the first boy was in store for you too.'

Josse made a move forward but instantly the knifepoint dug into Ninian's neck. 'Stay where you are,' de Loup warned.

Josse watched Ninian. The boy's eyes were closed and he was moving his lips; oh, God,

261

Josse thought, he is praying – he believes his life is about to end and he prays for forgiveness of his sins! But then the blue eyes shot open and looked straight at Josse. Amazingly, Ninian smiled. Then he went limp.

De Loup, feeling the sudden weight of the body sagging in his arms, was taken off guard and bent with the load. Ninian slipped to the ground, de Loup crouching over him. Then, as de Loup put out both hands to support himself, Ninian shot up and kneeled on the older man's chest, his hands pinning down the arms.

De Loup stared up at him, his face suddenly impassive. 'So,' he sighed, 'again you evade me.'

His deadly pale face was beaded with sweat and his breath came unevenly. He is dying, Josse thought. Ninian must have seen it too, but he did not relax his hold.

'You are fortunate in your allies,' de Loup said with a sigh, 'for you attract better fighters than I do.' The white face twisted into a smile. 'Two against so many, back at my tower on Oléron, but then one of those was rather special.'

Josse was puzzled; the two must have been Piers and Ninian himself, and he had had no idea that Piers had been a great fighter. On the face of it, it seemed unlikely, but then a man did not always display his full prowess until he had to. 'Piers of Essendon was a surprising man, then,' he said.

Both Ninian and de Loup turned to stare at him. Ninian looked guilty; de Loup was laughing softly.

'Shall I tell him or will you?' he asked Ninian. The boy did not reply, save only to tighten his grip on de Loup's arms. 'Very well,' de Loup said, smiling, 'I shall.'

He turned his head so that he could meet Josse's eyes more comfortably. 'Piers protested the moment we took the first boy and tied him to the altar,' he said, his voice pleasant and conversational, as if he were speaking about what he had eaten for supper. 'The Knights of Arcturus are not what they were. As you have seen for yourself, many of us are old and feeble. Nevertheless, restraining Piers was well within our capabilities and we made him witness what we did. We dispatched the first boy and were in the middle of our preparations for the second when we were interrupted.' He sighed heavily. 'The intruder burst into the upper chamber and took us by surprise,' he went on. 'He released Piers, pushed him on down the stairs and kept us at bay with that great sword of his. That's the problem with a narrow stair,' he added, frowning. 'Such things are built, naturally, for those within to defend themselves, for of course only one attacker at a time can advance. By the same token, however, they also help those who retreat. He kept us there while Piers released his boy and fetched a couple of horses. He wounded three of us and that had the effect of discouraging the others. By the time we got down the stairs, the three of them had escaped.'

'And they raced across the island to the waiting boat,' Josse said. He stared at Ninian. 'It was you – *you* were the slighter, shorter man, and Piers was the fair one!' Piers's hair had been light brown turning to grey; under the moonlight, he would have appeared fair.

That made two, and the third one had been the king.

Everything Josse had so painstakingly worked out suddenly fell apart. 'I thought ... I believed the king was one of the Knights of Arcturus,' he said. 'I thought Piers and Ninian escaped, and *you–*' he glared at de Loup – 'set off in pursuit with the king and another knight.'

De Loup calmly returned the stare. 'You were wrong.'

He shifted his position slightly and Ninian renewed the pressure of his knees on the older man's chest. 'King Richard did not care for our activities in the tower at the end of his mother's island,' de Loup said. 'He was always very fussy about what could and could not be allowed to go on in Aquitaine; Queen Eleanor brought him up in the firm belief that the whole country would be his one day and he acted as if that day had already come.' A sly smile creased his face. 'Still, you know what they used to say about him. He might have appreciated the particular nature of our ceremonies on any other night and it was sheer bad luck that— *Aaagh!'*

Ninian had shifted his right hand from de Loup's upper arm to his throat and he cut off the flow of words. He does not believe the filthy rumours muttered about the king any more than I do, Josse thought warmly. Good for him, he—

De Loup's freed left arm had slid like a snake across the grass and now he had his knife in his hand. He swept it up towards Ninian's belly and in the same instant Josse threw himself forward, pushing Ninian off de Loup's chest and landing with his full and considerable weight in the boy's place. The knife was between him and de Loup; he had time only for a very swift prayer.

De Loup groaned and coughed. Blood ran out of his mouth and he tried to draw air into his crushed chest. Josse moved off him; the knife lay flat against de Loup's stomach. Rapidly Josse inspected himself and de Loup, but neither of them had been wounded by the blade.

De Loup was struggling for breath, the white flesh around his mouth turning grey. His eyelids fluttered closed and he mouthed some silent words; with no breath, he could make no sound. After a few agonizing moments, the convulsive movements in his chest slowed and then ceased. Josse leaned down over him. Then, standing up again, he said, 'He's dead.'

Ninian found the black statue, carefully wrapped in one of de Loup's saddlebags. He was in favour of setting out for the coast, and a ship to take them back to England, immediately, but Josse knew they could not be so hasty. There were two more things he must do, and the first of them was right there.

With Ninian's grudging help, they dug a grave for Philippe de Loup. It was not as deep as Josse would have liked, but the ground was quite soft and they managed to cover the corpse with sufficient depth of earth for it not to attract predators. Josse was troubled by the lack of a priest to speak the necessary words; he mentioned this to Ninian, who said scornfully that de Loup would not have had any time for the priest or his prayers. 'He walked a very different path, Josse,' the boy added gravely. 'He must meet whatever awaits him in the same unorthodox way that he lived his life.'

There was nothing that Josse could think of to reply to that. When they had finished, Ninian stowed the figure in his pack and, leading de Loup's horse – for they could not leave the animal running loose – they set off back along the Eure. They did not follow the road all the way back to Chartres; as the city's walls appeared in front of them, the low, early sun making them appear to glow orange, Josse turned off to the north-west so as to avoid the city and they gave it a wide berth. Once they were clear, however, Josse led them back to the well-maintained road beside the river and they followed it as it meandered to and fro, all the time going steadily north.

Late in the evening, they neared the spot where the Eure joined the mighty Seine, looping and winding its way between dramatic limestone cliffs at the end of its long journey to the sea. Somewhere over to the east, Josse knew, was King Richard's Château Gaillard, his beloved 'saucy castle', bane of King Philip's life; the king, bless him, had declared in his usual single-minded way that the place was impregnable and when Philip had suggested the contrary, Richard had shouted colourfully that he would hold his beloved castle on the rock from his lifelong enemy even if its walls were made of butter. What a flamboyant, towering figure the world had lost with the king's death.

They made camp on an outcrop of rock high above the Eure, hurrying now as it approached the greater river. Ninian tended the three horses, while Josse made a simple shelter and set out stones for a hearth. He lit a fire and prepared a meal; their provisions were low, but with luck they would not have to last much longer. When they had eaten, they rolled in blankets and cloaks and were very soon asleep; it had been a long day, following an even longer night.

Josse woke from a deep sleep and lay quite still, wondering what had disturbed him. To his amazement, he thought he heard a baby crying, but the sound ceased and straight away he decided he must have heard a vixen's shriek, or a night bird's cry. Either that or the small sound had been part of a dream. He turned on his side and went back to sleep.

They set out early the next morning. Close to their destination, they stopped at an inn to eat breakfast and do what they could to wash themselves and brush the travel stains off their clothing. Then they rode on and, shortly before midday, came to Rouen.

Queen Eleanor had told Josse she would be in the city by mid-July. He was not entirely sure what the date was, but he thought June had turned into July a few days past. It was very likely that he and Ninian would reach Rouen before her, in which case they could find somewhere comfortable to stay and have a well-deserved rest. On the other hand, it might be later than he thought and she could be there already; it was because of this that he had insisted he and Ninian smarten themselves up.

They ate the midday meal at a busy tavern by the river. Josse listened to the chatter all around him and soon it became clear that a very grand visitor was in residence at the castle where she expected her son, the newly proclaimed King John, to join her at the end of the month.

Josse finished his meal and waited while Ninian wolfed down a second helping. Josse felt strangely calm: he had the answer he had gone searching for and he looked forward to revealing all that he had discovered to Queen Eleanor. He made himself concentrate on that happy prospect to the exclusion of everything else. He did not dare think about Joanna. The time would come when he would have to, he knew it, but he would try to wait until he was back home in England. There he could be sure of the support of people who loved him to help him through his grief.

Ninian had finished at last. Leaving the horses in the inn's stables, they set off for the castle.

Josse had explained to Ninian why they were in Rouen and what they had to do. The boy had accepted it without comment and Josse had believed he was not particularly anxious at the prospect of telling his story to the queen. If only, Josse mused, he knew ... But it was not his secret to tell and firmly he arrested the thought.

Now, however, as they waited in a huge anteroom for the summons to go before the queen, Ninian looked very nervous. He was probably reliving that terrible night in the tower, Josse thought. Such memories would be enough to make anyone look apprehensive.

The servant who had taken Josse's message to the queen returned and led the way up some wide stone stairs, along a corridor, up some more steps and into a large room sumptuously furnished with beautifully carved chairs, chests and tables, its walls hung with colourful tapestries whose general theme seemed to be the lauding of the Plantagenets and their deeds. Queen Eleanor was seated in a high-backed chair on a low dais. She nodded an acknowledgement to Josse's low, respectful bow and, dismissing both the servant and the two ladies who had been sitting beside her, beckoned him forward. Ninian remained by the doorway.

Josse kneeled before her, lowered his head and said, 'My lady, your son the late king was on the Île d'Oléron that night in March.' He heard her quick, sharp intake of breath. 'His purpose, however, was not to participate in what was going on in the tower at World's End but to stop it.'

There was a long silence. Josse did not dare look up. Presently the queen said, 'You are quite sure of this?' Her voice was low and oddly hesitant, as if, having steeled herself for bad news, she could not quite believe that it was not forthcoming.

'Utterly certain,' Josse said firmly. 'The ... er, the night's proceedings were under way and someone was being held there awaiting ... well, waiting to be taken to the upper chamber. King Richard found out what was going on – indeed, what had apparently been going on for some time, for the men who were there that night met often – and he recognized that what they were doing was an outrage that abused your territory and must not be allowed to continue. He broke up the ... er, the meeting and rescued the person who had been imprisoned.'

The queen did not speak for a moment. Then she said, 'Sir Josse, look at me.'

Reluctantly he raised his head and stared into her deep, dark eyes. 'My lady?'

'We both know what went on in that tower,' she said very softly, 'and I applaud your reserve in not going into details. What you are telling me is that my son prevented the grave misuse and death of a young man?'

'Aye, he did.' There was no need to mention the first poor lad, tortured and killed before the king got there.

'And you have spoken to this man? He has told you himself that my son saved his life?'

Josse risked a smile. 'Aye, my lady. Better than that, I've brought him with me so he can tell you himself. May I present him to you?'

Her eyes were looking over his head towards Ninian, standing unbowed at the back

271

of the room. 'This is the man? Sir Josse, he's little more than a boy!'

'He is fourteen, madam.'

'A boy,' she repeated under her breath. Josse, watching her, saw her expression and wondered if she was only now appreciating the full horror of what they had done at World's End. Then, with a curt nod, she said, 'Bring him forward.'

Josse beckoned to Ninian and watched as he walked gracefully up to the dais and bowed before the queen. As he straightened up, the queen stared down into his face and Josse thought he heard her give a tiny gasp. Then, recovering, she said, 'What is your name?'

'Ninian de Courtenay, my lady.'

'And where do you come from? I feel that I recognize the name but I cannot place it.'

'It is the name of my mother's kin, madam.'

The queen was still staring at him, a faint frown deepening the creases on her brow. 'De Courtenay ... I believe I once met a Marie de Courtenay, but she would have been too old to be your mother – your grandmother, perhaps.' She shook her head as if to free it from that thought and, with an obvious effort, smiled at Ninian and said, 'But we are not here to discuss your grandmother. You have something to tell me, I am told?'

With a shining and very apparent honesty, Ninian told his tale. Josse noticed with interest and approval that the boy too obeyed the same instinct as he had done himself not to risk distressing the queen. Like Josse, he did not speak of the true horror of what had happened that night.

'And King Richard took you and your master out to his ship?'

'Yes, my lady.'

Josse went to say something but stopped himself. You did not speak to a queen; you waited until she spoke to you.

She must have sensed he had something to add. 'Sir Josse?'

'Madam, it was the man who rowed the king, the boy and his master to the ship who disclosed the secret of the king's presence on Oléron that night,' he said. 'He spoke the truth, my lady.'

The queen smiled. 'No need to remind me, Sir Josse,' she said with discernible irony. 'I promise I shall not have the man arrested and his tongue slit for telling lies.'

Josse hung his head, but the queen said, 'Sir Josse?' and he looked up at her. She studied him for a few moments. 'Thank you,' she said. 'You have removed a terrible fear from my mind. Now I shall indeed be able to let my son rest in peace.' There was a short silence, as if all three of them were paying silent homage to the dead king. Then Eleanor said, 'So where now, Sir Josse?'

'I shall return to Hawkenlye Abbey and tell the abbess that—' Too late he realized what he was saying; to reveal to the queen that he was going to relate the outcome of the matter to the abbess implied that he had told her about it, and Eleanor had sworn him to secrecy.

But she was laughing softly. 'It's all right, Sir Josse,' she said. 'I think I always understood that, for you, sharing a confidence with Helewise of Hawkenlye was almost the same thing as talking to yourself.'

He was not entirely sure what she meant, but there was no time to work it out. She had risen to her feet and, taking this as an indication that the interview was over, Josse began backing away, nudging Ninian to make him do the same.

Eleanor, however, had not quite finished. Reaching beneath her chair, she pulled out a leather bag. It was quite large and clearly very heavy. 'You have no doubt been put to considerable expense in this mission,' she said smoothly. 'Allow me, if you will, to recompense you.' She handed him the bag.

Josse took it, too taken aback to comment other than a muttered 'Thank you, my lady.'

Then with one final, long look at Ninian, she dismissed them.

Josse reined in his impatience until he and Ninian were back in the stables, collecting their horses. Then, while Ninian stood guard, he untied the laces that fastened the leather bag. Within there were gold coins: a lot of gold coins. With shaking fingers Josse tried to count them, but he made a mistake. He must have done, for the total seemed to come to a sum that was sufficient to build a fair-sized house.

Part Four

The Great Forest

Sixteen

Helewise had not realized just how disruptive it would be to have even a modest and simple chapel built so close to the abbey. She had imagined that an added advantage of siting the new building outside the walls would mean that the community could go about its daily round in peace; this, however, proved not to be the case. Everyone, from the most senior and dignified nuns down to the youngest, newest lay brother, was suddenly preoccupied with thinking up excuses that took them out beyond the gates and past the workmen hard at work at the top of the slope on the edge of the forest. They did not content themselves with a quick look to check on progress; instead, Helewise noticed, quietly fuming, they would stand there in what looked like a light trance, wide eyes fixed on the apparently fascinating sight of a mason chipping away at a chunk of stone.

She was not immune from the draw of the new chapel, but she forced herself not to waste time during her working hours; instead, she made a daily visit to the site just after vespers, when the workmen would be packing up for the day. Quite often she took Meggie with her, and the little girl seemed to enjoy the special time together as much as she did. Meggie appeared to be happy enough, although frequently she stopped and looked around, as if searching for Josse, or, indeed, Helewise thought with pain, for her mother. Everyone made a pet of the child, Helewise included, for she was easy to love and a cheerful companion, which made the evening visits to the new chapel all the more enjoyable. Helewise would exchange a few words with Martin and one or two of his team and then, once they had all gone, walk slowly around, seeing for herself the day's progress.

Slowly, almost unaware of it, she fell under the spell of St Edmund's Chapel. It was not large: perhaps twenty paces from the west wall to the rounded apse behind the place where the altar would stand, and a fraction over half that distance from the north wall to the south. Beneath the nave, a crypt had been hollowed out; it was there for a specific purpose. It was odd but every time Helewise thought about what that purpose was, something seemed to fudge her thoughts and she would find her mind had been turned to something else.

The chapel's entrance was in the south wall, and the apse extended under the trees at the very edge of the forest. There would be three small windows glazed with plain glass set high up in the apse, so that the morning sun would shine down on the altar. The west end faced the abbey, which was wonderful because Helewise was to have her wish. Martin had told her that the two strong buttresses that would stand at either end of the west wall were there for support. She had looked blankly at him, not understanding. 'We'll strengthen that wall, my lady,' he explained, 'because then we can leave a great big space in it.'

'But—'

'And we'll fill it with glass,' he finished.

Not just any glass; Helewise discovered as Martin showed her the drawings that Queen Eleanor had been very specific. She must have seen for herself what was planned for Chartres and she wanted something equally beautiful for the new chapel built for her son. The west window in Hawkenlye's St Edmund Chapel would have a huge stained-glass illustration whose central panel depicted the saint on horseback, sword raised to strike down the enemies of the Lord. If St Edmund was tall, auburn-haired and blue-eyed and bore a resemblance to the queen's favourite son, then it would be a hard-hearted person who failed to sympathize and understand.

Helewise was amazed at how quickly the building was going up. June turned into July and the team made the most of the long sunny days. Construction always came to an end in October, she well knew, when any incomplete structures would be carefully padded with bracken or straw to prevent damage by winter frosts. Such a measure, she slowly came to realize, would not be necessary here, for unless some unforeseen setback occurred, the chapel roof ought to be on long before the autumn set in.

She talked at length with Martin concerning the chapel's interior. They were in agreement that the walls should simply be whitewashed; anything else would detract from the glorious colours of the west window. Martin persuaded her to have a rood screen. The master carpenter produced a sketch of a plain structure made of local oak and consisting of a series of arches, two narrow ones on either side and a wider one in the middle, giving access to the choir. The altar was to be a large block of sandstone, quarried locally and dragged up to Hawkenlye on a massive cart drawn by a whole team of oxen. Martin's masons were already working on it, shaping and smoothing it to form a rectangular cube.

Helewise readily immersed herself in every detail. Apart from anything else, it helped to take her mind off her abiding, gnawing anxiety about Josse.

She went into the abbey church very early one morning, following an almost sleepless night. Alone in the dim dawn light, she prostrated herself in front of the altar and begged the Lord to protect Josse and his young companion. They had been away for over three weeks and she was finding it very difficult to keep her fears at bay. They have gone after one man, she reminded herself again and again; the threat that they faced was no more than that. De Loup was from Aquitaine, and Josse might have had to follow him all the way there. Such a journey was not done quickly and, even having found de Loup, Josse would have to talk to him at length in order to persuade him to give up the black figure. It was foolish, she concluded, to imagine Josse and Ninian could possibly be safely back already. There really was no need to worry.

Yet.

And now, disconcertingly, Meggie had taken to keeping watch for her father by the abbey gates. It was as if she too felt that his return was sufficiently long overdue for it to be worrying. It might have been easier had the child expressed her fears in tears and demands for reassurance, or even in bad behaviour. Any of those would have been understandable; after all, both her mother and now her father had disappeared out of her life. Instead she kept up her vigil and barely said a word. It was heartbreaking.

Helewise dropped her face on to her folded hands and, for a few precious moments, let the Lord carry all her desperate anxiety.

When presently she rose and slowly left the church, she thought that the burden did not feel quite so heavy.

Early in July, Hawkenlye Abbey received a visit from the kin of Sir Piers of Essendon. Helewise had sent word to them of his death and they had promised to come for his body once arrangements had been made. Since his death, Piers had lain in his sealed coffin down in the crypt of the abbey church; Helewise was well aware that several of the nuns who had nursed him often slipped away down there to sit with his gentle spirit.

She had not known the composition of his household, although Josse had said he believed him to be a widower. So it proved, for the deputation who came for his body consisted of a daughter, Adela, her husband and four attendants. Helewise received the couple in her room, taking the chance to tell the woman quietly of her late father's last hours.

She had braced herself for some hard questions, for Adela had already been informed that her father had been murdered. It would only be natural for her to demand why Hawkenlye had not offered him better protection. When no such questions materialized, Helewise finally said, 'We believe we know whose hand it was that ended your father's life. Our local sheriff has been alerted. In addition, Sir Josse d'Acquin, a

284

friend both of your father and of this community, has gone after the man and will do his best to see that he is brought to justice.'

Adela seemed strangely unmoved, merely giving a shrug as if the matter was of no concern. Perhaps she was in shock, Helewise thought, instantly sympathetic. 'Would you and your husband like to stay at the abbey for a day or two?' she asked kindly. 'You could talk to the nuns who cared for your father and, if anything occurs to you that you'd like to ask, you could—'

But Adela was already standing up, commanding her husband with a jerk of her head to do the same. 'No,' she said. 'We'll take him and bury him. Then we intend to get on with our lives.' She drew herself up and there was a glint of avarice in her steely eyes. 'Essendon is ours now.'

Silently Helewise saw them out to where their horses waited, beside a cart on which the coffin now rested, the servants standing around it and uneasily shuffling their feet. She watched the couple mount up and lead the way out through the gates, the cart trundling along behind. She stood there until all that could be seen of the party was the cloud of dust hanging over the road.

As finally she returned to her room, she was consoled by the thought of Ninian. Piers had cared for Ninian; if the boy had returned that affection, then at least Piers had died knowing that somebody would grieve for him. Although she knew she must not judge, she could not help thinking that his hard-hearted daughter was too busy enjoying her inheritance to waste a moment mourning her father.

It was very sad.

July crept on, each day seeming to pass with painful slowness as Helewise and the Hawkenlye community waited for Josse to return. The chapel continued to rise up on its shady site in front of the trees and word of it had spread far and wide, causing a large increase in the number of visitors to the abbey. The monks and lay brothers in the vale were kept busy looking after them, as were the infirmary nuns. For many people, it was rare indeed to make the journey to Hawkenlye, and those with nagging complaints and chronic illnesses took the chance to speak to a healer while they were there. Meggie was in demand in both the vale and the infirmary, and she divided her time between the two. Sister Euphemia reported that even at the tender age of six and a half, the child had a way with the sick.

Helewise too had more than enough work to keep her occupied. Nevertheless, she found time each evening to collect Meggie and go up to the new chapel. One evening as she and the little girl were setting out, Sister Tiphaine hurried to join them.

'My lady,' she said, bowing deeply, 'I have

been commanded to ask if you will go into the forest before you visit the chapel. There is someone there who wishes to speak to you.'

Helewise regarded the herbalist levelly. She was long past telling her that as a vowed nun she obeyed commands solely from her abbess; instead she said, 'Very well. Is she there now?'

Sister Tiphaine smiled. 'You know to whom I refer.'

'I do.'

'Yes, it's her, and she's waiting. Shall I lead the way?'

I know the way, Helewise thought, but she nodded.

The Domina was standing in the middle of the clearing. Sister Tiphaine took Meggie off to show her a red squirrel's drey and, as soon as they were out of earshot, the Domina said, 'He is on his way home.'

Helewise's eyes widened. 'Josse?'

'Yes.'

For a moment she could not even form the words of a prayer; she just repeated silently, over and over again, 'Thank you. Thank you.' Then, calming, she wondered how the Domina knew. Perhaps other forest people had seen him and knew he was nearly home. It did not matter; just knowing that he was safe was enough.

'He brings the black goddess with him,' the

Domina told her.

'I knew that he would,' Helewise replied, realizing the truth of this as she spoke. She smiled. 'I've been watching Martin make a niche for her in the crypt beneath the new chapel and it never occurred to me that he was wasting his time.' She paused, for what she wanted to say made no sense. Then she remembered to whom she was talking. 'I've seen her there,' she said dreamily. 'I've stood there with my eyes half closed and it's as if she is already in her special place.'

The Domina too smiled. 'She has great power,' she observed. 'Perhaps she has already affected you.' She studied Helewise intently. 'You are changed, Helewise. Your mind encompasses more than it used to.'

Helewise considered this. 'Yes. I've been thinking.'

'Thinking can be dangerous.' The Domina's tone was neutral.

But Helewise knew full well what she meant. 'I love the Lord no less,' she said swiftly. 'He is the pinnacle for me, the one shining example of a perfect life whose teachings I shall always strive to live up to, but there is more...' She trailed off, unable to put into words the deep, disturbing possibilities that had crept through her mind as she contemplated that black goddess with her swelling belly.

'Do not try to hurry it,' the Domina advised. 'It will come or not, in its own time.'

'I am a vowed nun,' Helewise muttered, distress filling her mind. 'An abbess!'

'But you are also a woman who thinks for herself,' the Domina said. 'Soon you will find that your Church begins to frown on such a person, especially if she is female.'

'What do you mean?' Helewise tried to sound affronted but she did not think she had succeeded. The Domina's words were all too true an echo of what Helewise had observed for herself.

The Domina sighed. 'I have recently been in France, with many of my people. Some of them were with me in the Shining City; others travelled far and wide to meet men and women like us and hear what is happening in distant lands. The story is always the same: the Church marches with a new determination to rout out all those who do not see the deity as they order that their God must be seen. They command men and women not only what to believe but how to believe it; faith, they would tell us, is an intellectual process through the head and no longer a loving, powerful inspiration through the heart. They set out rules of what is and is not permitted, and the least deviation attracts severe penalty.' She paused, breathing hard, and waited until she was calmer. Then she said very quietly, 'Helewise, there will come into being a new and terrible institution whose sole purpose is to suppress heresy. You who have seen with your own eyes will comprehend the ferocity with which this battle will be fought. Thousands, hundreds of thousands will die for nothing more than that they view the creating spirit in a different form from that which the Church stipulates.'

A shiver of fear ran through Helewise. How would such an institution deal with the forest people? With the Domina? With Joanna? With dear old Tiphaine, who despite being loyal to Helewise and a first-rate herbalist had always kept one foot in her pagan past? How would they deal with me, she wondered, horrified, if they knew I planned to place a black statue of the Great Mother Goddess in the new chapel?

'Wh–what will the members of this institution do?' she whispered.

'They will round up all those who do not conform. They will have no difficulty finding these people, for others will betray them. Some will be acting out of misplaced solicitude, genuinely believing the priests when they say that, in turning away from the rules of the Church, their friends and neighbours risk eternal damnation. The majority of informers will simply be settling old grudges. If your neighbour is taken away to be tortured and burned at the stake, nobody will notice if you quietly move the disputed boundary fence. And what better way of getting even with the innocent old woman whom you blame for the death of your cow than seeing her kept awake for days, stripped, prodded and beaten, then led out naked to her terrible death?'

'But the Lord told us to love each other.' Helewise's eyes were full of tears.

'I know, Helewise,' the Domina said on a sigh. 'I know.'

Helewise was thinking, as she had often done recently, of the Cathar woman Aurelia and her companions. She remembered her priest, Father Gilbert, telling her of a planned Crusade against the Cathars, launched by the Church and the king of France and fuelled by their combined hatred, greed, power and vast resources. More pain; more death; more families torn apart; more helpless, hopeless, lost souls.

She wondered if this Crusade had already begun. The Domina must have picked up the thought: 'Not yet,' she said. 'But within a decade, it will come to pass.'

It will come to pass, Helewise repeated silently, bowing her head as the intolerable images filled her mind. My Church will do this. In the name of the vast body to which I have given my life and my soul, people will be hunted down and killed because they refuse to acknowledge any man's right, even that of a priest, to tell them what to believe. What am I to do, I who, if I were put to the test and somehow found the courage to answer honestly, might be cast out with the heretics?

She did not know.

She looked up to speak to the Domina but she had gone. Helewise stood alone in the clearing enduring the agony of her thoughts.

Seventeen

Josse and Ninian made their way up to the coast by the network of paths and tracks that spread out from the meandering Seine as the river made its stately way westwards to the sea. Josse felt strongly that they must remain out of sight, and keeping off the main roads ensured that few people would remember, if asked, a big man and a lad riding good horses and leading a distinctive grey.

He told himself his caution was in case any of the surviving Knights of Arcturus were on their trail, determined to take back the black figure, but he knew in the depths of his mind that this was not true.

He was not sure what he feared. Sometimes when he was very tired he thought he heard a baby; sometimes it cried; sometimes it made gurgling sounds of contentment.

It just went to show, he thought, how grief, anxiety and fatigue could play tricks.

They left the river and headed off north

towards Fécamp. Josse knew the little place and had decided it was a better option than the bigger ports such as Le Havre or Dieppe. As they approached the sea, calm and silvery-grey under the bright afternoon sun, he saw that he and Ninian need not even advertise their presence in Fécamp for, ahead of them on the shore, he spotted a small fishing hamlet where a cluster of wooden-framed dwellings made a semicircle round a jetty stretching out into the sea. Tied to the jetty was a small fleet of fishing boats and some larger craft. He drew rein, signalling to Ninian, and, wheeling Horace round, headed back into the shade of a small copse through which they had just passed.

'Stay here with the horses,' Josse said, 'while I go down to the shore and ask about passage over to England.'

Ninian nodded, already jumping down to take Horace's reins. 'Be careful, Josse,' he said. He looked worried. Josse nodded an acknowledgement.

He trotted over the short, wiry grass, pleased to be using different muscles after so long in the saddle. In the hamlet he quickly found a seaman happy to take two people and three horses over to Pevensey. The price was steep – with no competition, for his boat was the only one available that could transport horses, the seaman could ask what he liked – but Josse agreed. They would sail on the evening tide.

Josse bought a flagon of cider, some fresh bread, a large creamy cheese and two small onions from the seaman's wife and hurried back to the hiding place in the trees. He and Ninian consumed the food and most of the cider, and then Ninian curled up in the shade and went to sleep.

Josse sat with his back to a birch tree, staring out over the distant sea and listening to the natural sounds all around. Birds sang; a soft breeze stirred the leaves. The three horses, their tack removed and hobbled to prevent them straying far, tore at the grass. Ninian snored gently. No baby sounds now, Josse reflected.

I imagined those little cries, he thought. My half-aware mind heard an animal or a bird and, because I am tired and grieving, translated it into a human sound. I must not give way to such fancies.

Firmly he turned his mind to Philippe de Loup and the Knights of Arcturus. He had not liked leaving the dead man out there in his lonely grave; it went against everything he believed in. No prayers were said over de Loup; no marker told others where he rested. Even thinking about it now gave Josse a shudder of abhorrence and he vowed that he would have prayers said for de Loup's soul as soon as he was back at Hawkenlye.

But what else could I have done? Josse asked himself. Aye, I could have returned to Chartres and found a law officer to tell him there was a dead man out on the road beside the river, and that would have brought down on my head such a barrage of suspicious questions that I should have been driven to my knees. Moreover, it would not take a genius to connect de Loup with however many of the knights were found in the cathedral crypt, dead or too badly injured to escape. I would probably have been accused of laying out the night watchmen too.

Even if Josse had been prepared to risk his freedom, going back to Chartres would have involved Ninian. Josse could have tried to make the lad go on alone, but he knew Ninian would not have left him. The boy had a loyal heart.

Ninian. Josse took another mouthful of cider and thought back to the eager boy he had met seven years ago. They had liked each other straight away, he and Ninian; even before Josse fell in love with the lad's mother, he had taken to Ninian for his own sake. When Josse did what Joanna asked and found a place for the boy, in his fellow knight Sir Walter Asham's household, he had swallowed the pain of leaving the lad with no expectation of ever seeing him again. Unlike Joanna, Josse had no scrying glass. But then – it was funny how life worked out – their paths had crossed once more. Now Ninian seemed to have attached himself firmly to Josse's side, as if, with Piers dead, he had turned into Josse's squire.

What should I do with him? Josse wondered, the question instantly answered with
a slightly mocking echo. *Do* with him? He
will not be done to; he will decide for himself.

Ninian had said he did not wish to return
to Sir Walter. Had he not been happy there?
Josse did not know. What else would the boy
do? Once he had returned the black goddess
to Hawkenlye, then what?

Josse had not yet found the right moment
to tell Ninian about Meggie. He glanced
across at the sleeping boy. I will do so this
night, he vowed. Before we set foot on
English soil, I will tell him. Joanna would be
happy, he thought, to think of her son and
her daughter meeting at last.

Joanna ... There was something that had
been nagging at him ever since the night in
the cathedral. Now, at last, he let himself
think about it. She had been saying goodbye;
until now, even approaching that aching
moment had threatened to undermine him
totally. Even now, tears filled his eyes as he
pictured her. He had asked if she wanted to
go and she had said it was the only way,
whatever that meant. She had told him she
loved him and her children, and that she
could only bear to leave them because she
knew Josse would care for them. She must
have known Ninian was there, he thought –
of course she did! – for then she had said
something about Meggie being able to see

her and speak to her and added that she hoped this was the gift she left to any of her blood. Ninian too, she seemed to be saying, would be able to commune with her in whatever form she now took.

He saw but could scarcely take in the obvious conclusion: Joanna wanted Josse to take care of Ninian as well as Meggie. Why else, he asked himself, with a sudden lift of the heart, why else say, it is only because I know you will look after them so well that I can leave them? She said 'them', not 'her'; she meant both her children.

I must not force this on to Ninian, Josse thought. For my part, I am overjoyed at the prospect of becoming Ninian's guardian, but I must make quite sure he feels the same.

He drank some more cider. The fierce, sharp pain of thinking about Joanna and picturing her pale, tired face was already lessening, softened by the images of a life with Joanna's children. My children, he thought drowsily, living in my household; Meggie because she is of my blood and Ninian because all of us wish it so.

The empty mug fell from his hand as he slipped into sleep.

Josse woke up to be faced by dazzling orange as the sun went down in the west and the shining sea reflected the brilliant sky. He stretched and yawned, watching Ninian as the boy packed their gear with neat, economic movements. His face was set, and his eyelids were pink and puffy, as if he had been crying.

'Ninian?' Josse asked tentatively.

The boy looked up swiftly, then bent once more to his task. 'I'm all right.'

But you're not, lad, Josse thought, any more than I am. Still, if a stern façade was the boy's way of keeping his emotions under control, it was not Josse's place to attempt to get beneath it.

Ninian ran out of jobs to do and, after a brief hesitation, came to sit beside Josse. 'How long till we go?' he asked.

'Our boat sails two hours after sunset,' Josse replied. 'We've a while yet.'

Silence fell. Josse, very aware of Ninian beside him, sensed strongly that there was something the boy wanted to say. He'll need to speak of his mother, Josse thought, praying for the strength to respond without breaking down.

When Ninian finally rounded up his courage and broke the silence, it was not at all what Josse had expected. 'Josse,' he began, 'I feel really bad because I lied to you.'

'Eh?'

'I think Sir Piers did too, but I'm sure he didn't want to any more than I did. It was to protect someone else, you see, and no matter how much we liked you there just wasn't any choice. I hope you're not disappointed in me.' He hung his head.

Josse thought carefully before speaking. 'It's perhaps a little like attacking in self-defence, isn't it?' he said eventually. 'You and I had to hurt the knights down in the crypt because they were trying to kill us. Some-times you have to do something that's usual-ly regarded as bad because the alternative is even worse.'

'Yes, that's it, sort of,' Ninian said eagerly.

There was a pause, heavy with the weight of things unsaid. Josse waited.

'I think I can tell you now, Josse,' Ninian said in a low voice. 'You see, we were pro-tecting someone's good name. He – this person – was doing a good thing, but every-one would have thought he was involved in a very bad one.'

Josse began to understand. 'You're talking about what happened on the Île d'Oléron.'

'Yes. De Loup told you that the king was against the Knights of Arcturus and every-thing they were and did, and I could see that it came as a complete surprise to you and you'd had no idea until that moment. Well, Josse, *I* could have told you ages ago, only Sir Piers and I vowed that we would not men-tion King Richard's name at all. We knew what the gossips would say – it's funny but people always want to believe the worst possible interpretation of events, don't they? – and we decided it was safer to pretend that our saviour was an unknown knight. We were convinced that de Loup and his knights

299

would keep quiet about King Richard's involvement that night – it would not reflect well on them that one man fought off all of them to rescue me and Sir Piers – and we swore to do the same.' He sighed. 'But now the king is dead, Sir Piers is dead, the knights have lost their treasure and, with their leader and driving force also dead, are probably in disarray.' He raised his clear blue eyes to Josse. 'You know, anyway, so now I can confess that I told you a lie and hope you forgive me.'

'Of course I do,' Josse said warmly. 'You had no choice, Ninian, and what you did was right and honourable. If the king had not had the moment of carelessness that allowed the guard who rowed the three of you out to the ship to see his face, the secret would never have emerged.' He paused, thinking hard. 'But it is better this way,' he concluded. 'Now, if by some devious means the tale of what went on in that tower should ever be whispered again, Queen Eleanor will know the truth.'

He had imagined that, having confessed and with his fault off his conscience, Ninian would have relaxed, but instead he seemed even more tense. Again, Josse waited.

'Josse?'

'I'm listening, lad.'

'Josse, you know about Thorald of Lehon?'

'Aye, I do.' He was wary at the mention of that name. Thorald of Lehon was, in the eyes of the world, Ninian's father. The truth was a closely guarded secret which Ninian might not know...

'He's dead,' Ninian went on quickly. 'He wasn't my father, even though he was married to my mother.'

'Aye.' For a wonderful moment, Josse wondered if Ninian was bringing up the subject of his fatherless state because he envisaged Josse in that role.

'I found out something,' the boy said. 'When I was ten, Sir Walter took me and lots of the other boys to a mêlée. It was really exciting. We watched heaps of mock battles and there was this one knight who was so good he— But that's not important.' He paused, taking a steadying breath. 'There were some great names at the tournament and Sir Walter had to have us drilled and coached so that we did not let him down in front of the lords and ladies. Anyway, this old couple were watching the fighting from a box up in the stands and they kept staring at me. The woman was muttering to her ladies, and other people were looking too. I didn't like it and I slipped away on a pretend errand, only then I thought I'd really like to know why they were so interested in me, so I crept round behind their box and listened.' His face was red and he did not meet Josse's eyes.

'The old man had gone back to watching the sport, but the lady and her women were still muttering, and one of them said something about fun and games and pretty girls slipped into chambers to warm the beds. I didn't understand – then – and I thought they meant servants with warming pans. Then the old woman said, "I asked and he was ten last September, so he'd have been got that Christmas at Windsor," and she mentioned something about fine new apartments and enough room for lots of women, and she talked about people called Bellebelle and Rosamund.'

Josse had heard the tale before. Lost in the past, he saw Joanna, her face as scarlet as her son's was now as she confessed her shame and humiliation.

'Then–' Ninian's voice was sharp with anguish and Josse was jerked back to the present – 'then she said, "The lad's got the look all right and those eyes are unmistakeable."' He put his hands over his face.

Josse said carefully after a moment, 'Did you know what she meant?'

'I guessed she was referring to me, but I didn't understand the rest. Some of the older boys must have heard the rumours because that night they cornered me in the stables and pulled off my hat so they could look at me. They made me stare at them and they started jeering and saying I was a nobody and blue eyes didn't make me a ... didn't prove anything. I got really angry and I threw off the boy who was holding me

302

down. Then I grabbed a pitchfork and swung it at him and the others, and I hit one and made a big cut over his eye. One of them said I had the temper to go with the eyes, and then one of the squires heard the rumpus and came out and we all got a beating.' He had removed his hands and was sitting up straight, shoulders squared. 'I fought them off, Josse, and they didn't taunt me any more. One of them who was nicer than the rest explained.'

'You know, then?' Josse asked gently.

Ninian turned to look at him. 'Yes, Josse, I know.'

'Don't think ill of your mother,' Josse urged. 'She was young and inexperienced, and her cousin manipulated her and made it happen.'

Ninian's clear eyes showed no shadow of doubt. 'Yes, I understand that. The squire who sought me out to tell me explained what it was like back in those days.' Then, curiosity in his voice, 'How did *you* know?'

'Your mother told me.' For a precious moment he gave the lovely memory full rein. Then, carefully storing it away again, he added, 'I've known since the three of us were together in the house in the woods, all those years ago.'

'You never told anyone?'

'I told Abbess Helewise of Hawkenlye but nobody else. As for your mother, I understand she told just one other person. It was

303

her secret, Ninian, and now it's yours.'

Slowly he nodded. Then, his voice so tentative that it made Josse's heart ache, he said, 'Do you think *he* knew too?'

Josse had to think for a moment. 'King Richard, you mean?'

'Yes.'

Did he? Josse wondered. Apart from his understandable wish to rout out the evil things that were being done on his mother's island, had the king found out the identity of one of the knights' intended victims? Had his fear for the boy urged him on in that dash across Oléron, that furious attack on the tower at World's End?

Perhaps. It would be typical of Richard to adopt a cause for a sentimental reason and pursue it as vigorously as only he knew how. On the other hand, he was not renowned for acts of kindness for his full siblings, so was it likely he would have fought so hard for a half-brother? Then again, King Richard's full brothers were in the habit of conspiring against him, whereas Ninian was not. Perhaps...

'I don't know, lad.'

Ninian nodded. 'Well, you weren't there,' he said fairly. '*I* think—' He stopped, reddening again.

'Go on. What do you think?'

He raised his head proudly. 'I think he did know that we shared a father. He took such care of me, Josse. Sir Piers was going to take me on the horse he'd grabbed, but the king wouldn't let him. He said I'd be safer with him. It was stormy that night and the wind was howling, and the knights were yelling and I was really scared, but I *thought* I heard him say something about brothers sticking together.' He raised his chin as if defying Josse to contradict.

In that moment he looked so like Henry II of England that it was unmistakeable. If he had cause to adopt that particular expression that night, Josse thought, then King Richard would have known the truth in that instant even if he had not done so before.

Did it matter? he asked himself. If it helped a grieving boy to get over a terrible period in his life, then would it hurt to let him believe that his royal kinsman had deliberately set out to save his young half-brother's life? It might well be the truth, in any case...

'Then,' he said, reaching out to put an arm round the boy's shoulders, 'you're probably right and he *did* know.' Smiling, trying to lighten the intense mood, he said, 'Lucky for you, young Ninian, that he was there.'

With that the matter was settled. He and Ninian exchanged a deep look, as if sealing a bargain. And he knew that neither of them would refer to it again.

Eighteen

When it was fully dark, Ninian saddled the horses and they rode down to the shore. The seaman with whom Josse had negotiated their passage was waiting, and he and two of his hands helped Ninian settle the horses in the hold. Josse took their packs and went up on deck, where he found a spot up in the stern for himself and Ninian. It was a warm night and a light wind blew steadily from the south-west. The crossing ought to be relatively smooth.

Ninian came up to join him and they leaned on the rail watching the sailors as they prepared to haul in the gangplank and the heavy ropes that had tethered the boat to the quay. They appeared to be waiting for something, and presently some more passengers came hurrying along the shore: a young man and a woman, each carrying a baby. Twins, Josse thought, as the couple came into the circle of light cast by the ship's lanterns. No wonder the parents look so exhausted. Hoping that the babies would not cry all night and keep him awake, he turned to watch the captain organize the departure.

Before Josse could even try to go to sleep, there was something he had to do. It was strange; he had known for a long time that he could not avoid this obligation, but there had never seemed any urgency to get it done. Until now when, settling down with Ninian beside him as the ship swiftly left the land behind and, sails billowing, set out into the open sea, suddenly he knew the moment was right.

'Ninian, lad,' he began, 'we were talking earlier today about that time when you and your mother and I were together in the house in the woods.'

'Yes,' Ninian agreed tentatively.

Josse had asked himself over and over again how he would tell Ninian what he had to know. In the end he had decided on a simple statement of facts. 'Your mother and I fell in love,' he said. 'We lay together and she conceived a child, a little girl who was born the following October.' He waited but Ninian made no comment; Josse could sense his tension and the boy hardly seemed to be breathing. 'I did not know about our child for quite a long time,' he went on. 'For her own good reasons, your mother did not tell me. I met my daughter – she's called Meggie–' Ninian gave a gasp of recognition and Josse remembered his references to *that little girl* – 'when she was sixteen months old and, although she continued to live with her mother out in the forest, she and I have had regular contact ever since.'

There was a long silence. Then Ninian said, 'Why did you not marry my mother?'

Josse had expected the question. 'I wanted to and, in a way, so did she, for our love was true and enduring, but she was not willing to abandon the strong voice that called her to her life in the wild, and it was not a life that I could join.'

'Why not?'

'She lives with people like her, Ninian. They are not like me.'

'Are they like me?' Ninian spoke intently but so softly that Josse had to strain to hear.

'Your mother is of their kind, as was her mother,' he said. 'Mag Hobson, your grandmother, was one of the Great Ones of the forest people, as indeed is your mother. I do not know, lad, but I imagine that your inheritance on the distaff side would make you welcome out in the wild, if you chose to go.'

'I was looking for my mother when you and I met,' Ninian said. 'You did not ask why that was.'

'That's true.' Josse thought back. 'I had imagined it was because you were concerned about her.'

'I was only worried *after* I'd looked for her and been unable to find her. I went looking for her because I wanted to ask if I could go and live with her.'

But you were too late, Josse thought, pain

308

ripping through him. Your mother would have done all she could to persuade you back to the life she thought you ought to lead but, in the end, she would have let her heart rule and given you the best, biggest and most loving welcome any lad ever had.

He did not think it would help either of them to say so.

'What now?' he asked gruffly.

'Now? I do not know.' Ninian sounded far too world-weary for a boy of fourteen.

'You could return to Sir Walter,' Josse suggested. 'He would be pleased to see you, I'm sure, and you could continue your training with—'

'No.' Ninian spoke the single word with utter conviction. 'Sorry, Josse. I know you are trying to persuade me on down the path my mother envisaged for me, but I don't want to take it any more.'

'What *do* you want?' Josse hardly dared to ask.

Ninian gave him a very sweet smile. Then, settling down on his folded blanket and wrapping his cloak round him, he said, 'I'll tell you tomorrow.'

Josse listened to Ninian's breathing, deepened by sleep, and wondered why the soporific sound was not making his own eyes heavy. Sleep, though, was far away; quietly he got up and walked along the deck until he was standing directly behind the figurehead up in the prow. He looked at the carved wooden face and torso, faded by years of sun and saltwater. She was bare-breasted, her long hair flowing around her shoulders, and the expression on the strong face was fierce and proud. An image of the black goddess, wrapped in Ninian's pack, floated into Josse's mind. Soon she'll be safe, he thought. Soon we shall—

'May I join you?' A soft voice spoke beside him.

Turning, Josse saw that it was the young man who had come aboard with his wife and twins. 'Aye,' Josse said with a smile. 'I'd have thought you'd be grabbing some sleep while your babies were quiet,' he added.

The man returned the smile. 'Yes, it is true that the presence of young makes sleep a rare commodity.' There was a short silence. Then he said, 'You are Josse d'Acquin.'

'Aye.' And you, Josse thought instantly, are of the forest people, for they do not use worldly titles but call a man simply by his name. Hard on the heels of that realization came another: his companion might bring word of Joanna.

'I bring you news that will gladden your heart,' the man began, 'although it is not that which you yearn to hear.'

'Joanna is not ... She's...?'

'I can add nothing to what you already know,' the man said, with an air of stopping further questions. 'I am sorry but that is not why I am here.'

'You were following me?'

'Yes. We know you went to Rouen, and Deidre and I – she's my woman; I'm called Ruis – were sent after you. We've been watching you and this afternoon, after you had arranged to cross the narrow seas on this ship, I bought passage for us too.'

'Why?'

Ruis paused for some time. Then he said, 'You saw Joanna, both before the great ceremony and on that night when the power was raised.'

'Aye. I ... Aye.' Josse found it both a joy and a pain to remember and it was hard to speak.

'You did not lie with her when you met in the cathedral?'

'No. We ... She had to return to her encampment.'

'You observed her face on the night we raised the power?'

'Aye.'

'How did you think she looked?'

He pictured her, pale, with grey circles round the eyes. He recalled how he thought she looked exhausted, as if the ordeal had taken all her strength. 'She was tired. Very tired.'

'Yes,' Ruis breathed. 'She was.'

'It was taxing, what she had to do?' Josse asked, desperate to know.

'Very, although she was fully prepared for it and the extreme exaltation would have provided her with all the strength and energy she needed and more.' He paused. 'Josse, she was weary before the ceremony began.'

'Why?' The word shot out of him, for he was suddenly angry, so angry, with this calm young man who spoke for the strange people whom Josse could not understand and never would. 'Just what was it you'd made her do?'

Ruis laughed softly, but Josse could not begin to imagine what was amusing him. 'Neither we nor anybody else made her do anything. The days when Joanna could be forced into any act against her will were long gone.' He turned to look at Josse, his eyes bright in the light of the stars and the slim moon. 'She had a rare power,' he added. 'She was a great gift to us, and we shall honour her always for what she has done.'

'What has she done?' Josse whispered.

Ruis's smile spread, as if he were suddenly suffused with joy. 'She and the entity known as the Bear Man gave up their essence that night and merged themselves in the cone of power. It rose up to the heavens and drove down deep into the ground in that place that has always been sacred to us. The force that lies within the earth answered and it opened up to admit them. The power is now great – greater than it has ever been – and nothing can destroy it. Now and for ever we and what we believe will stay there.'

'But what of the priests?' Josse demanded. 'They will finish their great cathedral and it will—'

'Yes, indeed they will,' Ruis agreed serenely, 'but it does not matter. They cannot stop what now breathes through the very stone, wood and glass of their building. It will be there as long as the world lasts, for even if the cathedral falls, the power will remain. It was there at the beginning; it will be there at the end.'

'And this ... this mission was for Joanna to fulfil?'

'With the one other, yes. It is what she was born for; her destiny was marked out for her.'

'She knew? She accepted this?' He had to ask.

'Deep inside her, she always knew. When she received her orders, she welcomed them with joy. Her acceptance would have been total except for one thing.'

'What was it?'

'You, Josse. You and her children. She loved all of you dearly and did not want to leave you. It was only when we gave our solemn oath to do as she asked that her mind was set at rest.'

'What did she ask?' He could barely form the words.

'She wished you to raise them. Meggie is already yours and devoted to you. She will sorely miss her mother, but she has the consolation of being able to see and speak to her in the form that she now takes.'

'Aye, I know.' Josse had seen Meggie chattering with Joanna.

'Ninian, too, has found his way to you.' Ruis glanced up the deck at the sleeping boy. 'He will not return to his life as a squire, Josse. He will ask you in the morning if he may live with you.'

'I'll say yes, with all my heart!'

Ruis smiled. 'I know. I see the love you have for each other shining around you both. It began long ago and now this journey that you have taken together has reawakened it.'

'I'll have a family,' Josse said slowly, trying to envisage the life that now awaited him. 'I'll have two children to raise. Dear Lord, I've given my home to Dominic, Paradisa and *their* family! If only I'd known, I would have—'

'No you wouldn't,' Ruis said calmly. 'You gave away your house because you were lonely there and you knew others would come to love it much more than you ever did. It was never the right place for you, Josse,' he added. 'Now even more, it is not where you should be.'

Josse wondered what Ruis could mean by that, but his thoughts were interrupted, for the man spoke again. 'There is another place far more suitable, for it is both within the forest, where your children's blood calls out to them, and in the place where your own heart lies.'

'Where? What is this place?' Josse cried.

314

'It belonged to the children's mother. Now that she is no longer here, it passes to you and to them. Until they are of age, it is in your care.'

'You speak of the house in the woods?'

'Yes.'

'She wanted this, that I should live there with Ninian and Meggie?'

'She did.'

It was a great deal to take in. Josse stood silent, imagining...

As if the figure beside him were somehow putting pictures into his mind, he then saw the family that would live in the old house, waking it up from its long sleep with laughter and happiness. He saw Ninian grown tall and strong; saw Meggie with her healer's skill tending all who came, human and animal, in the way her mother and grandmother had done before her. In her hand he caught a sudden flash of brilliant blue as she dipped a precious jewel into a cup of water.

'Yes,' Ruis said quietly. 'You see true, Josse.' He gave Josse some moments to enjoy the vision. Then he said, 'There is one more thing.'

Josse's breath seemed to catch in his throat. 'What is it?'

Ruis took his arm and led him down the deck. In the stern, the woman Deidre sat wrapped in shawl and cloak. One baby lay beside her, fast asleep; the other was suckling vigorously at her breast. Embarrassed at being a witness to such a moment of intimacy, Josse turned aside.

'It is all right, Josse,' Deidre said gently. 'You may look. I do not mind.'

Josse looked; it seemed that his eyes were drawn to the spectacle of the woman and the babies almost against his volition. As he looked, he noticed something. Deidre's dark eyes met his; she smiled up at him and he thought she whispered, 'Yes.'

Ruis said, 'What do you see?'

'They are not twins,' Josse said wonderingly, 'for the one now at the breast is surely several months older than the other.'

'The one who now suckles is Iana,' Ruis said, 'and she is the daughter of Deidre and me. The other child, her milk brother, is not yet a month old. He takes little but his need is the greater, so Deidre feeds him first.'

'I have heard him!' Josse knew it; the small mewls and cries that had haunted him were the sounds of a newborn.

Deidre looked down at the tiny child, compassion in her eyes, but she did not speak.

'You have heard with your heart,' Ruis said, 'for although we have been following you, we have not been close enough for you to have picked up such tiny sounds.'

'But why...?' The question died before Josse could finish it.

He remembered holding Joanna, feeling the bulk of her satchel beneath her cloak. He saw her face as she was wound up inside the cone of power, fulfilment, exhaustion and a slow, deep happiness turning her expression to one of joy. He thought back to September when, after the equinox ceremonies, he and Joanna had spent their days together and their nights making love.

He heard the echo of Ruis's words: *You have heard with your heart.*

He stared down at the baby lying asleep in its soft blanket. His heart overflowed.

Ruis bent down, picked up the baby with gentle hands and placed him in Josse's open arms. 'His name is Geoffroi,' he whispered.

My father's name, Josse thought. She remembered.

Tears blurred his vision as he stared down into the face of his child. Settling the baby on the crook of his left arm, he touched the soft, rounded cheek with the tip of his finger. Geoffroi opened his eyes and looked up.

Josse had been told that newborns did not focus very well and he was willing to believe it. It must, then, have been some special quality in this third and last child of Joanna's that made the gaze so purposeful.

Josse and his son stared at each other. Josse might have been wrong, but he thought the small, sweet sound that chirruped from the baby might just mean that he liked what he saw.

Nineteen

Helewise knew they were near. Some newly awakened sense that seemed to wax within her whenever she went out to the new chapel put an image in her head of Josse riding with a boy that had to be Ninian. The boy led a rather beautiful white horse. Josse was holding a bundle – perhaps the black figure had been entrusted to him.

She went one evening to the chapel. The roof was to go on the following week; the team had worked very fast, taking full advantage of the continuing good weather. Helewise had carefully checked the finances and there was enough for a small additional request. She had commissioned Martin's men to build a tiny habitation immediately behind the chapel, on the very edge of the abbey land. It would consist of a single room, its walls of wattle and daub on top of a first course of stone and its roof of local rush thatch. There was no need for it to be any larger, for it would house a solitary inhabitant. It was the dwelling of an anchorite; one of those who lived in seclusion and whose solitary devotions, or so the country folk liked to say, helped to anchor the faithful in the faith. Helewise, who knew a little Latin, was aware that the word implied simply the act of withdrawal, but she thought the country folk's version might actually be more accurate. No such anchorite – or anchoress – was yet apparent, but Helewise thought that could change. Not yet, perhaps, but soon.

She stood inside the tiny room that would form the hermit's accommodation. No, she mused, hermit was not the right word, for the purpose of having someone living here between the abbey and the forest was so that those who came in need would receive not only the solace offered within St Edmund's Chapel but also a kind welcome, a mug of water and a bite to eat from the person who tended it.

It was not going to be easy; she knew that. Quite a lot of people would need a great deal of convincing. But she had made up her mind and she would not allow her vision to dissolve.

Meggie was calling. Helewise hurried out and stood before the chapel, waving. Meggie, running towards her and dragging a laughing Sister Caliste beside her, waved back.

'He's nearly here, my lady!' Meggie cried.

Helewise pretended not to understand. 'Now who on earth can you mean, little Meggie?' she asked. 'Would that be Brother

Saul, perhaps, or Sir Gervase de Gifford? Or – yes, *I* know! – it's Father Gilbert, coming for more of Sister Tiphaine's special rubbing oil for his sore back!'

Meggie was hopping from foot to foot with excitement, laughter creasing her pretty little face. 'No, no and no,' she chanted. 'It's my daddy! He's on his way and he's almost at the bend in the road!'

'*Is* he?' Helewise made it sound as if it was the most extraordinary thing. 'Well, then, we had better go and meet him!'

She gathered the skirts of her habit in her hands and, running as she had not done for years – amused, she noticed Sister Caliste's astounded face before the young nun picked up her own skirts and followed suit – flew down the shallow slope and jumped down on to the road. Meggie landed beside her, and Sister Caliste slithered down the bank on her bottom. Then, panting, flushed, the three of them turned to stare down the track to the spot where it bent away out of sight.

A reddish chestnut appeared first, its rider holding the leading rein of a grey. The rider – it was a boy of about fourteen – saw them and, with a shout, kicked the chestnut into a canter, the grey following behind. Then round the corner appeared another, larger horse on which sat the familiar, broad-shouldered figure of Josse.

As he approached he was partially hidden from Helewise's view by Ninian, but he was not hurt, she could tell that much at least. Not physically hurt, anyway, though he had lost Joanna, so the pain would be deep inside. And he would bear it for ever...

Her eyes were fixed on the bundle that he was holding so carefully, so tenderly, before him, cradled in the crook of his left arm. It could not be the black figure, for it moved. It wriggled, stretched, and then it let out a small cry that quickly escalated to a full-scale yell.

Josse was level with her now. Meggie hurled herself at her father and, pulling up the big horse, he let the reins go slack and reached down with his free hand, hauling Meggie up in front of him. She twisted round to gaze at the baby, eyes round with wonder.

Josse sat staring down into Helewise's eyes. She could not read his expression. In it there was pride, deep happiness and also a sort of guilt. Then she knew for sure that what she had begun, incredibly, to suspect was true.

Josse, detecting perhaps some slight relaxation in her face, smiled and said, 'My lady, may we proceed straight away into the abbey? I really hope that among your patients and visitors there's a recently delivered woman, for my son is hungry.'

She swallowed the threatening tears. In a voice surprisingly like her normal tone, she said, 'I am sure such a woman can be found, Sir Josse. If not, then the nursing nuns will come up with something. Come along!'

With her heart singing and a spring in her step, she led her small procession back to the abbey.

As soon as the little party arrived, news began to sweep through the abbey that Sir Josse was back and had his baby son with him. Sister Clare, who ran Hawkenlye's home for fallen women, approached Helewise and very shyly said that one of her regulars had just given birth to a healthy little girl and had more than enough milk for two. If the abbess thought Sir Josse would not mind his son sharing the breasts of a Tonbridge prostitute, then Jehane had said she'd be pleased to oblige.

'It is a very kind offer, Sister Clare,' Helewise said. 'I will speak to Sir Josse.'

Sister Caliste had taken Josse and the baby into the infirmary, where, in the absence of any lactating women, Sister Euphemia was trying to get the increasingly desperate Geoffroi to accept warm water with a tiny spoonful of honey melted in it. Helewise noticed as she approached that Sister Caliste, three nursing nuns and two elderly patients long acquainted with Josse were all standing around the infirmarer as she held the screaming baby, looking down adoringly and muttering helpful comments.

Helewise beckoned to Josse and, out of earshot of the others, said, 'There is a young mother in the fallen women's refuge. She has offered to share her milk with your son, although if you would prefer—'

He did not wait to hear her out. A huge smile creased his tired face and he said, 'My lady, I could kiss you! Oh, I apologize, I did not mean to be rude. I'll fetch Geoffroi and we'll go over straight away.'

Helewise escorted him to the fallen women's home, where Sister Clare presented a young woman with an oval face, a sensuous mouth and hazel eyes; she would have been lovely, Helewise thought with compassion, but for the scars and the world-weary, dejected expression that her way of life had forced on to her.

She was about to make some diplomatic comment to ease Josse out of letting his son feed off this poor wreck of a woman but, to her amazement, Josse had hurried forward and taken her hand in his. 'Jehane!' he exclaimed. 'I did not think *you* would be our saviour! How are you? It's ... what, six years since we met, in this very place? You have a new baby, they tell me?'

'I do all right, Sir Josse,' Jehane replied, a smile sweetening her face. 'And, yes, I've had another girl. She's sleeping.' Jehane looked back over her shoulder to where a baby lay in a cradle.

'Will you feed my son?' Josse asked. 'He is in sore need of milk, as you'll have noticed.' The child was crying ceaselessly now.

323

Jehane looked down into the tiny scarlet face. 'Of course,' she said softly. 'Give him here.'

Quite unabashed, Jehane took Geoffroi, sat down on the end of the nearest cot and, unfastening her gown, put him to her breast. He was desperate with hunger now and, for a few moments, too far gone in panicky fear to realize what was on offer. With a practised hand Jehane squeezed out a few drops of her milk and spread them on Geoffroi's lips. Scenting and tasting what he so desperately needed, the infant suddenly latched on to the nipple and, an expression of bliss on his face, closed his eyes and began to suckle.

Helewise stood beside Josse and Sister Clare. Josse's face, she noticed, was fixed in an absurd grin; Sister Clare looked almost as happy. Jehane looked up, her face alight. 'He'll do all right now,' she said. 'Took him a while because I smell different from whoever fed him afore, but he'll know me next time.'

That, then, was that, Helewise thought with a private smile. A hungry baby had found comfort; an anxious father had his problem solved; and, knowing Josse as she did, undoubtedly he would wish to employ Jehane as wet nurse for as long as his son needed her. So, Jehane would keep away from the back alleys of Tonbridge for a few precious months. Who knows, she mused, a time of living a different, better life might just persuade Jehane that there were alternatives to earning her bread on her back.

But perhaps that was asking for *too* much.

For the next two weeks, Josse and his family remained at the abbey. There were all at once many things clamouring for his attention. Helewise, watching and eagerly helping whenever she was asked, thought that perhaps he had made up his mind to keep busy in order to stop himself grieving for Joanna. He had told her, briefly and in a manner that suggested he did not want to be faced with any questions, no matter how sympathetically asked, that Joanna would not be returning. 'I have a task now,' he added, with a tentative pride that touched her deeply. 'I have my daughter and my little son to raise, and Ninian has expressed a wish to join my household.'

One of Josse's priorities, then, was to find out how he went about becoming Ninian's legal guardian. Watching the two of them together – Ninian actually made Josse laugh, something Helewise recognized as a minor miracle just then – she thought in a flash of illumination, the boy has treated Josse like a father ever since they met! The poor lad never knew his real father and he loathed his stepfather. Then, when he and his mother were on the run, along came Josse, a man to depend upon, admire and love.

Something occurred to her. Josse had told her that Ninian had been in the forest looking for his mother. Helewise thought that was not the whole truth, for she was certain that the person Ninian had been waiting for as he lurked on the forest fringes was Josse. Well, now they had found each other. Soon Ninian would be Josse's son in the law's eyes as well.

Josse had told her of the plan to set up home in the house in the woods. At first she had been greatly surprised; she had associated him with New Winnowlands for all the long years of their friendship and it was hard to envisage him anywhere else. As she grew accustomed to the idea, however, she realized that Josse had never truly been at home in his manor. It is too far away, she thought. He wants – needs – to be near both the forest and the abbey, and he would not have been so generous as to share New Winnowlands with my son and his family if the house had taken up a place in his heart.

As if to underline that his decision was final, Josse had a document drawn up that passed the estate of New Winnowlands unconditionally to Dominic Warin and his descendants. Then, as July ended and August began, he set out with Ninian, Meggie, the baby and his wet nurse, Brother Augustus and Brother Erse the carpenter to begin turning the house in the woods into a family home.

It was not far away – under an hour on foot and considerably less than that if you went through the forest instead of following the track around its perimeter. One morning, burning with curiosity to find out how Josse was getting on, Helewise set out to see for herself. She took Sister Tiphaine with her, and the herbalist, a frequent visitor to the forest, unhesitatingly set off on the shorter route.

'Joanna's hut is just over there.' Tiphaine jerked her head to indicate a faint path through the undergrowth.

'What will become of it now?' Helewise found she was whispering.

'The forest folk will look after it. They'll keep it safe as long as they're here to do so.'

'As long as ... You mean they're going away?'

Sister Tiphaine looked at her, sorrow in the deep eyes. 'The world's changing,' she said. 'Soon there will be no more wild places. The coming men will not have your tolerance, my lady, for people who kneel before a different deity.'

Helewise fell silent. They strode on and, deep in thought, it came as a mild surprise to find they were already at their destination. Josse and his companions had been busy. All the windows and doors of the old house stood open to the sunshine – someone had been felling and pruning, cutting back the surrounding trees and bushes so that there was now a clearing of perhaps ten paces all around the buildings – and as Helewise went up into the hall, she was greeted by sweet smells and a shiningly clean stone floor.

Josse came hurrying to greet her and took her on a tour of his new domain. His man Will had come over from New Winnowlands to lend a hand; Josse confided that he had asked if the move could become permanent, being too long in the tooth, as he had said, to get used to a new master. He and his woman, Ella, were going to join Josse's household as soon as Dominic had found replacements.

There was another addition to the household; with a smile and a firm hand on the young woman's sleeve preventing her from turning tail and fleeing as she was brought before Helewise, Josse presented his new housekeeper. 'This is Tilly,' he said.

Helewise stared at her. Tilly was perhaps twenty years old, lean and thin-faced with brown hair drawn severely back under a white cap. Her pale eyes looked frightened. Helewise, wanting to reassure her, said kindly, 'Hello, Tilly. Have you come to answer Sir Josse's prayers?'

'Don't know about that,' Tilly whispered. Then, raising her head and, with a visible effort, summoning her courage, she added in a rush, 'Jehane sent word that 'e needed a maid and Goody Anne, she says 'e'd done 'er enough favours over the years and it were high time she did 'im one back, so 'ere I am.' Flushed at her own boldness, she hung her

328

head again.

'Thank you, Tilly,' Josse said.

Sensing herself dismissed, Tilly dropped a bob curtsy and scurried away.

'She comes from the inn at Tonbridge?' Helewise asked.

'Aye.' Josse smiled. 'She loves it here. I did wonder if she would settle out in the woods so far from everything she's ever known, but it seems she's a countrywoman at heart. She's doing wonders with my hens.'

'Hens?'

'Aye.' The smile broadened. 'Ninian's made a fox-proof run and we have fresh eggs every morning. He's also got a pair of hounds and a cat with kittens. He and Meggie apparently share a passion for every sort of living creature the good Lord ever made. Meggie's rescued a dove with a damaged wing, and most nights we have badgers feeding on the bank beyond the house.'

'And Geoffroi is thriving?'

Josse's expression softened. 'Aye. Jehane too; without her paint and dressed in a less spectacular fashion, she's already looking more like the woman she was before ... er ... when...'

'I understand,' Helewise said. Another prayer answered, she thought.

'Come and see them!' Josse grabbed her arm. 'She's set up a nursery in a room behind the hall, although I really would like to build a solar. We do need the extra space.'

'I know a fine team of masons,' she said. 'They just happen to be finishing their present job. Would you like me to ask them to pay you a visit?'

He laughed. 'I would indeed.' He met her eyes. 'I have gold, my lady,' he said very quietly. 'Queen Eleanor was extremely generous.'

'I see.' She was glad for him. 'Lead on, Sir Josse – I want to see this son of yours!'

Geoffroi d'Acquin was baptized at Hawkenlye Abbey at the end of August. Helewise stood godmother, and Brother Augustus was godfather. The young man had asked Brother Firmin, who in turn had asked Helewise, if anybody thought it would be a terrible thing if he abandoned the life of a lay brother at Hawkenlye Abbey – where, he had said earnestly, he had been very happy, don't let anyone think otherwise! – and went to work for Josse. Helewise summoned him and told him very gently that there was nothing terrible about discovering that his calling was no longer where he had believed it to be. She undertook to set about the necessary steps that would release him from the abbey.

Josse told her in private that Gussie had fallen in love with Tilly. The young man believed nobody but he knew of his sweet anguish – until he was released from his lay-brother status, he had not admitted his feelings to anyone, least of all Tilly – but Josse had been reliably informed that, when the time for revelation finally came, Tilly would not turn him down. According to Josse, she had put on some much-needed weight and was blossoming into a rather lovely young woman.

Josse's new household, Helewise reflected, was proving to be a healing place for more than just its master.

St Edmund's Chapel was completed as September drew to a close and the mists of autumn began to appear. It lay empty over the winter months, for Queen Eleanor had asked the new king, her son, to attend the service of consecration and he was fully occupied over in France, where he had inherited his elder brother's enemy, King Philip. But then, early in the new year of 1200, King John paid a lightning visit to England – rumour had it that he was only coming to raise some much-needed cash – and word was sent to Hawkenlye announcing that he would fulfil his mother's request.

The chapel looked beautiful. The plain white walls threw the glorious glass into prominence. Sun shone through the jewel-bright colours of the window and danced on the stone flags of the floor; the pale oak of the rood screen glowed like gold. Helewise, performing a solitary final inspection the night before the king was due to arrive, tried to see the chapel as it would appear to someone new to it, someone who had not been witness to its long birth. It will impress, she decided; it cannot fail to do so.

The king was unlikely to notice that one of the flagstones was in fact a trapdoor leading down to the crypt, where the black goddess sat in her niche down in the darkness. Helewise visited her regularly, as, she well knew, did various others. The king would not be told about her; neither would the vast party of clergy summoned to the ceremony. What they did not know could not hurt them. She left the chapel, carefully closing and locking the door. In time, there would be no need for a lock.

She walked over to the little habitation, now also complete. Martin's men had built it to her exact specification. Its new inhabitant would not take up residence yet – not this year and perhaps not the next – and Helewise would look after the simple dwelling until the time came.

She went outside into the evening air. It was growing cold – there would be a hard frost tonight – and she wrapped her cloak more tightly around her. She stared down at the lights of the abbey, shining out into the night like a beacon of hope. It is a good place, she thought. It will be one of the last places to succumb, but succumb it will. She sighed, for the thought made her sad. But the future was not entirely bleak – far from it.

Her eyes roved on and she stared at the distant vale. Josse was down there, with Ninian, his adopted son, and Meggie and Geoffroi, the children of his blood. They were staying in the monks' quarters and, like everyone else, were excited at the prospect of tomorrow's ceremony. It was not every day, after all, that a chapel right on your doorstep was dedicated to a warrior king. Josse's entire household had accompanied him, although Will, Ella, Gussie and Tilly had only just arrived and would have to go back to the house in the woods immediately after the ceremony to see to their duties.

For now, though, they were all here at Hawkenlye and Helewise revelled in their company. She was now a regular visitor in Josse's house, welcomed by everyone with such warmth that it always moved her. Sometimes she would meet other loved ones there; Josse's building programme had been forced to halt back in the autumn, but he had plans to expand as soon as the new season started. For now, guests such as her elder son Leofgar and his wife Rohaise, and Dominic and Paradisa, seemed perfectly happy to muck in with everyone else. From living a lonely life at New Winnowlands, Josse was now the treasured head of a diverse household who were united, if by nothing else, by their love for him.

She sensed that he was happy. She hoped and prayed that he was, that the pain of the deep wound left by the loss of Joanna was, if not healed, then at least assuaged by the company of everyone else who loved him.

She set off down the path to the abbey. One of these days, she thought, I must ask him.

Twenty

Ten Years Later, June 1210

The abbess sat in her little room staring down at the thick cream parchment unrolled on the table before her. She held it down and read through every word that was written on it, absently running her fingers over the outline of the heavy wax seal at the bottom of the page. She had no need to study it in such detail, for she knew what the wording said and she had long been expecting it. Nevertheless, to see this vital document before her eyes was still a shock, for its import was momentous; for her, for Hawkenlye Abbey and, most important, for the person to whom the document referred. Despite all the reassurances, she knew very well that from now on, nothing was going to be the same.

She sat back in the great throne-like chair,

thinking back to when it had begun. Well, to be honest, she did not really know, for who can read another's deepest thoughts? She could calculate readily enough when the first external signs had become apparent, but that was not to say that the process that led ultimately to this moment had not been set in motion months – years – before that. Indeed, this had in fact been intimated to her.

The first signs became apparent ten years ago, when Queen Eleanor commanded that St Edmund's Chapel be built at Hawkenlye to commemorate her son King Richard. The abbess smiled, as she always did when she thought about the chapel, for in every respect it had succeeded beyond her wildest dreams. From the start it had attracted numerous visitors; increasingly, the ordinary people were overawed by what the Church was becoming and many preferred the simple building on the forest fringes to the magnificent abbey church. From the time that there had been someone living in the little dwelling place beside the chapel, a steady stream of the hungry, the distressed, the grieving and the troubled turned up every day, to kneel in prayer within the plain white walls of the chapel, stare in wonder at the beautiful window and, hopefully, spare a thought and a prayer for the late king, before going outside to be greeted with a smiling face, a kind word, a bite to eat and a sympathetic ear for whatever ailed them. Often they would gently be redirected to the infirmary, or the monks in the vale; sometimes, comforted, they would simply melt away.

The abbess sighed. Life had always been hard for the poor of England; now, for many, it had turned into a battle for survival.

King John's reign had become increasingly oppressive. Even the nobility suffered, for the king's constant need for more funds had led to a sharp increase in the frequency with which he demanded money from them. His favourite means was to impose the tax known as scutage, which vassals paid in lieu of military service. He had overseen a ferocious tightening of the forest laws – the imposition of severe fines was another way to increase the flow of money into his coffers – and yet there seemed little to show for everything he demanded. The king had proved an ineffectual military leader; far from following in his warrior brother's aggressive footsteps, John had done little but lose Continental territory to his enemies. The last strongholds in Anjou and Normandy had gone; Poitou was teetering on the brink. Now, with cruel accuracy, they called the king 'Soft-Sword'.

King John had taken a new bride soon after coming to the throne. Typical of he who knew no half-measures, he had seen and fallen for the fourteen-year-old daughter of the Count of Angoulême when her father was paying homage to him, ruthlessly breaking off her betrothal to another man, who, incensed, appealed to Philip of France for justice and witnessed with satisfaction the French king forfeit John's Continental fiefs. The young Queen Isabella had fulfilled her prime duty: already there were two little princes in the royal nursery and the queen was said to be pregnant again.

Although she tried not to listen, the abbess had heard what the soothsayers predicted. The king's heir, Henry, they whispered, would be a fat, witless weakling and England would not be great again until his own mighty son came to reign. She sighed. I doubt I shall live to see those times, she thought. I must do the best I can with the days I do have.

Oh, but it was hard. Five years ago, the king had quarrelled with Rome over who should become Archbishop of Canterbury. John had selected the wrong adversary, for Pope Innocent III was even more determined than the king and, when John refused to back down, he laid an interdict on England suspending all church services. John still did not come to heel and last year the Pope had excommunicated him. Church and State were at loggerheads and all England suffered.

I barely recognize the Church I once loved, the abbess thought sadly. It is no longer a supporting and loving helpmeet; it is a moneymaking giant whose chief aim appears to be the acquisition of land, money and power. As if this devastating quarrel between the Pope and the king was not bad enough – surely, *surely* two men who had been put on earth to serve their God and their people ought to have been able to do better! – there was now the terrible Crusade against the Cathars. In the south, they said, the towns were burning with the people inside them. The Pope had joined forces with the king of France and, although the excuse was the stamping-out of heresy, everyone knew full well that both Church and State would emerge from the fight immensely the richer.

It was not right.

And here I am, the abbess reflected sadly, trying to fulfil a role set out for me in a world where the old rules no longer apply and everyone seems to have gone mad. Old Queen Eleanor, that great levelling influence and supporter of Hawkenlye, had died peacefully in her sleep at Fontevrault. Sometimes it seemed to the abbess that more than an eighty-two-year life had gone out of the world that April day.

Abruptly she let go of the ends of the parchment and it flew back into its roll. She retied its ribbon and carefully stowed it away in the cupboard let into the wall. Then, squaring her shoulders, she went out to break the news.

In the house in the woods, Josse bent over his spade and, ignoring the vague pain in the small of his back, made up his mind that he would finish the row before Meggie came back. He had promised to dig over the empty area in her herb bed, for she wanted to plant more of her little seedlings this evening. The moon, apparently, was in a condition that favoured vigorous growth.

He smiled as he thought about his beloved daughter. She was seventeen now and in his eyes she was quite beautiful, with abundant, shiny dark hair that had kept its youthful curl and brown eyes that shone with golden lights. She worked too hard, he kept telling her; she was up early hunting for flowers, leaves and roots for her herbal remedies, and she never turned away anyone who came to her for help. In October two years ago, on her sixteenth birthday, she had inherited the powerful heirloom that Josse's father, Geoffroi, had brought back from Outremer. It was a huge sapphire set in gold and it was known as the Eye of Jerusalem. It held a strange power within its deep blue depths for, in the hand of its rightful owner, it warned of the presence of enemies and, dipped in water, made a febrifuge that possessed the power to stop bleeding. It also detected poison in an apparently innocent drink.

It had come into the family with the

sombre prediction that one of Geoffroi's descendants would one day wield it. A great sorcerer had told Josse that the jewel would in time pass to one possessing the innate psychic power to make it come fully alive and, when that came to pass, for the first time in two thousand years the Eye of Jerusalem would come into its full potential. At the time Josse had not even known of his daughter's existence, but it was she to whom the sorcerer had referred and now the Eye was hers.

She used it rarely and only at grave need, for its power was extraordinary and she admitted that she had barely begun to comprehend it. In her struggle for understanding she was not alone: the Domina, immeasurably wise, very old now and deeply revered by all her people, was there to help her. Slowly, painfully, Meggie was coming to terms with her extraordinary inheritance. It had already started to change her life, for with the gift came responsibility, and Meggie, true child of both her parents, was not one to turn aside.

Josse dug on and his thoughts moved to his son. Geoffroi, named according to his mother's wishes after Josse's father, was ten years old and Josse's boy through and through. It was likely he had inherited his mother's strange powers – inevitable, really, since both her other children had done so – but so far he was nothing more than a solid,

cheerful, funny little boy who adored his
elder sister and half-brother, especially when
Meggie let him help her prepare the sweet-
smelling herbs and Ninian showed him how
to mend a wild animal's hurt.

Ninian was twenty-four and in love with
Little Helewise, daughter of Leofgar Warin
and his wife, Rohaise. The girl was not yet
sixteen, but she was mature for her years and
it was plain to anyone with eyes in their head
that she adored Ninian. Time would tell; if
they married, Josse would go on his knees all
the way to St Edmund's Chapel to cry out a
prayer of thanks.

He and Ninian had never once referred
again to the young man's parentage. His
half-brother was busy ruining England, so
perhaps it was just as well.

Josse's former manor, the estate of New
Winnowlands, was flourishing, thanks to
Dominic's talents as a landowner. Dominic
now concentrated on sheep and he was
growing rich. In truth, everything he earned
was the result of his own hard work, ably
supported and assisted by the many-talented
Paradisa, but Dominic had not forgotten
that fourteen years ago Josse had given him
and his new wife a home at New Winnowlands, and he insisted that a fair share of his
profits went to Josse and those who lived
with him in the house in the woods. Josse,
who lived frugally with his largely self-
supporting family and still had most of the

gold given to him by the late queen, was quite embarrassed by his own wealth.

He was almost at the end of the row. Hearing voices, he straightened up, a hand to his back, to see who it was. Gussie was striding out towards him, two of his three children running beside him and laughing at something he had just said. He was already holding out a hand for the spade. Josse watched him, smiling. He had filled out from the skinny boy he used to be and now, a man in his prime, he was broad-shouldered and starting to look a little stout. Tilly, his wife, had become an excellent cook.

'Tilly says you've been out here far too long already and you'll pay for it with a sore back tonight,' Gussie said, taking the spade from Josse's hand. 'Give me that – I'll finish for you.'

Meekly Josse handed it to him.

'Horsy, horsy, Josse!' said the younger child, a little girl.

Josse sat down on the low bank that enclosed Meggie's herb garden and, drawing up his legs to make a pretend horse's back, picked up the child and set her on his knees. 'I had a little pony,' he sang, and instantly she and her brother joined in: 'His name was Dapple Grey. I lent him to a lady, to ride a mile away.'

The children yelled the words, their light voices blending with Josse's deep baritone, and as the song wound up to its inevitable climax, with the pretend horse rearing and shooting its small rider into the soft grass, all three shouted with laughter.

The happy sounds, soaring into the summer sky, echoed beneath the protective circle of trees so that the forest itself seemed to be laughing.

The woman striding along the narrow forest track heard the merriment and smiled in response. Not far now, she thought.

She had been sitting quietly in the chapel when the abbess had come to find her. As the familiar black-clad figure had stood in the open door and beckoned, she had got up and gone outside with her. They stood side by side in the sunshine and the abbess said, 'It has come.'

A moment of stillness; this moment, so long anticipated, was nevertheless surprisingly disturbing in its power, for this was the final step of a journey begun a very long time ago and her life would never be the same again.

Others had preceded her. She was by no means the first. It helped, a little. This was her choice; she had no more doubts now. As the portent of the abbess's words sank in and were absorbed, she began to smile.

'I have no need to ask if you are ready,' the abbess said softly.

She smiled. 'No, my lady. I have left everything neat and tidy. Whoever follows me will find the little house welcoming.'

'I know,' the abbess said with a smile.

'Have you a candidate in mind?'

'Yes. She is eager but she is young, and I am not entirely convinced that she understands the demands of the role.'

'A term of trial, perhaps?'

'Just what I had in mind. Can I help you carry your belongings? I will walk with you, if you wish it.'

'Thank you, my lady, it is a kind offer, but I prefer to go alone.'

The abbess studied her. 'I thought you might say that,' she murmured. Then, stepping forward, she took the older woman in her arms and they exchanged a long, close embrace. Then the abbess let her go. 'Goodbye. May God watch over you.'

'I will be back, my lady,' the woman murmured. 'I shall be under an hour's walk away, after all.'

'You always go by the forest paths now,' the abbess remarked. 'You are fully at home there, I think.'

'Yes. I often meet the Domina, and Tiphaine, although I sense that they will retreat from their ancestral lands here soon.'

'Soon?' The abbess looked dismayed.

'Oh, it will not happen yet. But the world changes, my lady, and there is nothing we can do to stop it.' She sighed. 'Already men encroach on the forest fringes, for despite our king's best efforts, still families manage to prosper and grow, and they need room to spread. It is the way of things.'

'Yes,' the abbess said slowly. Then, sadly, 'Nothing lasts for ever.'

Her companion put an arm round her waist. 'Some things do,' she said softly. 'Love. Memory.'

'Memory,' whispered the abbess. 'Ah, yes.' Then, brushing at her eyes, she said, 'Go on, be on your way before I start weeping! This is a joyful day and I would not spoil it.'

The woman smiled, a deep, serene smile born of utter contentment. 'Nothing could do that,' she murmured. Then, making the deep reverence that was her abbess's due, she had shouldered her small pack and strode off into the forest.

She was close now to the house in the woods. She could hear his voice and silently she called out to him. He must have heard; she saw his head and his broad shoulders appear over the tip of the low bank that surrounded the little settlement. Not so little now, she thought, for over the years as children had been born he had built on and the house extended outwards on both sides. It was still a lovely house, she thought. A happy house and, thanks to him, full of love.

He had caught sight of her and, his face lighting up, he hurried to meet her. She broke into a run.

★ ★ ★

Josse had sensed her approach. He had been waiting for this moment for so long and he could scarcely believe it was here at last. He had always known what he wanted; the difficult choice had been hers. They had talked long and he knew why she had finally made up her mind. He accepted what she said, although he was not sure he entirely understood. Not that it mattered, as long as she was happy.

He stared at her as she ran towards him. He saw a tall woman, leaner now than she used to be – the years had been hard – dressed in a simple black robe. She was bare-headed, the short, springy reddish hair now turning grey. She was smiling, and he caught the glint of tears in her eyes.

He stood quite still and opened his arms. She walked into his embrace. They stood without speaking for a while.

Then she said, 'You've been digging again. I can tell from the way you're standing that your back's aching.'

'Meggie will be home soon,' he replied serenely. 'She'll rub on some of her magic oil and the pain will melt.'

'That's as maybe, but you still do too much. I thought I'd come and help you, if you can do with another pair of hands.'

He rested his hands on her shoulders and stared into her eyes. She spoke lightly but he knew the profound meaning behind the levity.

'You'll stay?' His voice broke on the words.

'Yes,' she whispered. 'Abbess Caliste received the document this morning.'

Josse lifted his head and, eyes closed, said a swift silent prayer of thanks. It was over; she had done it.

He took her hand in his and led the way up towards the house. Helewise, who had stepped down as abbess when Queen Eleanor died and had for the last six years lived alone in the little house beside the chapel, walked beside him.

She loved him; she had loved him for twenty years. She had told herself that ordinary human love was not hers to enjoy, for she had heard and answered a different calling, but the voice that had called and went on calling had subtly altered and it no longer emanated from the Church, for the Church itself was no longer the same.

She had seen him love and lose another woman; she had seen him master his grief and pick himself up, making a refuge in this house in the woods not only for his own two children but for his adopted son and for all the others who came to him because they loved him and wished to be with him.

And now, she thought, now I am doing the same. She leaned against him as they walked, squeezing his hand...

And he squeezed back. Helewise, he thought, his heart overflowing. Here with me, at last.

They reached the low bank and together they climbed over it. As they approached the house, its old stones glowing golden in the summer sunshine, a burst of laughter from the children rang in the warm air.

It was like a blessing.